REST IN PIECES

"This thing that's come up, Mr. Clarke," Hudson began. "As I mentioned on the phone, it's connected with your family lot and very unpleasant, I regret to say. No one seems able to account for it—"

The funeral director hesitated. He didn't seem to know how to go on. Then his melancholy look deepened as he resumed, "The superintendent of Hillside Cemetery got out the map and it showed two places unoccupied in the Upton lot, one of them beside your father's, Mr. Clarke. They met with no obstruction when they had it sounded and the superintendent arranged to have it opened this morning. When they got down a few feet, however, they came across a human skull."

John Clarke stared at him blankly.

"A human skull," Hudson repeated firmly. Then his voice fell away. "A bullet dropped out of it—"

DORIS MILES DISNEY
HERE LIES

Kensington Publishing Corp.
475 Park Avenue South
New York, NY 10016

ZEBRA BOOKS
KENSINGTON PUBLISHING CORP.

ZEBRA BOOKS

are published by

Kensington Publishing Corp.
475 Park Avenue South
New York, NY 10016

First printing: May, 1988

Printed in the United States of America

Chapter 1

"I can't believe it's so hot," Kitty Clarke said, shifting around on the seat. "It must be close to ninety."

"Nowhere near that," her husband said. "It's the sun on the car roof."

"Even so, New Hampshire's got no right this time of year. It's September. It's the day after Labor Day."

"Law against it?"

"Well, I think of it as all forests and mountains and lakes. I expect it to be cool, especially up here in the northern part of the state."

"It'll cool off fast enough at nightfall," John Clarke said. "We'll be in Collingswood, though, long before that. Haven't got much more than an hour to go."

Kitty wiped her damp face and neck with her handkerchief. "I hope the inn is nice and comfortable. I'm looking forward to a long, long shower, a couple of ice-cold martinis, and a good dinner."

"Sounds wonderful," her husband said.

She glanced at him. He looked tired. He'd had little sleep last night and almost none the night before, after the shock of his mother's sudden death.

Now they were on their way to Collingswood to bury Phoebe Upton Clarke in the Upton family plot.

"Want me to drive for a while?" Kitty inquired.

He shook his head. "No, thanks. I'd just as soon drive as sit."

There was silence for an interval. The car windows and ventilators were open but whatever the actual temperature at 3:30 in the afternoon, the sun was still high and hot. It wasn't a day that could be mistaken for midsummer, though. The distant mountains showed patches of flame and yellow, the corn had been harvested in the fields on either side of the road, and woodbine on an old stone wall had started to turn red.

"This is a beautiful valley," Kitty said. "And always the mountains to look at. But I should think it would be a lonely place to live. You were never up here much, were you?"

"Only once when I was a child."

She consulted the map on the seat between them. "Collingswood must be the metropolis of this whole area. Berlin is the largest town north of it. How old were you the time you came?"

"Six or seven. It was around Memorial Day, I think, because I remember going to the cemetery with my mother and that all the graves seemed to have flowers on them. It's an old cemetery. Goes back to when the town was just a little outpost, a few houses and a fort, designed to repel French-Indian attacks from Canada. I remember my mother pointing out soldiers' graves from the 1760s." After a pause John Clarke added, "I don't suppose the cemetery or the town have changed much since I was there a good forty years ago."

"I hope you've made the right decision bringing your mother back here to be buried," Kitty said. "It seems so far away from Woodbridge where she spent most of her life. After all, she left Collingswood over fifty years ago."

"But she had my father buried there in the Upton lot with her parents and grandparents and an aunt."

"That's six. She'll make seven. It must be an eight-grave lot. There wouldn't be room for us."

"No, you needn't worry about being put there yourself." John Clarke's tone was dry. "I'm not that much of an ancestor worshiper." He slowed down on the outskirts of a village made up of a few scattered houses, a gas station and a general store.

As they left it behind Kitty said, "It's too bad that she never said where she wanted to be buried."

They had been over this subject yesterday. John Clarke had no desire to go over it again. "Her place is with my father," he said briefly.

"But think how long ago he died. She told me once she'd almost completely forgotten him. After all, they'd only been married three or four years when he and your grandmother were killed in that accident. I've forgotten, did they run into the train or were they crossing the tracks in front of it?"

"They skidded onto the tracks when he tried to stop. It was sleeting, my mother said, when he left for the railroad station to meet my grandmother. The streets were a glaze of ice . . . Light me a cigarette, will you?"

Kitty lit one for him and one for herself. She said reflectively, "What a long time your mother was widowed. It's a pity she didn't remarry. She was lovely looking, from her pictures, and must have had

9

plenty of chances. We've been married twenty-six years, so she was in her forties when I first met her but still a very attractive woman. I know at the time I wondered if she wouldn't remarry when she found herself alone. Remember that man, the widower who lived near her—what was his name?''

"Hamlin, Hamilton, something like that.''

"Hamlin, I think. It looked for a while as if she might marry him. He certainly seemed very interested. But nothing ever came of it.''

"She had a full, active life of her own,'' John Clarke said. "It was what she wanted. It suited her.''

"Yes . . .'' Kitty spoke hesitantly and didn't add that now, when that full, active life was ended, his mother's body was being sent far away from the town where most of it had been spent, to be buried with a husband she could hardly remember who had been dead for the greater part of her own life span.

Sentiment, of course, dictated that a wife lie in death beside her husband.

No one would go near her grave, Kitty's thoughts continued pensively. John would place a standing order with their florist for a plant on Memorial Day and perhaps once or twice in the years ahead they would make a pilgrimage to it. That would be the end of it. Betsy and Sam, their children, wouldn't go at all.

Kitty sighed. She was sentimental about graves. She had wanted her mother-in-law buried in the Woodbridge cemetery where they could have stopped by sometimes on a Sunday drive. At Christmas they could have put a wreath on her grave and in summer watered the plants in dry weather. But John, when his mother died so unexpectedly—and with her good health, who'd ever dream that her heart would give out like that?—had insisted that she must be buried with his father in the town where she was born. It was his mother, his decision to make. Late last night the body had been sent by train to Collingswood Junction where a Collingswood undertaker would meet it. Tomorrow morning there would be a graveside funeral service conducted by the Congregational minister who was a complete stranger to the dead woman and her family. Then they would go home to Massachusetts and Phoebe Upton Clarke would be left alone for good and all . . .

Kitty sighed again. Presently she said, "I hope Grace and Mabel didn't keep the children waiting too long. They fuss around so, getting ready to go anywhere."

"They're old," John Clarke said. "Grace must be in her late seventies and Mabel's not much younger." He smiled at his wife. "When I hit my seventies I'll claim the right to dodder too if I feel like it. Keep that in mind."

"I will." Kitty smiled back at him. "But I'm only a year younger than you are so I'll be getting on myself. I guess we'll just have to take turns doddering."

"I bet you'll still look ten years younger than I do, though," he remarked on a note of pride.

It was justifiable pride in her appearance. Kitty, elegantly slender, hair fashionably silvered, her thin face holding its firm contours, didn't look almost forty-eight, the mother of a twenty-five-year-old son and a daughter who was twenty-one. She didn't look, at the most, more than forty.

John Clarke, white-haired, a little jowly, always heavy in build but heavier now than he used to be,

11

looked his actual age. He had a nice face, though, Kitty told herself, giving him an affectionate glance. Kindness, humor, firmness, too, showed on it. He had earned his look of firmness and authority. He was the senior member of the long established law firm of Clarke and Mason, a city councilman and member of the planning board, and a director of more organizations than she could keep track of.

They had a good marriage, she thought contentedly. A very good marriage.

"I wonder how far behind us Betsy and Sam are," she said next.

"Well, Fitchburg's not too much out of their way. If you allow half an hour after they arrived for Grace and Mabel to get themselves together, they shouldn't be over an hour behind us."

Kitty yawned. "We'll plan to go to bed early tonight. All that crowd at the funeral home last night was exhausting. Your mother would be pleased, though, if she knew how many people in Woodbridge came to pay their last respects to her. I'm just as well satisfied myself that we don't have to go through it again tonight in Collingswood."

"There'd be no point to it. There can't be a handful of people left in the town who remember her."

They were driving through another village. All around them were the level stretches and gentle slopes of the valley ringed by the distant mountains whose serrated peaks stood sharp against the clear blue sky.

Kitty subsided into her thoughts. She hoped that the elderly Clarke cousins, Grace and Mabel, weren't bickering all the way up here. Betsy wouldn't mind, would, in fact, derive a certain amount of entertain-

12

ment out of their querulous exchanges. But Sam, less patient with them, would have a fit. It was too bad to have to bring them at all but it couldn't be helped. They'd been quite hurt when Kitty had suggested that they might find the trip too tiring. They had known Phoebe, they'd said, since they'd met her at her wedding to their cousin Sam—young Sam was named for his grandfather—and they thought it only fitting that having welcomed her into the Clarke family on her wedding day they should say good-by to her at her funeral.

Perhaps she and John had better take the old ladies home in their car tomorrow. John, wanting to get up here as soon as possible in case the undertaker needed to confer with him about anything, had left it to Sam to pick up Grace and Mabel in Fitchburg. Perhaps that should be considered the end of Sam's responsibility for them. On second thought, no. John would be depressed tomorrow after his mother's funeral and shouldn't have to listen to the pair all the way back to Massachusetts. It wouldn't hurt Sam to put up with them again. He needed lessons in patience.

Betsy didn't need them. Since childhood she'd showed a remarkable understanding of people and had always been able to laugh at or excuse any number of things that irritated Sam. She understood him particularly well; and for all that he was nearly five years older, he often talked things over with her that he wouldn't even think of mentioning to his parents. That, of course, was the gap between generations revealing itself. Kitty could be thankful that it would lessen with time and that someday Betsy and Sam would draw closer to their parents again. She had found this happening with her own parents

13

in later years and with John's mother too.

She could recall with satisfaction that she had always got along well with the dead woman. They hadn't ever made John a bone of contention between them. Phoebe had been generous in relinquishing first place in her son's life. Kitty's own mother had wondered how it would work out, considering that Phoebe had been a widow so long and that John was her only child. But she had shown no possessiveness toward him. Indeed, Kitty, before she got used to her mother-in-law's ways, had thought her almost too detached, almost, well, self-centeredly so. Phoebe, who traveled a lot, had her own friends, lived her own life, and kept her hands off John's, extending this detachment to Kitty when she became his wife.

In the long run, though, it had turned out to be the surest way of holding their attention. Kitty would remember it when her own son and daughter were married, although she knew that she was a warmer, more affectionate person than Phoebe had ever been and that it would be harder for her to do. But she would try . . .

John Clarke's thoughts were also on the dead woman. Driving through the green countryside he found himself sorting out his earliest memories of his mother. They were associated with her furs. There had been a big fur muff he'd liked to bury his face in; a long fur coat, a jacket, and various neckpieces. She'd had a hat, too, with fur on it that he'd sometimes been allowed to stroke. She had always been scented with some perfume that had a very delicate fragrance. To this day he didn't know the name of it; he didn't think anyone used it nowadays. He had often meant to ask his mother what it was but hadn't got around to it. Now he would never find out; his mother would answer no more questions. But his early memories of her furs and perfume would remain far clearer than many a later memory of her.

She seemed always to have been on her way somewhere in those early memories. Sometimes she was in evening dress, rich satins and rustling taffetas and long white gloves, stopping in his room to say good night to him. Other times she was in street dress, sleek suits and furs or wearing flowing summery pastels. Whatever her costume she seemed always to be saying good night or good-by to him with a light kiss on his forehead or a pat on his cheek before hurrying away.

He had been jealous of her friends and activities in those far-off days. He'd been a lonely kid, he guessed, rattling around in the big house his great-grandfather Clarke had built soon after the Civil War. His mother had never given it up and had died in it two days ago. Now he would have the job of selling it and God knew who would want a great ark of a place like that. At least the stained-glass windows going up the stairs that had always somehow frightened him—was it because they had darkened the landing?—had long ago been replaced with clear glass and the heavy dark paneling painted white.

He couldn't remember why the hall had made him so uneasy. He'd got over the feeling by the time he was seven or eight but before that, when he couldn't avoid going through it, he had toiled up the stairs as fast as his legs would carry him and often sought the haven of his mother's bright rooms on the second floor. Not that she'd been in them much, on the go all the time as she was, but at least she'd provided substitute companionship. There'd been Lenny—for Lenora—his nursemaid and the other servants. He had adored Lenny and she had been kept on until he was eight or nine.

When he was twelve he'd gone away to school. His mother, in her middle thirties then, had paid him an occasional visit and had so dazzled the headmaster, a bachelor he disliked very much himself, that for a time he had been wildly worried for fear she would marry the man.

When he was at college his roommate had adored her and been outspoken in his envy of a mother so elegant and charming.

But in some ultimate sense—perhaps it was as a bulwark against the world—she had never been a mother at all. There had been moments in his married life when he had watched Kitty being loving and attentive to Betsy and Sam and had actually resented his own children's close relationship with her.

Eventually, however, he and his mother had become good friends. She had welcomed Kitty as his bride and taken more interest in her grandchildren than she had ever taken in him.

But she had kept a certain degree of detachment to the very end.

He would miss her, just the same; her cool, shrewd appraisal of problems, her faintly mocking humor, her alert awareness of the changing world around her.

He would miss her. She had not been the ideal mother but her death left a void, a sense of emptiness. He would miss her and now and then feel pangs of regret that somehow the deepest meaning of their blood tie had always escaped them both.

But wasn't that more his mother's fault than his? A child was molded into giving love through having love given to him.

His mother had not been a generous giver.

Well, all that was in the past now, over and done with. There was nothing more to be said of her but *requiescat in pace . . .*

The road took a turn that brought it to the Androscoggin River and followed its course between stands of birches that Kitty said looked like a fairyland with their graceful spread and chalk-white bark.

At five o'clock they reached the outskirts of Collingswood. They passed a paper mill and were caught up in the homegoing traffic coming out at the gate and farther on merging with the traffic from a leather-goods factory and a woolen mill strung out along the river. In another few minutes they reached the tidy, busy center of Collingswood, Kitty viewing everything with lively interest on this, her first visit to the town in which her husband's maternal forebears had settled almost two centuries ago.

They passed the Collingswood Trust, colonial brick, and turned off onto a tree-shaded side street, lined with old houses, handsome and well kept. A block from the center, John Clarke stopped in front of the Collingswood Inn, a three-story building painted white with a porch across the front, whose counterpart could be found in any New England resort area.

They had reserved four rooms, two doubles for themselves and the Misses Clarke and two singles for

Betsy and Sam.

A boy came out to take their luggage. John Clarke registered at the desk and was told that there had already been a call for him from Hudson, the Collingswood funeral director.

They were shown upstairs to a large corner room with twin beds and a view of the mountains. It was clean and comfortably furnished and when Kitty had inspected the bathroom she expressed satisfaction.

Her husband picked up the telephone and called the funeral home. Hudson was not in at the moment but was expected back shortly and would call him. His next call was to room service for ice and soda. While Kitty was taking a shower he mixed drinks for them from the bottle in his suitcase and carried his into the bathroom when he went in to take a shower. While he was toweling himself the phone rang. It was Hudson, who asked if it would be convenient for him to come over right away.

"I'm just out of the shower," John Clarke said. "Can you give me half an hour?"

"Well . . . yes."

John Clarke caught the hesitant note in the other's voice. "Is it something important?"

"Yes, Mr. Clarke. It's connected with your family lot but it's something I'd rather not go into on the phone."

"All right, I'll be downstairs in twenty minutes." John Clarke hung up and reached for the fresh underwear his wife laid out on the bed.

"There's some hitch about the lot," he said. "I can't imagine what it is."

18

Chapter 2

Betsy and Sam arrived with the Clarke sisters before their parents were ready to go downstairs. Nothing was said about the problem connected with the family lot, Kitty limiting herself to the comment that they had made good time.

Sam, solidly built like his father but with his mother's dark good looks, rolled up his eyes to indicate how trying the elderly pair had been. Betsy said firmly that they'd all found the drive easy and pleasant. She was lighter than her brother, a compromise between her father's fair complexion and her mother's brunette cast. She had hazel eyes and light brown hair worn in a simple cut that eschewed any form of the bouffant. She smiled tranquilly at her parents and the Clarke sisters who were exclaiming over how little Collingswood had changed since their last trip in 1915 to attend the double funeral of John Clarke's father and his grandmother.

"Of course there are those two motels coming into town," Grace, the elder said. "And I'm sure that leather-goods factory has been built since then. I don't remember the department store on Main Street, either."

"I do," Mabel, the younger, put in promptly. "I remember it very well. It had a different name and was more like a dry-goods store. I'd lost one of my black gloves and I went in and bought another pair."

"No, that wasn't the place at all," Grace contradicted. "You bought them in a women's-wear shop near where the department store is now. But it wasn't even in existence then."

"Now, Grace, I ought to know where I bought my own gloves. Phoebe was with me and I remember saying to her—"

"Mabel, it frightens me the way your memory's going. I distinctly recall that you and Phoebe came back to her mother's house together and you said—"

"Why don't you all go to your rooms and freshen up," Kitty intervened. "We'll meet you downstairs after we've seen the funeral director and then we'll think about dinner."

"That's fine with me." Sam moved with alacrity to open the door for the two old ladies. "See you downstairs in about half an hour."

Still arguing about whether or not the Collingswood department store had existed in 1915 the Misses Clarke went across the hall to their room with Betsy trailing after them to her room next door.

"That's the way they've been carrying on since we left Fitchburg," Sam informed his parents in a long-suffering tone. "Betsy thinks it's funny. I think they're a couple of old bores."

"No more so than plenty of people who come into our office," his father said.

20

"At least we get paid for putting up with it there," Sam said.

"Bickering stimulates them," Kitty said. "Now go take your shower and change. We'll be downstairs."

The phone rang as Sam left the room. It was the desk clerk.

"Mr. Hudson is here, Mr. Clarke," he said.

"Thank you, I'll be right down."

"You'll find him in the sitting room at the foot of the stairs. He asked to speak to you privately and I said no one would disturb you there."

"That's very kind of you. Thanks again."

John Clarke hung up the phone. He was still in his shirt sleeves. His wife had hung up the dark jacket he would wear tomorrow. While he was putting it on he said to her, "I think you'd better come downstairs with me and meet Mr. Hudson."

"All right." She applied a last touch to her hair and stood up from the dressing table.

She was wearing a dark silk dress. Not black, which she didn't particularly like, but charcoal with an almost invisible plaid pattern. Packing it that morning, she had thought that with a black hat and shoes it would be suitable for the funeral. She pulled on short white gloves and picked up her pocketbook. After a last glance in the mirror she preceded her husband to the door.

They went down the wide staircase side by side, suddenly quiet, suddenly aware of the purpose of this trip that would see Phoebe Clarke left to her final rest on a New Hampshire hillside.

Their expressions were solemn as they entered the sitting room at the foot of the stairs. Hudson unfolded himself—he was startlingly tall and skinny with a long melancholy face—from a sofa and advanced to shake hands with them. His manner seemed even more constrained than the occasion demanded.

John Clarke asked if his mother's body had arrived at the expected time.

"Oh yes. It came in to Collingswood Junction on the 2:30 train and I was there to meet it. No problem at all about that—"

He hesitated. He didn't seem to know how to go on.

"Shall we sit down?" John Clarke said. He didn't ask what had shaken the funeral director's professional aplomb. He had a lawyer's habit of waiting for a client to tell his story in his own way. He would wait for Hudson's.

They sat down, the Clarkes on the sofa, Hudson facing them.

"This thing that's come up, Mr. Clarke," he began. "As I mentioned on the phone, it's connected with your family lot and very unpleasant, I regret to say." He paused. "No one seems able to account for it—"

"Yes?" John Clarke said.

"When Mr. Atkins called me from Woodbridge he instructed me that you would like your mother buried beside your father. Was that correct?"

"Yes."

Relief that at least that much of the proceedings were in order flickered across the funeral director's face. Then his melancholy look deepened as he resumed, "The superintendent of Hillside Cemetery

22

got out the map and it showed two places unoccupied in the Upton lot, one of them beside your father's, Mr. Clarke. They met with no obstruction when they had it sounded and the superintendent arranged to have it opened this morning. When they got down a few feet, however, they came across a human skull."

"But—"

"A human skull," Hudson repeated firmly. Then his voice fell away. "A bullet dropped out of it—"

"A bullet?" John Clarke stared at him blankly.

"Yes." With the worst told Hudson's voice regained firmness. "The workmen notified the superintendent. He called the Collingswood police and then called me. I went right over. This was about ten o'clock. Dale, the police chief, got there ahead of me and had the men keep digging. They found the rest of the skeleton mixed in with some rotted boards and a few rusty bits of hardware from a coffin. It looked like a man's skeleton when they got it all laid out on the ground. Too tall to be a woman's."

Kitty's hand, concealed by a fold of her dress, sought and found her husband's. He pressed it reassuringly and said, "Could the body have been buried there by stealth when it was in a coffin?"

"Dale mentioned that too. He had to see the map himself before he was convinced that the grave was marked unoccupied. We've been wondering if you'd have any suggestions to offer that would help to identify the skeleton and clear this thing up."

"I haven't the least idea how it got there." John Clarke's tone held crispness as if to disassociate himself from the affair. "If the body was buried legitimately, then the only answer is that it got into the Upton lot by mistake. It belonged in a lot nearby or one where the name was similar or something of that sort. Are the cemetery records being checked? There can't be very many people buried there who died from a bullet in the head."

"We thought of all that." Hudson allowed himself a faint note of reproof. "It isn't the answer. The records have been checked."

"Oh." John Clarke's crispness diminished.

"Did you ever hear of anyone in the Upton family who was killed by a bullet—an accident, perhaps, or a suicide?"

"Not that I know of. But I should add that this is only the second time in my life that I've been in Collingswood. My mother left here in 1912 when she was married. Her mother died three years later and after that she only came back once that I know of. I was with her on that trip and we did not come to attend the funeral of some connection who was shot or had shot himself. In fact, she had no relatives left in the town."

Her husband's tone was again too crisp, Kitty thought. It made him sound too much on the defensive. But who could blame him? On the eve of his mother's funeral he was asked to explain how a skeleton with a bullet in the skull had got into the family lot. It would upset anyone, most of all John, who sought order and regularity in his affairs.

He said next, "What are the police doing about it?"

"Well, when we couldn't find out anything from the cemetery records Dale called the state police and they sent some of their technicians. They took the skeleton and the bits from the coffin to their lab for examination. The fact that there was so little of the coffin left made them think that the burial took place a good many years ago. The absence of a vault is another indicator that it goes pretty far back." Hudson came to a halt and then said, "I'm very sorry about this, Mr. Clarke. It just makes things that much more difficult for you."

"Yes. Where does it leave us on my mother's funeral tomorrow?"

"The police would like the grave we intended to use left open for the time being. They didn't settle the question of what they were going to do with the skeleton when they were finished with it."

"I don't want it back in the Upton lot," John Clarke said. "It has nothing to do with our family."

The undertaker cleared his throat. "Well, let's see what develops. Regardless of the final disposal of it, your mother's resting place was the immediate concern. I had the remaining grave opened for her. It isn't next to your father's but it was the best I could do."

"Yes, of course. I wouldn't want her in the other grave even if it could be arranged." John Clarke stood up and walked across the room, halting in front of a window. More to himself than to the others he said, "I can't understand this at all. Not at all . . ." He turned to face his wife. "I wonder if Grace or Mabel ever heard any family tale that would account for it." For Hudson's benefit he added, "My father's cousins. They came up here with us. I'll have to talk to them about it."

Hudson stood up to leave. "In the meantime,

25

though, the service is to go forward as planned?"

"Oh yes."

He ticked off the arrangements on his fingers. "Then you'll be at the funeral home tomorrow morning at ten. The body will then be placed in the hearse and we'll have the limousines ready to follow it; one for you and your family and the other for the pallbearers. Mr. Brewer, the Congregational minister, will meet us at the cemetery."

"You ordered a fresh blanket of flowers for the coffin?"

"Yes, it's to be delivered at eight tomorrow morning. I'm afraid none of the flowers that were sent on from Woodbridge will be usable by that time. They didn't stand up well under the train trip."

"The fresh blanket will be all that's necessary."

"Well, if there's anything else just let me know, Mr. Clarke. And by the way, you'll have a visit from the police chief later. We thought it best that I should see you first, but naturally, he wants to see you too."

"After dinner, I hope." John Clarke looked at his watch. It was twenty minutes to seven. "We've had a long day and now this on top of it. Would you mind calling Dale and asking him if he'll wait until after eight o'clock? I want to talk with my cousins, anyway, before I see him."

"I'll be glad to take care of it." With a last murmur of sympathy for the distressing complication that had been added to the sadness of the funeral, the undertaker withdrew.

Husband and wife stood looking at each other. He made a grimace. "Isn't this the damnedest?"

"It'll work out somehow." Kitty linked her arm

through his. "Let's get the others and have a cocktail and dinner."

They were given a window table in the dining room. The rib roast, a specialty of the inn, was delicious but only Sam and Betsy ate with real appetite. John Clarke's emotions were mixed. He was worried but resentful, too, that his grief over his mother should have this strange and vaguely threatening factor intruded upon it; that what should be a simple, dignified service tomorrow would be overshadowed by the gaping grave that was supposed to have been hers; and that the skeleton removed from it might involve them, innocent bystanders though they were, in an unpleasant investigation.

He found Betsy and Sam irritating. They took an academic interest in the skeleton and were all too ready to advance theories to account for the bullet in its skull and its presence in the Upton lot. Betsy's tended to become lurid. Her mother quelled her.

The Misses Clarke were just as trying as he had known they would be, casting around in the Upton family history as they had heard it from his mother, arguing, contradicting each other, and introducing irrelevant bits from the annals of the Clarke family. And it was all for nothing. Neither one had ever heard of any Upton connection who had died from a bullet wound, suicidal, accidental, or homicidal. The suggestion of homocide, coming from Betsy, shocked the old ladies.

The only person at the table who didn't get on John Clarke's nerves was his wife. Unobtrusively attentive to his needs, she did her best to quiet the others. When all was said and done, her husband reflected gratefully, a wife like Kitty, to whom he could always look for understanding and sympathy, was a blessing beyond price.

At ten minutes after eight they left the dining room. A man talking with the desk clerk turned toward them. There was nothing noteworthy about his appearance. He was in his early forties, of medium height and build and neatly dressed in conservative civilian clothes.

He singled out John Clarke. "I'm Dale, the police chief," he said.

The old ladies fluttered in the background. As Kitty herded them into the inn parlor with Sam and Betsy they were exclaiming that at least the man wasn't in uniform to embarrass them in front of the other guests. Even so, they said, they certainly hadn't expected to be involved with the police when they set out this morning to bury dear Phoebe.

Chapter 3

Once again John Clarke found himself in the sitting room where he had talked with the funeral director. Dale, to insure their privacy, closed the door. Slow and methodical, he took his time getting settled in a chair. Then he said, "I'm sorry this had to happen, Mr. Clarke, when you've come up here to bury your mother. It's the queerest thing I ever came across. I can't remember anything like it in all the years I've been on the force."

"It's a pretty upsetting thing," John Clarke informed him grimly. "Completely beyond me. According to Mr. Hudson, the logical explanation— that a mistake was made when the body was buried in the Upton lot—isn't the correct one."

"That's right. We've checked the cemetery records very carefully for similar names and lots in the same section without finding a thing. It wasn't a promising theory, anyway. The burial must have taken place at least twenty or twenty-five years ago when there were still people alive, including the old sexton, who knew the Uptons and knew who belonged in their lot. For that matter, it might go

29

back even farther to when your grandmother was alive or before your mother got married and moved away. There's no telling yet when it happened. But however far back it was, I can't imagine the body being buried where it was by mistake. Not in a town this size where everybody knows everybody else's business."

John Clarke turned the police chief's words over in his mind. At last he said, "Well, I've got nothing else to suggest. I've never heard of any Upton who died from a bullet through the head. I've talked with my father's cousins whose memories go back a lot farther than mine and they've never heard of anything like that either. How about old-timers here in Collingswood? There must still be people who remember the Uptons."

"Yes, there are. I've had a man working on it since this morning. He hasn't picked up anything, though. There's some who went to school with your mother and he's talked with one old woman in her eighties who remembers your grandmother. But her memory's not very reliable. She mentioned that you had an aunt. Everyone else said your mother was an only child. You ever have an aunt on your mother's side?"

"No, she was an only child."

The police chief nodded. "That's what people said. Hudson gave me her date of birth and I had the town clerk look it up. Her birth record says she was the first child of Harold and Christina Upton, born in 1891. I wondered if there was a younger sister."

"No, there wasn't. Her father died when she was a child."

"And then, when your mother got married, she moved away. Did your father always live in Woodbridge?"

"Yes. He practiced law there."

"You a lawyer too, Mr. Clarke?"

"Yes, I am." John Clarke smiled faintly. "It seems to be turning into a family tradition. My son Sam was graduated from law school last year and he's come into the office with me."

"That's nice for both of you," Dale said.

"It's working out well." Dismissing family tradition, John Clarke reverted to the family burial lot. "What will you be able to do about all this?" he asked.

"Well, as you no doubt know, the state police removed the skeleton to their lab. They've already said it belonged to a male and when they've made a study of it they'll tell us a lot more; the man's age and race, his height, his approximate weight, and whether or not the bullet wound could have been self-inflicted. They'll find out what kind of a gun the bullet was fired from; and if we can't get the information somewhere else, they'll work out an estimate from the coffin remains of how long ago the man was buried. They won't be able to pin it down very closely but it will be better than nothing."

Dale paused to take out his pipe and get it filled and lighted. Then he continued, "It will take a little time, of course. Meanwhile, I'll do what I can here. I stopped at the town clerk's house on my way to see you tonight. I asked him to start going through the old burial books first thing tomorrow morning. I thought I might as well give myself plenty of leeway so I asked him to begin with 1900 and work up to 1945, making a list of every man or boy who died of a bullet wound. If I don't get a lead from that I'll have to try something else."

"What about death certificates?"

"I could try them, but the burial books are quicker, the town clerk said; the death certificates include people who died in Collingswood but were buried somewhere else. I'm only interested in people who were buried here."

"If you don't find a man who matches up with the skeleton, what's your next step?" John Clarke inquired.

Puffing on his pipe, the police chief eyed him thoughtfully. "I'll broaden it out until I find someone it does match up with, no matter what he was supposed to have died from."

John Clarke considered the implications of this statement. "You mean murder with the bullet wound passing for something else?"

"Yes, although God knows how."

"Then, if we leave out the coffin—after all, the police lab hasn't examined the pieces yet—isn't it possible that the man was buried illegally with the Upton lot picked by chance?"

Dale replied, "The soil retained an outline of the coffin and the hardware we found was coffin handles, Mr. Clarke. But leaving that aside, I can't see a murderer getting rid of his victim in a cemetery. He wouldn't dare risk the sexton spotting a new grave where there shouldn't be one."

His dispassionate tone made it plain to John Clarke that it was no use grasping at straws to explain away the skeleton in the Upton lot. Nothing connected with it would be made that easy for him.

Soon thereafter the police chief took his leave. If he felt disappointed that the interview hadn't been more fruitful, he concealed the feeling as he shook hands and said he would like to talk with him again tomorrow after his mother's funeral.

"I'll have a couple of men on hand at the cemetery in the morning," he added. "They'll keep any curiosity seekers at a distance."

"Oh. Thank you. I haven't had time to think about that. Word of the skeleton is all over town, I suppose."

"It's got beyond that. It was on the six o'clock news broadcast and we're beginning to get some calls from newspapers. It looks as if it will get quite a play from them."

John Clarke nodded resignedly. He said good night to the police chief and went back to his family feeling baffled and uneasy. He hoped that his mother, who'd had formidable dignity in life, wouldn't go into her grave tomorrow with a total lack of it. She would have hated whatever publicity lay ahead. Although she had been a social and civic leader in Woodbridge as far back as he could remember, she had made every effort to avoid the limelight, professing the old-fashioned belief that a lady shunned it.

Well, it would shine on her tomorrow, he feared; but at least she would not know it.

The morning papers gave the skeleton space on the first page under such headlines as: STATE POLICE LAUNCH PROBE OF MYSTERY SKELETON and BULLET FOUND IN SKULL OF MYSTERY SKELETON. The late Mrs. Samuel Clarke's wealth and social standing in Woodbridge were stressed. Her only son came into the story as a Woodbridge city councilman and senior member of the law firm of Clarke and Mason. His refusal to talk to reporters who had begun calling him late the night before had been translated into the statement that he had no theory to account for the skeleton's presence in his ancestral burial lot.

The afternoon papers would have time to write up other cases of mystery skeletons and gather local background, John Clarke reflected; they'd probably find plenty more to say about it.

At the peaceful, tree-shaded old cemetery there was nothing like the crowd of curiosity seekers he had expected; he had overlooked the small-town tendency to respect the mourners' privacy at a funeral. A number of older people turned up but they had known Phoebe Upton Clarke in her youth and could be considered to have a legitimate reason for being present. Those who came only to gape were kept at a distance by the police officers detailed for that duty.

A tarpaulin covered the open grave from which the skeleton had been removed. Standing beside the dead woman's coffin the young minister read the committal service with tender reverence. Betsy and Kitty and the two old ladies were in tears. Sam's solemn face indicated that he was close to tears himself. John Clarke managed to put out of his mind the anxieties and vexations that had been thrust upon the occasion and turned his thoughts to the fact that he was saying a last good-by to his mother who was gone irrevocably from his life.

The original plan he had made was to leave for home immediately after lunch; but that plan had been discarded last night. When they were back at the inn he said, "I don't know what's going to come up next. I hope we can leave tomorrow but I'm not going to count on it. Sam, you'd better call the office and tell them to expect us when we get there. Have Margaret cancel all my appointments for tomorrow and tell her that if anything unexpected comes up she'll have to take it to Frank or young Mason."

When Sam went to the telephone his father turned his attention to the old ladies. "I'm sorry about all this but I'm afraid it can't be helped," he said. "I shan't be able to get you back to Fitchburg today and I'm not even sure about tomorrow. If you feel you should get home, though, we'll check into bus schedules."

For once in their lives Grace and Mabel Clarke found themselves in agreement. Leave in the middle of this extraordinary affair and go tamely back to Fitchburg? Indeed not. As one voice they said, "Don't give us another thought, John. Our next-door neighbor is feeding Suky and the parakeet, so it doesn't matter when we get home."

Betsy and her mother exchanged an amused glance behind the old ladies' backs.

There were reporters waiting in the lobby when the family went down to lunch. John Clarke told them he knew no more about the skeleton than they did and was firm in his refusal to speculate about it.

The police chief appeared soon after lunch and offered no objection to John Clarke's suggestion that

Sam should join them in the sitting room.

"We've made the identification," he said, when he had closed the door and seated himself. "It's the skeleton of a man named Melvin Arthur Scott from Chatham, Connecticut. Ever hear of him?"

"Melvin Arthur Scott . . ." John Clarke shook his head. "No, I can't say I have. Or of anyone named Scott in the Upton family."

"According to the burial book, he was the husband of Eliza Jane Upton Scott. Ever hear of her?"

"Not that I—wait a minute, though. My great-grandmother was Eliza Jane Upton. I noticed it on the monument in the cemetery but I don't think her maiden name was Scott. She died in the nineties. Was the man buried that far back?"

"No indeed. He died October 5, 1918. His wife must have been named for your great-grandmother."

"Yes." John Clarke looked puzzled. "Funny I never heard of her. She must have been a distant cousin."

"Not too distant," Dale said. "There she was in Chatham, Connecticut, but she knew about the family lot up here in New Hampshire and was able to authorize her husband's burial in it."

John Clarke was slow to reply. Sam said firmly, "Dad, it stands to reason."

"That's right," the police chief said. "She either knew the cemetery people, the minister or the undertaker—they're all dead now so we can't check it with them—or by some other means they were satisfied that she had the right to bury her husband in the Upton lot. It was forty-four years ago, Mr. Clarke. There were people in Collingswood at the time who

36

knew who she was."

"There must have been," John Clarke conceded. "But why wasn't the grave marked on the cemetery map?"

"I had a talk with the superintendent about that a little while ago. He thinks that the date of burial, October 8, 1918, comes into it. It was during the flu epidemic and the records show that the man who was the superintendent then died of it himself the previous week. Other people were dying of it, too, and somehow, with the superintendent's death and a little delay before a new one took over, there must have been confusion about keeping the records and the map up to date. It sounds likely enough, don't you think?"

John Clarke nodded. He felt relief. Eliza Jane Upton remained as an unknown factor but at least the skeleton was accounted for. "The war was still going on in October 1918," he said. "Was Scott killed in it and his body brought back or what? How did he come to die of a bullet wound?"

"We don't know." Dale spoke without emphasis. "Spanish influenza was given as the cause of death. There's no mention of the bullet wound."

"No mention . . ." John Clarke's voice trailed off into silence as the implications of this statement came home to him.

Dale continued, "The Collingswood undertaker was a man named Butterfield. His son, who still runs the business, looked it up in their records. It was just jottings that indicated the same sort of arrangement as when your mother's body was sent from Woodbridge. Butterfield received instructions on October 6 from the Morton Funeral Home in Chatham. Scott's body would arrive on October 8 at Collingswood Junction on the 9:30 A.M. train for interment in the Upton lot the same day. Apparently the body was taken straight to the cemetery. Mr. Ketchum, the Congregational minister, officiated at a graveside service. That's all Butterfield put down in his records."

"No undertaker could miss a bullet wound," Sam said. "Were bodies always embalmed in those days?"

"Oh yes," the police chief assured him. "I asked Butterfield's son about it. He was only a kid himself at the time but he remembers hearing his father mention how very particular they were about embalming during the flu epidemic. He also said that the burial and transit permits—a transit permit would be required to ship the body to Collingswood—wouldn't have been issued unless the body was embalmed."

"How was the burial permit signed?" John Clarke asked.

"James Henning was the undertaker's name. He must have worked for the Morton Funeral Home. The state police sent a teletype inquiry on him and the Scotts to the Chatham police this morning as soon as we identified the skeleton. They got an answer back and called me just before I came over here. The Morton Funeral Home is still in existence but under a different owner. Morton and Henning are both dead. It's about what you could expect after forty-four years. They're going to try to locate Mrs. Scott. But"—Dale shrugged—"she could have moved away or remarried or she could be dead too.

And the doctor who signed the death certificate."

"What else does the burial book have on Scott?"

"Well, it's copied from the death certificate so it has exactly the same information. He was thirty-one years old and born in Boston. His parents' names are given, including his mother's maiden name, but God knows they're dead for sure, he'd be seventy-five himself if he were still alive. His occupation, salesman, is no help, either. Much too vague, His address is listed as Walnut Street, no house number, Chatham. Mrs. Scott is named as the informant. That's about it."

"What have you heard from the state police lab?" John Clarke asked next.

"They're working on the skeleton but it will take a few days for their complete report. The bullet, they said, smashed through the occipital bone in the back of the head, went through the brain and almost came out over the left eye; at least it dented the bone there. From the path it took, it would have caused almost instantaneous death. The bullet is a .22 but it's not from any make of gun they could identify right away."

There was a silence following this statement from the police chief. Sam was the first to speak. "A bullet through the back of the head rules out suicide."

"Yes. Although the lab people say it's just possible a man could shoot himself that way. But that's what I call quibbling. If it were suicide or an accidental shooting there'd have been no need to put down Spanish influenza as the cause of death." The police chief came to a halt and then said, "From now on we'll treat it as suspected murder."

"It doesn't seem to have taken place in Collingswood, though," John Clarke said.

"No. The indications are that Scott was killed in Chatham, Connecticut. We'll keep in touch with the police there and when we get together all the information we can from this end we'll dump it in their laps. Particularly, anything we can find out about Mrs. Scott."

Sam glanced at his father. "Things don't look so good, Dad, for this unknown relative of ours. Or the undertaker."

"Now you're jumping to conclusions. You didn't learn that in our office or in law school."

"Okay." Sam grinned and subsided.

"I guess I need that reminder, too, Mr. Clarke," Dale said. "I'm inclined to jump to conclusions myself but I'm trying to keep them under control. The first step is to locate Mrs. Scott if she's still alive and find out what her story is. If she's dead, too, I don't think anything much can be done with the case."

Dale lapsed into thought, his pleasant unremarkable face wearing a slight frown, his gaze fixed on a painting of Mount Washington on the opposite wall as if he expected it to offer assistance.

Presently his gaze shifted to John Clarke. "I wish we could get hold of someone in your family who at least knows how Mrs. Scott is related to you. What about the two old ladies you brought along? Couldn't they help?"

"They're on my father's side. Still . . . Sam, why don't you go and talk to them about it? Ask if they ever heard my mother mention an Eliza Jane Upton who became Mrs. Scott. Have them give it some thought."

Sam left, closing the door after him. John Clarke said as if thinking aloud, "I wish I could figure out how the woman is related to us. My Upton grandfather was an only child, so was my mother, and so was I." He smiled. "I broke the tradition by having two children. But the point is, we're not a prolific family. The only way I can account for Eliza Jane is through my grandfather's first cousins."

"Did they live in Collingswood?"

"No, it was somewhere else in New Hampshire. If I ever heard the name of the town I've forgotten it. It was my impression that my mother lost track of them after she was married."

The police chief shook his head in his slow, methodical way and said, "She couldn't have. She'd have the say about who could be buried in the Upton lot and must have given permission for Scott to be buried there. Eliza Jane wouldn't have had to say that her husband had died from a bullet through the head. And neither one of them would have known that the grave didn't get marked on the cemetery map."

"No, but it still seems strange that I never heard of the woman."

"Maybe your mother had lost track of her by the time you were old enough to take an interest in your relatives."

"Well, yes, that could be the answer. My mother wasn't much inclined to keep in touch with stray relatives. Or, for that matter, with her home town." John Clarke went on to say that he planned to show the Upton house to his family but couldn't remember

41

from his one childhood visit just where it stood.

The police chief supplied the address and the name of the people who owned the house now.

Sam returned, shaking his head as he entered the room. "They're absolutely certain that Gran never mentioned Eliza Jane Upton under her maiden name or as Mrs. Scott to them. But what a time I had pinning them down to it."

"The usual argument?" his father inquired.

"The whole works." Sam eyed him quizzically. "I knew you sent me so that you wouldn't have to listen to it yourself."

"You're a lot younger than I am," his father replied placidly. "I've had to put up with them all my life. Now it's your turn. Too bad, though, that they couldn't help."

His glance went to Dale. "Do you think the town clerk would let me have a look at the burial book, Chief? I'm getting more and more interested in finding out about this woman."

"I don't know why you shouldn't see it, considering what the situation is." Dale got to his feet. "Why don't you both come along with me? I want to stop in there myself to see if a thought I had about your grandfather has come to anything. I took the date of his birth and death from the monument in the cemetery and asked the town clerk to check from the time he was about eighteen on until his death to see if he fathered an illegitimate child. In the old days, the town clerk says, when a girl named a man as the father of her child, quite often they'd put the name on the birth certificate. I thought that might be the case with Eliza Jane."

"It's quite an idea," John Clarke said.

"Well, if he acknowledged her, maybe it would have given her some kind of a claim to bury her husband in the Upton lot."

Sam laughed. "I can't imagine entertaining ideas like that about my great-grandfather."

Dale shot him an indulgent glance. "Great-grandfathers were just as human as anyone else."

The Clarkes followed Dale to the town hall in Sam's car. But the expedition proved futile. During the nineteen-year span between 1880 when John Clarke's grandfather turned eighteen and 1899 when he died, he had not been named as the father of any illegitimate child born in Collingswood; and a study of the burial book added nothing to their knowledge of Eliza Jane Upton.

It was late afternoon by the time they left the town hall. Dale said that he could see no particular reason for their staying on. He had John Clarke's address and his home and office phone numbers and would get in touch with him if it became necessary.

Father and son, comparing notes on the way back to the inn, discovered that while they were pleased at the prospect of going home in the morning, they shared uneasy feelings about the unfinished business they would leave behind them.

Chapter 4

"Well, I finally located Dr. Young," Casciello, detective third grade on the Chatham police force, announced, reporting back to Lieutenant Egan in his office. "He moved to West Hartford after he retired in 1938 and died there in 1946."

"Oh. Sit down."

Casciello sat down. "The whole thing is nuts. The Chatham undertaker is dead. The undertaker in New Hampshire is dead. The minister who buried the guy is dead. Now it's the doctor who signed the death certificate. Are we supposed to start interrogating tombstones?"

"We don't know about Eliza Jane Upton," Egan reminded him. "She may still be alive."

"Yeh. All I know is that I can't find her or her husband in the phone or city directories for 1918 or for ten years before or after. I can't find them through any of the Scotts listed at the time. Or through tax records or voters' lists. Or under her maiden name."

Casciello's tone was understandably sour. It was Friday afternoon and since Wednesday morning when the first teletype inquiry came in from New Hampshire, Casciello, assigned to the investigation, had been putting in long hours on it. He regarded his

44

superior without enthusiasm. It was all very well, he reflected, for him to sit there on his can and dream up new sources of inquiry but it was Casciello who had to ring doorbells and wear out his eyes poring over the faded ink of old records. Well, maybe that wasn't entirely correct. Egan had run a check on the Morton Funeral Home himself. Just the same, though, the whole thing was nuts, trying to get evidence of a murder that belonged in the history books. But Egan was intrigued by the case. It had caught his interest the moment the teletype was laid on his desk.

Casciello settled himself more firmly in his chair, planted his elbows on the wooden arms, and took on the appearance of a man who was going to rest his feet for a while.

Lieutenant Egan, slumped down in his own chair, began to hum "Loch Lomond" off key. Casciello, who had true pitch himself, gritted his teeth to bear it.

Presently, Egan switched across the Irish Sea to hum "Kathleen Mavourneen." Those two were his favorites. He was slight in build, almost skinny. Tough, though, and wiry, he was the best judo man on the Chatham force and also renowned as the best marksman. He would never see forty again but could pass for ten years younger except for his gray hair. His bright blue eyes were turned on his subordinate but he wasn't looking at him. He went on humming deep in thought.

A high note wavered and flattened. Casciello winced and gritted his teeth harder.

At last he broke off and said, "Let's see, what was in the obituary?"

His subordinate repressed a sigh. "It was in the

Chatham *Free Lance-Star* for Monday morning, October 7, 1918, and got about five or six lines. It said that Melvin A. Scott, Walnut Street, died at his home on Saturday, October 5, from Spanish influenza. He was survived by his wife, Mrs. Eliza Jane Upton Scott and his burial would take place in Collingswood, New Hampshire, with the Morton Funeral Home in charge of the arrangements. That's all it said but like I told you, there were so many dying of the flu that they had to keep their obituaries short. Even so, there was a whole page of them that day and the next."

"No children. I wonder where they were married. The Collingswood police ought to check to see if it's on record there."

"Well, it's certainly not on record in Chatham. I went all the way back to 1900 just in case you asked me if they didn't get married when Scott was fourteen. Nothing at all. And no birth certificate for Mrs. Scott back to 1880."

The lieutenant nodded absent approval of his subordinate's thoroughness. "It would help if they'd had street numbers on Walnut Street in 1918."

"Amundsen, who lives down the end of the street, says it was more like a country road in those days. Within the city limits in name only. R.F.D. mail until long after the first war was over. The street's at least two miles long and there weren't more than twenty houses or so on it in 1918, according to Amundsen. So it figures that nobody was living in their neighbors' laps."

"Considering how few there were, a fair percentage of them stayed put."

"Home owners."

"The Amundsens, the old maid, Miss—?"

46

"Dunbar. Miss Bessie Dunbar. Henry Reilly, who was only a kid at the time, and Mrs. Snyder, twice married and living there with her first husband in 1918."

"You're sure it's less than twenty years ago that he died?"

Casciello nodded. "The Amundsens back her up on it. Miss Dunbar too."

"What's she like?"

"Little old maid. Honest and reliable, I'd say. They all seem to be."

"And none of them ever heard of the Scotts."

"That's right and they're all that's left to ask. Everyone else who lived on Walnut Street then is dead or moved away a long time ago. But I've got no reason not to believe the ones still there when they tell me there was no Mr. and Mrs. Scott living on the street in 1918 or any other couple where the husband died suddenly or dropped out of sight. Can you think of any reason why they'd all be lying about it?"

"No."

"That's how I figure it."

"I've been looking at the city map," Egan said next. He took the map out of his desk. "Have you noticed that all the streets running off South Main are named after trees in alphabetical order? Ash, Beech, Cedar, Chestnut, and so forth. Walnut's the last one right on the city line. Spruce is the one just before it and then comes Pine. Henning lived on Pine Street in 1918."

"Where'd you find that out?"

"From a 1918 city directory. I called the Municipal Building and one of the girls looked it up for me. James Henning, embalmer."

"It's nice to be able to pull rank," Casciello remarked. "Anything I want to know, I have to go and look it up myself."

"You need the exercise."

Casciello chose to ignore this. He said, "So Henning was a neighbor of the Scotts. But they weren't living under that name on Walnut Street. No matter what name they were using, it's funny no one remembers them, the husband of the couple dying suddenly or dropping out of sight. I even put it on the basis of a couple who moved away in a hurry with the wife telling the neighbors that her husband had gone on ahead to take a new job or something. Nobody remembered anything like that. It's a long time ago, but still—"

"We must be missing a different kind of a setup or else Mrs. Scott told a fancier story," Egan stated. "She had to account for her husband's disappearance somehow."

"Maybe there was something going on between her and Henning," Casciello suggested. "When did he get married? Maybe he married her."

"Well, that's a thought. But if Mrs. Henning was Eliza Jane Upton, she's dead. Henning died four years ago. D'Amato, who bought the funeral home from her, said she died about two years ago."

"They have any children?"

"Two daughters, both married for years and no longer living in Chatham." Egan reached for the phone book, looked up the number of the funeral home and dialed it. He asked to speak to D'Amato and when he came on the line, said, "Lieutenant Egan, Mr. D'Amato. Do you happen to know when the Hennings were married?"

Casciello sighed. He could see himself on his way back to the Municipal Building to look up the marriage certificate.

"Early twenties, you think?" Egan said into the phone. "Well, that's close enough. One more thing: do you know what Mrs. Henning's maiden name was?"

D'Amato, Casciello gathered, didn't.

Lieutenant Egan hung up and said, "It shouldn't be hard to track down. Start with 1920 and work up."

"Maybe they were married somewhere else."

"Maybe," Egan agreed cheerfully. "Wait a minute, though. There's an easier way to do it. Mrs. Henning died in Chatham two years ago. Her death certificate will give you her maiden name, the date and place of her birth, and all the rest of it."

Casciello got to his feet. "I hope she was Eliza Jane Upton. That would bring the whole nutty case to an end, wouldn't it?"

"I suppose so. But if Mrs. Henning wasn't Eliza Jane, I have another thought about Scott's occupation. He was supposed to be a salesman. We could try some of the bigger firms around here. Or we could begin with the department stores."

"Don't they call their help clerks?"

"They call them salesmen or saleswomen too." Egan's tone was firm. Casciello foresaw that the department stores would be included in his rounds—unless Mrs. Henning's maiden name had been Eliza Jane Upton.

He picked up his hat and left.

He was back within the hour, so soon that Egan thought the case was about to be closed with Mrs. Henning identified as Eliza Jane.

But Casciello's announcement was to the opposite effect. "Her maiden name was Boone," he said. "Gladys Ruth Boone. She was born in Chatham in 1896, daughter of Andrew and Gladys Johnson Boone. Don't know why the mother wanted to name her daughter after herself. I don't like Gladys for a name. I looked up the marriage certificate too. She married Henning in September 1922."

"How old was he at the time?"

"Twenty-nine. Must have been born in 1893."

"He bought the funeral home from Morton just before he was married. The summer of 1922, D'Amato said. But it was long before his time. Well, anyway, the case is still alive."

"It's got a new twist, though."

"Oh. Let's hear about it."

Casciello sat down. "When I got over to the town clerk's office today I watched the girl who works there look something up for someone else. If you can give her the name and the exact date, she'll whip the book open to the right page and read it off to you. That's what she did the other day when I had her look up Scott's death certificate. Today I got to thinking about it and I asked her to get out that book again and let me look at it myself just to make sure I hadn't missed anything."

Casciello paused and couldn't help looking pleased with himself as he continued, "It was all like she read it off to me, but she'd just looked at that one name. They're listed for each month by the date of death and all she'd looked at was Melvin Arthur Scott. On the opposite page there was a Malcolm Arthur Scott who died the same day of Spanish influenza. Henning was the undertaker and Dr.

50

Young signed the death certificate. Malcolm Scott was forty-five years old and lived clear across town from Walnut Street on Carmote Avenue."

"Well," said Egan. "Malcolm Arthur Scott, Melvin Arthur Scott. Same cause of death, same doctor, same undertaker. No wonder we haven't been able to pick up any trace of them. Sleight of hand with the death certificates?"

"That's what I thought. I asked to see the burial book. Malcolm Scott was buried here in Chatham. His wife's name was Hilda Reid Scott. She was the informant."

Casciello stopped to light a cigarette, missed the ash tray on Egan's desk with the burnt match, and resumed, "You know how doctors handle death certificates, Lieutenant. They fill in the name of the deceased and the cause of death. Then they sign it and give it to the undertaker to get the rest of the information from the next of kin. I had the girl get out the original death certificates on Malcolm and Melvin Scott and studied Dr. Young's handwriting on the two names. The ink was faded and all and the doctor's writing was like hen scratches, anyway, but the more I studied the name Melvin the more it looked to me like it had been changed from something else. If a handwriting expert looked at it, I'm sure he'd back me up."

Egan started to hum "Kathleen Mavourneen," checked himself, and said, "That would mean that all the information on the certificate for Melvin Scott is probably false. Henning was free to put down whatever he pleased. I don't suppose he had any trouble getting the second certificate. He'd just have to tell Dr. Young he'd lost or mislaid the other one."

Casciello nodded. "No reason why the doctor would give it a second thought. He didn't have time to, right around then. You should see the deaths from the flu in October 1918. Pages of them. Like I said about the newspaper obituaries."

"I remember hearing my mother talk about it. She was a nurse. People were dying on the steps of the hospital and doctors dropping in their tracks from exhaustion trying to keep up with their calls. Coffins in such short supply that carpenters were nailing boxes together; undertakers working day and night, going from one place to another to help each other out." Egan shook his head. "It was a hell of a time, I guess. I'm not surprised that Henning got away with what he did. He probably wouldn't have dared try it under normal conditions."

"Funny, how that flu epidemic spread all over the world."

"It was the war, my mother always said. Crowded camps and troopships, and a lot of moving around among civilians. But let's get back to the death certificate. Incidentally, I'll m ake sure you get credit for a nice job on it."

Casciello tried to look modest. "I'm just glad I don't have to waste any more time looking for Mr. and Mrs. Melvin Scott."

"I don't know what's going to be any easier about it," Egan said. "We don't even know the victim's name now. All we have to go on is Eliza Jane Upton's maiden name. I wonder if it would do any good to try to locate Malcolm Scott's family."

Egan made this suggestion halfheartedly. The only likely connection Malcolm Scott had with the case, he thought, was that his death certificate happened to be immediately available to Henning; any other would have served as well.

His thoughts turned to the information put down on the altered certificate. All of it must be presumed false except for the age which would have had to come close to the truth. Henning would have used his embalming skills to conceal the bullet wound but whoever had assisted him in moving the body wouldn't have missed a noticeable age discrepancy. The man who had been buried under the name of Melvin Scott had been somewhere around thirty years old.

Casciello's thoughts were still on Egan's remark about locating Malcolm Scott's family. "I can't see any point to it," he said.

"I guess there isn't." The lieutenant picked up the phone and dialed D'Amato's number again. "I'd like to find out how bodies were handled in 1918," he said. "Can you help me?"

D'Amato laughed. "I was in my cradle back then, Lieutenant, but I'll give it a try."

"Good. Let's start at the beginning. When a call came in, did they always send out two men to collect the body the same as they do today?"

"In most cases, they didn't bring it in to the funeral home at all. The embalming was done in the house and the body put in the coffin and laid out in the house. It was generally the custom for people to be buried from their own homes in those days."

"What happened when someone was being buried out of state?"

"Well, I suppose the body was taken from the house to the train. Or from the church if they had a service there. And don't think of it as a horse-drawn

53

hearse if it came from Morton's. I've heard Henning say he learned to drive while he was still in his teens and that Morton's had a motorized hearse around 1915."

"But when it was just to do the embalming, they didn't send the hearse at all, did they?"

"No, not until they were bringing the coffin."

"Just one more question: Can anyone embalm a body alone or does it take two people?"

"No, one man can handle it all right."

When the lieutenant hung up he reviewed the conversation for Casciello's benefit. It had been possible for Henning to go alone to Scott's house—lacking his real name, they would have to go on referring to the man as Scott—and embalm his body. Once that was taken care of, Egan said, there was no reason why the suddenness of Scott's death wouldn't have passed without question. People sometimes died within hours after coming down with the flu. For all they knew, Eliza Jane might even have had a wake for him.

Another thought occurred to Egan. "Wait a minute, though," he said. "We're thinking of Eliza Jane as Scott's wife because that's what it says on the death certificate. Maybe she was his mistress. Maybe she had a jealous husband who killed him and forced her to help cover it up."

"Or if she was married to the man, maybe she was playing around with Henning and he had a hand in killing him." Casciello's broad face broke into a grin. "Plenty of maybes," he said.

"Yes," Egan said. "We're long on them and short on facts."

54

Chapter 5

As it turned out, they didn't have to look for the Scott family. The center of interest in the mystery skeleton was shifting to Chatham, and Lieutenant Egan, dogged by reporters, gave them a handout the next day on the duplicate death certificates. It was hardly in print before an indignant phone call came in to police headquarters from the former Mrs. Malcolm Arthur Scott demanding to know what they were up to, spreading her first husband's name all over the newspapers when he himself had been lying decently at rest in a Chatham cemetery for over forty years and had never had any connection with a Melvin Arthur Scott.

Casciello was sent out to see her. Widowed for the second time, she was close to eighty but still bright and alert and ready to be co-operative, once her ruffled feathers were smoothed down. But she had no recollection of any unusual incident being related to her first husband's death certificate. A young under-taker—presumably Henning—had come to see her the morning after her husband's death, she said, and she had supplied whatever information he had requested for the death certificate. That was all there was to it.

But Mrs. Scott was a side issue. In the meantime, Lieutenant Egan had phoned John Clarke in Woodbridge and was given an appointment at his home Monday morning. Apparently, Egan thought, he regarded the skeketon as a personal problem that should be kept out of his office.

At 10:30 then, Monday morning, Egan arrived at the big brick Georgian house. Set back from the street, it had a serene and solid dignity, a look of permanency, symbolic of a way of life made possible by the money behind it.

Parking in the turnaround near the front door Egan said to himself, "Nice to be rich. Oh well . . ."

A maid answered the door and took him to John Clarke's study at the end of the hall. It overlooked a terrace where a very pretty girl—it was Betsy but Egan didn't meet her—was stretched out on a chaise longue taking the September sun.

When they were seated the maid served coffee and toasted muffins with jam. Egan ate with relish, his glance surveying the rows of books, the massive old writing table and Sheraton side chairs, and finally coming to rest on John Clarke who was giving no thought to his surroundings at the moment. Under its crest of snowy hair his face had a worried expression. But he limited himself to small talk until Egan finished eating.

Then he said, "About an hour ago, Lieutenant, I had a call from the trust officer of the Collingswood bank. He had some news for me that came as a bolt from the blue. Eliza Jane Upton is my half-aunt. My grandfather Upton was married twice and she was the child of his first marriage which ended in divorce. Then he married my grandmother and my mother was born to them. Both wives were from Boston where my grandfather worked back in the eighties and nineties. My mother told me that he and my grandmother were married in Boston so I assume that he also married his first wife there. If that marriage had taken place in Collingswood I think it would have been so generally known there that it would still be remembered by someone."

"Yes." Egan looked puzzled. "I wonder why your mother never mentioned it to you. It was past history; it had nothing to do with her."

"I know. The only reason that occurs to me is that there was some scandal connected with the first marriage or the divorce. Divorce itself was scandalous enough in those days. Whatever it was, it concerned her father and perhaps she wanted the whole thing to be forgotten."

"But Eliza Jane was your aunt, her half-sister. She kept the very existence of this close relative from you too."

"Yes," John Clarke said. "It's a queer little story, isn't it? It came as a shock to me. I felt that my mother should have told me about it long ago. But from what Jamison, the trust officer, said, it came as an even greater shock to her when her mother died. After all, it hit closer to home with her. Eliza Jane was her half-sister; they had the same father."

"Your mother never knew she had a half-sister until your grandmother died? When was this?"

"In 1915. My grandmother and father were killed

57

in the same accident. Then the bank told my mother about the trust fund my grandfather had set up in his will for Eliza Jane."

"Wait a minute." Egan was making notes. "Let's get the trust fund straightened out."

"There were two of them, one for my mother and one for Eliza Jane. They were for five thousand each. In later years my mother mentioned hers to me. She received the money from it when she became twenty-five."

"And Eliza Jane's?"

"That was a different situation. She was living with her mother and my grandfather apparently had no contact with her. Her whereabouts were unknown at the time my grandfather's will was drawn and at the time of his death."

"Did this trust officer mention what efforts were made to find her?"

John Clarke nodded. "Their file shows that they advertised for her in the Boston papers—her last known place of residence—every year for the first five years after my grandfather's death and less regularly thereafter. Their last advertisement was inserted twenty-five years after he died. Ever since, Jamison said, they've been just sitting it out waiting for the trust to terminate."

"How was it set up?"

"Because her whereabouts were unknown, it was established for what is known as life in being—that is, normal life expectancy—plus twenty-one years."

Egan, turning to a fresh page in his notebook, was interested. "I didn't know they had life expectancy tables that far back."

"Well, according to Jamison, there's quite a bit of correspondence in the file on it. The first ones, the American Experience Tables, came out in the 1860s, but apparently weren't regarded as very accurate by the late nineties when my grandfather was establishing the trust fund. They gave Eliza Jane a life expectancy of only forty-six or -seven years. My grandfather added ten years to what the tables said."

John Clarke was consulting the notes he had made himself while he was on the phone with Jamison. He smiled. "Jamison thought my grandfather was quite smart about it, anticipating the first modern tables that came out around 1900. Based on those figures, Eliza Jane had a life expectancy of fifty-six years. She was born February 5, 1887."

"So she's seventy-five now if she's still alive." Egan, doing mental arithmetic, added, "Fifty-six plus the twenty-one years makes seventy-seven. The trust fund runs out on her seventy-seventh birthday?"

"Yes, in another sixteen months. February 5, 1964."

"How large is it now?"

"Jamison didn't have the exact figures. He'll give them to me later. He's been away for a couple of weeks and just got back to the bank this morning. He apologized for the delay. He'd called the Collingswood police chief and told him who Eliza Jane was before he got in touch with me. It was my impression that the Upton trust fund has been gathering dust in their files so long that no one else at the bank knew much of anything about it."

"No wonder," Egan said.

"Yes, no wonder. He gave me an approximate

figure, though. Somewhere around fifty thousand. It's been conservatively invested, of course." John Clarke smiled wryly. "It's fascinating to think what it would have grown to with less conservative handling and with all the dividends reinvested. General Motors, say, or the big utilities."

Lieutenant Egan laughed. "Looks big enough to me as it is. If Eliza Jane isn't found, who does the money go to when the trust is terminated?"

John Clarke's wry look deepened. "It reverts to my mother or her heirs, so it would come to me. Which puts me rather on the spot to have her found or the fact of her death established so that the money can be turned over to her heirs, if any."

He sighed audibly. "It's bad enough to have her wanted for questioning in a suspected murder but it's going to get much worse when it hits the papers that she's my aunt and that I stand to profit financially by it if she isn't found. God knows in view of what she'd have to face, I'd just as soon she never is. But I can't let it go at that. I'm in a cleft stick. No matter what comes of it, I've got to try to help find her."

Egan nodded. Clarke, apparently, could afford to be an upright man. Fifty thousand dollars didn't mean enough to him to allow it to cast the least shadow of doubt on his good name.

The value placed on any sum of money was always a relative thing, of course. Last spring Egan had investigated a murder committed for a five-hundred-dollar insurance policy.

He asked, "Did this man Jamison say anything about how your mother felt when she was told she had a half-sister?"

"There was a letter from her in the file written not long after she first heard about it, asking the bank to advertise more often in the Boston papers and to try the New Hampshire papers too. This was done but nothing ever came of it. My mother was never able to locate Eliza Jane."

"The trust fund was the only mention of Eliza Jane in your grandfather's will?"

"Yes. Jamison read a copy of the will to me. Aside from the two trust funds established for her and my mother, his entire estate when to my grandmother. I might add that he was in comfortable circumstances but not a man of considerable means."

The real money, Egan reflected, had come from the Clarke side.

"Eliza Jane must have been ten or eleven years old when your grandfather died," he remarked. "Did Jamison say how long it had been since he'd known her whereabouts?"

"The file indicates that he lost contact with her when she was two or three years old."

Egan, not knowing the whole story, the circumstances of the divorce, or the amount of bitterness engendered by it, refrained from passing judgment on the father's neglect of his older daughter.

Whatever the rest of the story was, he felt that John Clarke had no thought of a cover-up but had told him all that he knew of it.

It was the lieutenant's turn. He spoke of their first fruitless efforts to find some trace of Eliza Jane and Melvin Scott and then brought up the duplicate death certificates that left them with the skeleton once again unidentified and only Eliza Jane's maiden name to go on.

"Doesn't look very promising," John Clarke said. "You don't know her married name or her husband's name—assuming it was her husband. The man could have been her lover."

"Yes. One or the other, I should think."

"What's your next step?"

"Well, we've already looked for Melvin Arthur Scott in our 1918 missing-persons file. When New Hampshire sends us a full description we'll check again and go into 1919, too, for anyone at all like him. We'll try the state police, although I don't know if their files go that far back. Never had any occasion to find out."

He shook his head. "Nothing quite like this has ever been handed to me before. I have no proof that it was a murder or, whatever the nature of the crime, that it was committed within my jurisdiction. And look how long ago it happened. I don't know the victim's name or anything about Eliza Jane except her maiden name. I don't know if she's still alive; all I know is that everyone else connected with the case is dead."

Egan paused to lend emphasis to what he was going to say next. "What I'm getting at, Mr. Clarke, is that I can't spend much of my time or the taxpayers' money on it, however intriguing I find it myself."

He smiled and added, "From the police point of view, we have plenty of contemporary crime to keep us going twenty-four hours a day. It's fresh and immediate with witnesses, suspects, evidence, the whole works."

"You mean you'll just drop this investigation?"

"No, not quite that. We'll check whatever we can, like the missing persons files. When we get a report from ballistics in New Hampshire we'll work on the gun. We've got a raft of old records and permits stashed away and we'll see if we can get anything from them. But that's about all we can do."

John Clarke was silent when the lieutenant finished speaking. At last he said, "If that's all that can be done, I don't think Eliza Jane will ever be found. I understand your position, Lieutenant, but it doesn't lessen the difficulties of mine."

Egan hesitated and then replied, "There are reliable private investigators. Would you consider hiring one? If you got hold of a good one who could give it his full time, you might get results from it. For instance, the New Hampshire end needs a lot more attention. Your aunt had some kind of a connection with Collingswood or she wouldn't have known there was an Upton burial lot with room in it for her husband or whatever he was. Maybe that could be tracked down. Or possibly Vital Statistics in Boston or tax records would offer something. There are a number of angles a private investigator could follow up. I should think the bank would be ready to pay a share of the costs out of the trust fund. It would be carrying out the provisions of your grandfather's will."

John Clarke thought about it and said, "It's worth considering, at least."

"If there isn't anyone you'd want to go to around here, perhaps I could recommend someone in Chatham to you."

"Well, as a matter of fact, my firm occasionally requires the services of a private investigator and we've always found the Hughes Agency in Worcester very satisfactory. Owen Hughes heads it up and I understand his son Griff went in with him a couple of years ago. He's acquainted with my son who thinks he has a lot on the ball. There'd be no harm, I guess, in talking it over with them."

They left it at that. Egan went back to Chatham. John Clarke, already late for an appointment, went to his office. When he had a free moment he put in a call to the Hughes Agency in Worcester. It was arranged that Owen Hughes and his son would pay him a visit at eight o'clock that night.

Chapter 6

"Well . . . some joint," Griff Hughes commented as he turned onto the Clarke driveway. "So this is where Sam lives."

"Why not? Somebody has to live in these big places." Owen Hughes got out of the front seat on the passenger side, a man not very tall with gray hair receding from his forehead, shrewd dark eyes under projecting brows, a craggy face, and a figure that matched except for a distinct little pot at the waistline.

Griffith Hughes, never called anything but Griff, stood only two inches taller than his father but had the leanness of active youth. His hair and eyebrows were almost black, his eyes unexpectedly light gray in his dark-complexioned face. He had big white teeth that just escaped being prominent and a generally rough-hewn face that would be as craggy as his father's when he grew older.

He had begun to work for his father the last two summers he was in high school and had continued during college as interest in it had gradually got into his blood. It was often plodding stuff; the agency's chief clients were insurance companies, law firms, and business offices. Owen Hughes wouldn't touch a divorce case or anything that looked the least bit dubious to him. The lack of glamorous ladies seeking their services was a worn-out joke between father and son. In spite of this lack, Griff conceded that there was a challenge running through the work. One started with a problem; more often than not it could be solved routinely; but not always; and one could never be sure what case might take a sudden turn that demanded the most intensive efforts.

It was only two years ago when he was a year out of college that Griff had applied for his license, thereby acknowledging to himself and his father that his future lay with the agency. Last year he had started going to law school nights, not with the thought of entering into practice but because much of the agency's work tended toward the field of insurance cases, the investigation of accident and liability claims where legal knowledge would be a particular asset.

Owen Hughes was very happy to have his son come in with him. They had always been close. Griff could barely remember his mother, who had died in his early childhood. His father had never shown the least inclination to remarry.

Owen Hughes was rather an elderly father, thirty-six when his only child was born. Now, at sixty-one, he had to watch his diet and blood pressure and had begun to delegate more and more responsibility to Griff. He employed two other investigators and a stenographer-bookkeeper. These comprised his full-time staff although he had a loose working arrangement with other agencies in key cities in the area. He had been a licensed investigator for thirty-three years; Griff had the greatest respect for the store of knowledge and experience his father could draw upon.

It was twenty-odd miles from their home in a Worcester suburb to Woodbridge. They had just wound up a case for a bonding company involving the head bookkeeper of a firm who had been juggling the books and had rehashed it on the way. Owen Hughes made it a rule not to discuss ahead of time a case they might be asked to take; such discussion, he maintained, would tend to color, however slightly, their approach to it.

Sam came to the door. He had met the elder Hughes before. He said, "How are you, sir?" as they shook hands and then to Griff, "How's it going?"

"Just fine. Any day now they'll be after me to head up the CIA."

"To sweep the floors," Griff's father added.

Sam laughed. "Come on in. Dad's got the whole family lined up for you. He feels that this concerns all of us and that we might all have an idea or two we could contribute."

They went into the spacious center hall with a wide graceful staircase curving up from it. On his right Griff looked into a living room that took up almost the full length of the house. But the conference was not to take place there. Sam led the way past it to his father's study.

The Hugheses hadn't met Kitty before and the elder Hughes hadn't met Betsy either. Griff, who

67

hadn't seen her in years, greeted her with surprise and pleasure. With her poise and piquant prettiness she bore little resemblance to the awkward, shy kid sister he remembered running into occasionally in Worcester with Sam some years ago.

"Well, Betsy." He adopted a paternal tone as they shook hands. "Seems as if you've grown up while I just turned my back."

"Yes, Grampa." She gave him a demure smile.

She'd developed a wild crush on him when she was sixteen and he had all but ignored her. Not now, though. There was sudden interest in his glance. An old wound to her vanity began to heal.

Kitty didn't miss the little byplay. It amused her but she gave Griff an appraising look. She tended to appraise every young man who came within Betsy's orbit. Her husband had pointed out that Betsy would make her own choice when the time came but Kitty had replied that she still had the right to make her own appraisal and went on doing it.

John Clarke made drinks all around. Glancing at the elder Hughes and Griff he said, "I talked this over with my family tonight and we're all in agreement that we should have our own private search made for Eliza Jane Upton and that we'd like your agency to undertake it."

Owen Hughes smiled. "It sounds like quite an assignment, Mr. Clarke. Suppose you tell us the whole story and then we'll see where we stand."

John Clarke sat down and told it, beginning with his arrival in Collingswood and ending with Lieutenant Egan's visit to him that morning.

The elder Hughes sipped his light bourbon and

water. Griff took notes that would be useful to his father when he dictated a summary of their new case to the stenographer.

John Clarke finished his story. His family supplemented it on a few points.

The elder Hughes's shaggy, overhanging brows were drawn together in thought. "Lieutenant Egan is quite right about the New Hampshire end needing more investigation. Does Collingswood have its own newspaper?"

"Yes, an afternoon one."

"Do you know how old it is?"

"It seems to me it goes back pretty far. At one time it was a weekly, I think. My mother used to get it by mail when I was a kid."

Owen Hughes nodded. "A lot of smaller papers began as weeklies. Your grandfather's two marriages may have received mention. I'd also like to know what his obituary said and your great-grandparents'. Eliza Jane would have to come into them as a surviving daughter or granddaughter. Melvin Scott must have had an obituary notice too."

He fell silent for a moment and then continued, "If both your grandfather's marriages took place in Boston they'll be on record there; and also his divorce from his first wife—who brought the suit and on what grounds and when it was granted. Once we have the date the newspapers can be checked to see if it were any sort of *cause célèbre* at the time. An agency in Boston that I've worked with in the past would take care of that end."

He fell silent again and looked at the other man questioningly. "There could be considerable effort and expense involved in this thing, Mr. Clarke. Aside from that, you might not like what we found when we got to the bottom of it. Are you sure in your own mind that you want to go ahead with it? Some things are better let alone, you know. They more or less demand oblivion.''

"Have you seen the afternoon papers, Mr. Hughes?" John Clarke's tone was dry. "They're having quite a field day with the trust fund and the fact that I have an aunt I didn't know existed.''

"Most of them just gave the facts. The tabloids were more sensational, I'll grant.''

"Indeed they were. One I read all but came right out and said that the Clarke money would be used to sweep the whole mess under the rug, cover up a murder and make sure the trust fund comes to me.''

"I asked you not to read them, John," Kitty said.

"I told you I wanted to know what they were saying. Here I am, I've always had a good reputation, I've never been mixed up in anything questionable in my professional or private life and yet I'm made to look like some shyster out to hoodwink the law and get my hands on the trust fund.''

His voice had sharpened. Kitty got up and went to sit on the arm of his chair. She stroked his forehead. "Take it easy, darling. At least here in Woodbridge everyone knows the papers are printing nonsense about you and this is where we live and where it matters. We can't worry about the rest of the world. You're getting much too upset about it.''

He glanced up at her. "It would upset me a lot more not to get to the bottom of this thing.''

"I know." Her hand dropped to his shoulder.

"Just think," she said ruefully, "only a few days ago we'd never heard of Eliza Jane Upton."

Betsy, curled up in a big leather armchair, said, "I feel as if she's been a part of my whole life, that I've known her since the day I was born. I want her found, no matter what comes of it. That is," she gave Griff a lightly challenging smile, "if she can be."

"We'll see," he said.

The talk moved on to what could be done in Chatham. When the conference was over, John Clarke wrote a check for a retainer. The elder Hughes informed him that Griff would do the actual work of the investigation but that he himself would be in over-all charge and that John Clarke could always reach him at the agency office. "I don't do much outside myself any more," he explained. "Getting older. My blood pressure too."

"He sits and thinks up leg work for me," Griff contributed.

"Aren't we lucky, Mr. Hughes?" John Clarke remarked with a smile. "We have our sons following in our footsteps."

"That's right. And imitation is supposed to be the highest form of flattery."

"Listen to them," Sam said to Griff.

The night had turned chilly with the promise of autumn in it. Driving home, Owen Hughes, a devoted gardener said, "I hope we're not going to get an early frost. Did you hear the weather report tonight?"

"No, I didn't. Do you think we'll find her?"

"Sure we will." The father spoke with comfortable assurance. "One way or another. If she's dead we'll

71

find her grave."

"I wonder if she had children."

"We'll find that out when we find her. The first step is for you to get up to New Hampshire tomorrow. Hinkel can take over the Risley case. It's just a matter of a few loose ends left, isn't it?"

"That's about it."

They went over the possible lines of inquiry Griff could pursue in Collingswood and then, hinging on what they revealed, in Chatham. For the most part, Owen Hughes said, it would have to be played by ear.

They were nearly home when Griff remarked, "You'd think Mrs. Clarke would at least have told her own son that she had a half-sister."

"Whatever it was that made her keep it to herself— if it was connected with her father's divorce we may be able to clear that point up—perhaps she hoped she would live until the trust was terminated and John Clarke would never have to know about Eliza Jane."

"Or perhaps she found out something about her half-sister—like a murder, say—" Griff broke off with a laugh. "I'm talking off the top of my head."

"A bad habit," his father said.

Chapter 7

Griff arrived in Collingswood at noon the next day and registered at the inn. After a quick sandwich lunch he made his first stop at the police station to see the chief. It turned out to be mainly a courtesy call except that Dale was firm in asserting that Eliza Jane Upton had never had any open connection with the town. All of the oldest inhabitants, including the old lady who had first mentioned an Upton aunt, had been questioned on that point and none had ever known her or heard of her being in Collingswood.

Griff went next to the *Gazette* office, housed in an old frame building on Main Street with a brick addition in the rear for the pressroom. The staff consisted of the genial editor-publisher and two reporters.

Griff was welcomed cordially and told that the editor had already taken care of one research project for him. The paper, he said, went back to 1926 as a daily and to 1879 as a weekly. He had looked up the October 10, 1918, issue and found Melvin Scott's obituary in it.

"I did a piece on it for today's paper," he added.

"The run will be coming off in about half an hour. If there's anything else you want to look up in our back files just help yourself."

He took Griff into a room off the office. It had one dusty window, a battered table with a drop light over it, and racks filled with bound volumes of the newspaper along the walls. The 1918 volume lay open on the table where the editor had left it.

Griff read the obituary. Under the head, COMMITTAL SERVICE HELD FOR EPIDEMIC VICTIM, it ran:

> Melvin A. Scott of Chatham, Connecticut, who died of influenza on October 5 was buried Tuesday in Hillside Cemetery. The Reverend Mr. Lionel Ketchum of the First Congregational Church officiated at the graveside ceremony.
>
> Mr. Scott, a native of Boston, Massachusetts, was employed as a salesman in Chatham where he had made his home for many years.
>
> He is survived by his wife, Mrs. Elizabeth (Upton) Scott.

"Elizabeth," Griff commented. "I wonder how she got away with that when it was Eliza Jane on Scott's death certificate."

The editor shrugged. "No problem there if she told the undertaker she used Elizabeth in preference to it and asked that it appear that way in the obituary." He laughed. "I guess her maiden name was the only word of truth in the whole thing."

He excused himself a moment later. "Just make yourself at home, Mr. Hughes. Anything you need, ask them in the office. I'll be out in the back shop myself."

Griff went to the racks to look over the volumes. They were in chronological order beginning with 1879. During the half century of publication as a weekly there was a volume for each year. After 1926, when the paper became a daily, there were quarterly volumes.

Griff put back the 1918 volume and took down the 1887 one. He found Eliza Jane's birth recorded in the February 10 issue. It read:

A daughter, Eliza Jane, was born Saturday, February 5th, to Harold and Agnes (Williams) Upton of Boston, Massachusetts. The proud grandparents welcoming their first grandchild are Mr. and Mrs. Barnabas Upton of West Main Street. 'Barney', Collingswood's popular storekeeper, states that his new granddaughter is a bouncing eight-pounder and is named for her grandmother. The equally proud papa, Harold Upton, has been making his home in Boston for the past four years. The *Gazette* offers its congratulations to the whole family.

He skimmed through the rest of the month—surprised at the amount of space given to national and international news in the four-page weekly—but came across no further reference to Eliza Jane.

Harold Upton had gone to Boston in 1883. Griff took down that volume next. Turning the pages he found various references to the Uptons. Mrs. Barnabas Upton was chairman of the cake booth for the church bazaar; she was elected president of her reading club; she gave a tea for a prospective bride. "Barney" Upton caught the first bass of the season; headed a fund-raising drive for new pews for the church; as chairman of the school board presented diplomas to the ninth-grade graduating class of Second District School. His ads appeared regularly as the owner of Upton's general store; a shipment of rubber boots of first quality received; a new line of dress goods; prime beef; a special on barrels of flour.

Mr. and Mrs. Barnabas Upton had been solid citizens, leaders in their community.

In July 1883 under the head, LOCAL MAN ACCEPTS POSITION IN BOSTON, Griff read that Mr. Harold Upton, son of Mr. and Mrs. Barnabas Upton of West Main Street was leaving the following Saturday to take up employment with a wholesale grocer in Boston.

Trying his wings or gaining experience to bring back to his father's store?

The question was left unanswered. Harold Upton had graduated from Collingswood Academy (no public high school in the town in those days?) four years ago and had since been employed by his father. In conclusion, the *Gazette* wished him luck in his new venture.

Four years out of school, he was about twenty-two when he went to Boston, Griff thought.

Skimming the next three volumes Griff found no reference to Harold Upton's marriage until he came to August 19, 1886, and then it didn't take the form of announcement. It appeared in a Social Notes column and read: "Mr. and Mrs. Barnabas Upton will

76

welcome friends at their home Sunday afternoon, August 22nd, to meet their new daughter-in-law, the former Miss Agnes Williams of Boston. She and her husband, Mr. Harold Upton, were married in Boston on August 10th. They will spend a few days with Mr. Upton's parents.''

There was no need to count on the fingers. It had been a shotgun wedding with the bride nearly four months pregnant when she made her bow in Collingswood. Had it begun to show and created an instant flurry of gossip? What kind of clothes were women wearing in 1886? His grandmother used to laugh about what she went through in her girlhood to achieve a wasp waist. Perhaps with tight lacing the new Mrs. Upton had been able to conceal her interesting condition in that far-off summer.

But everyone in the town must have been doing their arithmetic when the following February 5 came around.

Griff went on to later volumes, dipping and skimming, glancing at the social notes and the births, marriages, and deaths.

Harold Upton's divorce received no attention but in April 1890 a brief announcement of his marriage to Miss Christina Margaret Holt of Boston appeared. In August 1890 Barnabas Upton suffered a stroke. By December he was getting around in a wheelchair. In January 1891 the paper offered the item that Mr. Harold Upton had given up his position in Boston and was returning to Collingswood to take charge of the family store. A week later it was reported that he and his wife had arrived and would make their home with his parents.

In June 1891, a respectable fourteen months after her parents' marriage Phoebe Christina Upton was born to them.

Griff went on skimming. Upton store ads continued to appear and the Upton name figured in social and civic affairs. In March 1896 Eliza Jane (Brock) Upton, wife of Barnabas Upton, died at her home on West Main Street following a long illness. In addition to her husband, her survivors included a son Harold and two granddaughters, Eliza Jane and Phoebe.

In May 1898 Barnabas Gridley Upton died at the age of seventy, after having been confined to a wheelchair for several years following a stroke. In spite of the illness of his later years he had continued to take a keen interest in community affairs. He was survived by a son, Harold, and two granddaughters, Eliza Jane and Phoebe.

Harold Upton, Griff discovered in the next volume, had outlived his father by less than a year. In February 1899 his death was recorded under the headline: MERCHANT SUFFERS FATAL FALL, with a subhead, "Community Shocked and Saddened by Death of Harold Upton."

The story read: "Yesterday morning, following the sleet storm of the previous night, Mr. Harold Gridley Upton of West Main Street slipped and fell on an icy step at his home, striking his head on the cement walk. He lapsed instantly into unconsciousness and was carried into his house by neighbors. Dr. Charles St. Pierre was summoned but all his medical skills proved unavailing and after lingering in a coma for several hours Mr. Upton passed on at 4:45 P.M."

The story paid tribute to the business acumen and

industry of the deceased and continued with a biographical sketch of his family background and education, his sojourn in Boston—no mention of his first wife—and return to Collingswood after his father became an invalid. His survivors were listed as his wife, Mrs. Christina (Holt) Upton, and two daughters, Eliza Jane and Phoebe.

The next week's issue contained a detailed account of Harold Upton's funeral. Pallbearers, minister, prominent citizens in attendance, stricken widow, and grieving small daughter all received mention but not the older daughter, the twelve-year-old Eliza Jane, whereabouts unknown.

In September 1899 a story on the first page announced the sale of Upton's General Store to Silas Weaver of Manchester, New Hampshire. Griff, with a start, realized that Weaver's Department Store across the street from the newspaper office probably stood on the site of the original Upton's or nearby it.

He glanced through a few later volumes without finding anything but social notes about Mrs. Harold Upton and skipped past a dozen more to 1915. The paper had grown to eight pages during the years he had skipped and in format and general style seemed more modern.

The mid-February issue contained an account of the car and train collision in Woodbridge that had taken the lives of Phoebe Clarke's husband and mother and their double funeral at Hillside Cemetery.

It was an odd little coincidence, Griff reflected, that sleet storms should have taken the lives of Phoebe Clarke's father, mother, and husband. Her mother had died at fifty-one, her husband at twenty-eight. She was the only one of the four who had lived out a normal life span.

There was no mention of a stepdaughter, Eliza Jane, among Christina Upton's survivors.

It was what Griff expected. Eliza Jane's father and his second wife had, in a manner of speaking, erased her from the family records.

The editor had come into the room while Griff was poring through the back volumes. Today's paper was thrust into his hand and he read the story built around a verbatim account of the Scott obituary. It was almost five o'clock. He bought the editor two drinks at the nearest bar and went his way.

He hesitated getting into his car and then asked directions to the Hillside Cemetery of a passer-by.

The Upton lot, marked by a tall granite shaft, was easy to find. The names and dates of birth and death were already familiar to him. Phoebe Clarke's grave was a fresh mound among the others with the space next to it still open, covered with a tarpaulin and planks.

Griff didn't know why he had come. He stood looking at the graves, new and old and empty, for a moment or two and then turned away.

The sun was low in the west. It was after six o'clock. He might as well go back to the inn for dinner.

A girl with brown hair and hazel eyes sat at the next table. She reminded him a little of Betsy. It occurred to him that a week ago tonight Betsy must have had dinner in this same room.

The following morning he was on the bank's doorstep when it opened. He presented his credentials to the trust officer who brought out the Upton file. They went through it together but it told him nothing of any import that he hadn't already known.

When he mentioned the Scott obituary the trust officer agreed that perhaps someone at the bank should have caught the similarity between Elizabeth and Eliza Jane and looked into it.

"Although," he added, "the fund was already twenty years in being at the time and not necessarily familiar to all the employees. Whoever was handling it may have only glanced at the obituary, not recognizing the name or may not even have seen it at all."

This hypothesis was as good as any, Griff thought as he left the bank. It was all a thing of the past, anyway.

If there had been talk among the older residents of Collingswood about who Elizabeth Upton Scott was, it had not got back to the bank. Perhaps they'd been too busy talking about the inroads of the flu or the war, then in its last stages, to pay much attention to it.

Eliza Jane had found the time just right for burying her husband in Collingswood with a minumum of notice.

Why she had chosen to bury him there at all was another matter.

Griff was ready to leave Collingswood. Before he checked out of the inn he made a phone call to his father and gave him the dates related to Harold Upton's two marriages and divorce in Boston.

When he finished talking with his father he was ready to leave. It was a long drive to Chatham.

Chapter 8

He had lunch and dinner on the road. It was after nine that night when he arrived at the shiny new motor hotel on the fringe of downtown Chatham. As soon as he was settled in he phoned the police station to ask what time he could reach Lieutenant Egan in the morning. Eight o'clock he was told.

He took a shower and went to bed, tired from today's drive on top of yesterday's.

Sleep, however, was slow to come. There were no external reasons for its tardiness. His bed was comfortable and his room quiet, the area where the motel was located being all but deserted at night.

But Griff felt wide awake. He lay on his back, arms under his head, eyes fixed on the ribbed pattern of light on the opposite wall filtering in from the courtyard through the venetian blind.

He thought about Eliza Jane Upton. With the name Scott proved false, he thought of her by her maiden name. He thought about what kind of a girl she had grown up to be, cut off from her father's care and his solid New Hampshire family; and what kind of an environment her mother had provided for her;

and if it had included a stepfather. She had reached womanhood in an Edwardian world, safe and comfortable for people like the Uptons. Assuming that like called to like, Eliza Jane's mother had come from the same kind of world and had reared her daughter in it.

Eliza Jane had reached her twenty-first birthday in 1908. Sometime in the next few years she had probably got married. Most women had children but somehow he didn't think she was one of them. The only real reason he had for this thought was the man who had been killed. If he were her husband, and she'd had children, they wouldn't have been old enough in 1918 to be away from home and it would have been no easy thing to explain the sudden death of their father to them. They couldn't have been told he had died from the flu when he wasn't being buried under his own name; in fact, Griff could think of nothing plausible that she could have said to them. If she had put it on the basis that he had gone away somewhere, the very suddenness of it would have been equally hard to explain.

In any case, police inquiries on Walnut Street had turned up nothing of that kind.

If she'd had a lover who was involved with her in the murder of her husband, Griff couldn't see where it would change her basic problems at all.

Neighbors and children could be left out of the picture, however, if the man who was killed was her lover rather than her husband. He couldn't have lived in Chatham, though; the police would then have had some record of his disappearance.

Even if he'd been a drifter, he must have had a job

or other means of support and a roof over his head, a rented room, at least. When he disappeared he should have left some sort of a gap, a question asked somewhere.

Griff lighted a cigarette and smoked it in the dark turning all this over in his mind, wondering if Eliza Jane had killed the man herself or what role she had played in his death.

Whatever it was, she had got away with it, buried the victim, and come back to Chatham to resume her true identity.

Perhaps she still lived in Chatham, an old woman of seventy-five, the crime committed so long ago dim in her memory, a thing that had happened to someone else.

Perhaps she was dead and buried.

He hoped not. He wanted to find her and learn the answers to all the questions he was now asking himself, including the major one of her relationship with Henning.

Between them they had concocted a bold, resourceful plan for disposal of the body, that perennial stumbling block to successful murder. Eliza Jane had also shown plenty of nerve when she accompanied it to New Hampshire as chief mourner.

She had got away with it for forty-four years and it was only by the merest chance that she hadn't got away with it forever.

If she were still alive, the discovery of the skeleton must have hit her like a bolt from the blue. This very moment, wherever she was, she might be thinking about it, frightened to death that she would be found.

Griff yawned and stubbed out his cigarette, ready

to go to sleep. His last thought made him smile; whatever Eliza Jane was like in the past or the present, Betsy, her great-niece—or half-niece—was a doll. He looked forward to bettering their acquaintance.

He went to sleep.

Right after eight the next morning he called Egan and made an appointment with him for nine.

He had to wait a few minutes at the police station. Then he was shown into Egan's office.

They shook hands. Griff was seated. The lieutenant slumped at his desk, his bright blue eyes the only sign of alertness about him.

"So how's it going?" he asked.

"Oh, background stuff in Collingswood." Griff gave him an outline of it and went on to the inquiries his father was initiating in Boston.

"Detective Casciello's been making some inquiries here, as you probably know," Egan said finally. "But before we go into that—we got a report on the gun yesterday from New Hampshire. I'm not surprised they had a little trouble with it. It was pre-World War I vintage, a .22 derringer pistol, German make. A lot of foreign guns get into the country in wartime. Makes you wonder if the guy was in the armed forces."

"What makes were government issue?"

"Oh, Smith and Wesson .38, Colt .45. Some guys preferred their own. Or it could have been a souvenir."

"Only officers were issued sidearms, weren't they?"

Egan shook his head. "Had an uncle in a machine

gun outfit. They were issued automatics. Other outfits, too, for all I know. Cavalry, for one. I had another uncle who served in it."

Griff smiled. "It seems queer to think that it was used that recently."

"Both sides in Europe were using cavalry in the early stages of the war. You know what they say about general staffs always being ready to fight the last war. Now, of course, we're all real up-to-date with missiles. But in 1917 Fort Ethan Allen in Vermont was a cavalry post and my uncle was stationed there. I guess they had plenty more of them, too."

"Too bad to lose them. They had a lot of color and dash that we don't associate with infantry."

"Won't matter, the next big one. But getting back to this little private killing—a guy in the armed forces would be more apt to get hold of a German pistol than a civilian. He could have been shot with his own gun."

"October 5, 1918, came on a Saturday," Griff said. "Devens would be the nearest place if he were on a weekend pass."

"Let's not forget Ethan Allen. Plattsburg too. Both farther away but possible."

"Yes." Griff paused in thought. "But I'll still go slow on the idea. Plenty of civilians get hold of foreign guns, particularly in wartime."

Egan shrugged. "It's all conjecture at this point. Except for one thing: if the guy was in the armed forces he didn't come from Chatham. The Army or whatever branch of the service he was in, would have asked the Chatham police to look for him and there'd be a record on him somewhere in our files. I had them digging for it yesterday after I got the report on the gun and there wasn't a thing."

Egan went on to say that he had sent out letters to the state police in neighboring states asking them to check their missing persons files. "If they go back far enough," he added. "Not all of them do. I've got plenty of other work to do but I can't seem to let this thing alone. It's the stubborn Irish in me, I guess. You got any of it?"

"No, I'm Welsh descent."

"Well, the Irish and the Welsh have the same Celtic blood."

"And the same habit of getting licked by the English."

Egan chuckled. "And also of picking themselves up off the ground to start another rebellion."

"My grandfather used to belong to some Welsh society whose only reason for being, so far as I ever heard, was to drink to the downfall of the English."

"Zatso?" Egan looked interested. "I thought the Irish had a corner on that."

"Don't leave out the Scots. They got their lumps from the English too. I doubt that they mean it kindly when they call them Sassenachs."

"Nowadays the English are getting plenty of lumps of their own." Egan was laughing but then he shook his head. "I feel bad about it. Although my grandfather would turn over in his grave if he heard me say that . . . But here we are again, off on a tangent."

The lieutenant had taken a liking to Griff but was reminding himself that he had a busy day ahead. He said next, "Let me give you a rundown on what Casciello's picked up."

He gave it with the economy of long practice, Casciello's browsings in Vital Statistics, his inquiries on Walnut Street, his interview with the bona fide Mrs. Malcolm Scott.

He moved on to Henning, pausing to sort out the notes on his desk. "Casciello checked on him the other day. Let's see . . . Born in 1893, licensed as an embalmer in 1914. Father died in 1912, probate records show that his estate consisted of a house on Spruce Street valued at $3100.00, other assets totaling $2600.00, wife Elvira the sole legatee. First listed in the city directory, 1916, employed at Morton's, home address Pine Street. The trouble is," he interpolated, "they didn't have street numbers out that way in 1918. Or area maps. All they have in the town clerk's office is a file by streets with the owners listed. If we had a number for the house the man's body was removed from we might get somewhere tracing the owners or occupants at the time. Not that I have the men to spare for it. I've had to take Casciello off it. We've been having a rash of store breaks over in the West End lately and we had another one a couple of nights ago. I've got several men working on it. They have to be cleared up."

"Did he pick up anything else on Henning?" Griff inquired.

"He brought back an approximate figure on what Henning paid old Morton for the funeral home when he bought him out in 1922. The warranty deed on file with the town clerk just says something about a dollar and other considerations, but it was assessed at the time for eighteen thousand, fifty per cent of its appraised value. God, weren't taxes a cinch back in those days? Fifty per cent—it's sixty-five now—and the mill rate was fourteen compared to forty-nine today. I was figuring out what the taxes on my house would be if—well, that's neither here nor there."

"Nobody thinks of the police as taxpayers," Griff told him with a grin.

"That's right. We just hear about what an expense we are to them." Egan slid lower in his chair and clasped his hands behind his head. He went back to where he had left off on Henning. "He'd only been working for Morton a few years and couldn't have earned enough to save what he'd need for a down payment on a thirty-six-thousand-dollar business. His mother didn't have it to give him from his father's estate. He could have inherited it from some other relative or borrowed it, I suppose, but what interests me is whether he got if for embalming the man's body and keeping his mouth shut about the bullet wound. Did Clarke mention what D'Amato said about how easily it could be worked?"

"Yes, but nothing else that he told you."

"There wasn't anything else after we checked with him on the initial inquiry from the New Hampshire police. I've had a couple of phone conversations with him since but that's about all. I didn't feel there was much more he could tell us. He didn't start working for Henning until 1938."

"Still, maybe I'd better see him." Griff smiled briefly. "It's as good a starting point as any." He was silent for a moment, an inward look in his light gray eyes. Then he said, "If Henning got paid for what he did, he kept the money stashed away somewhere until he bought out Morton. I wonder if his bank would still have a record of it."

"Not of a safe deposit box. I don't know about a

savings account."

"He wouldn't just take it out of a safe deposit box and hand it over in cash to Morton."

"No." Egan started to hum "Loch Lomond," checked himself and tapped a pencil against his teeth instead. Presently he said, "No harm in asking D'Amato the name of his bank. Sometimes people use the same one all their lives. Henning's only dead a few years. With all this microfilming, they should still have some record of his account."

"They're not always so co-operative, though, with private investigators." Griff spoke from experience.

"If you get the name of his bank, give me a call and I'll see what I can do." The lieutenant paused and tapped his teeth with the pencil again. "Naturally, I'd like to hear whatever you find out from them."

"I'll let you know." Griff kept to himself the thought that if it were a current case that Egan had his own men working on, he wouldn't be so ready to hold out a helping hand to a private investigator.

They were both perfectly aware of that but would leave it unmentioned.

Griff had supplied himself with a city map at his motel. Egan marked the route to the funeral home for him and the different route to Walnut Street. He gave him the names and addresses of the people living on it who had been there in 1918. He had touched on Casciello's visits to these people but knew that Griff would want to see them himself.

His last word was that as soon as he could arrange it, he would have someone start going through their old gun permits. Just for the record, he added. He didn't expect much from it.

Chapter 9

The Morton Funeral Home was situated in a big Victorian house that had been its quarters since 1912. Except for the garage and parking lot in back of it, it hadn't changed much since Henning was first employed there in 1915. The street it stood on had changed greatly, though. It had once been an exclusive neighborhood with the funeral home the first to encroach upon it. Now nearly all the imposing properties had been made over into rooming houses or apartments with beauty parlors and other small businesses occupying part of the premises.

A card at the front door offered instructions to ring and walk in. Griff entered a large front hall of subdued decor with viewing rooms opening off it. He was instantly assailed by a heavy odor of flowers. There'd been a funeral that morning was his first thought; not necessarily, he thought next. The carpet beneath his feet, the walls, the woodwork, the furniture must be permeated with the odor. With sorrow, too, and echoes of heartbreak and weeping?

He shook his head at himself over this fancy.

D'Amato himself answered his ring, emerging from a room far down the hall. He looked to be in the middle forties and was short and plump with a broad, amiable face. He had blue eyes and light hair whereas Griff had expected him to be dark, but then remembered that there were fair-complexioned Italians from the north.

D'Amato permitted himself a sigh when Griff introduced himself.

"Well," he said, "come into my office, Mr. Hughes, and we can have a talk there."

Griff followed him down the hall past a smaller viewing room and into his office opposite it.

Aside from the limed oak desk and bank of files, it looked like a private sitting room with its fireplace and thick carpet and easy chairs. But even here the odor of flowers had seeped in. There were none visible. No doubt D'Amato couldn't stand the sight of them, Griff thought with an inner smile. He probably didn't allow one inside his own house and had nothing but green grass and nonflowering shrubs planted around it. When they were seated he said, "I don't know what I can do for you, Mr. Hughes. The police have already asked me about Henning."

"Yes, I know. I've just come from headquarters."

D'Amato sat at his desk. Two framed portraits, yellow with age, hung on the wall behind him. One showed a man with muttonchop whiskers and gates-ajar collar; in the other, the man had a heavy mustache and wore a high stiff collar.

He noticed that Griff was looking at them. "Henry Morton, who founded the business, and Henry,

Junior," he said. "Henning's on the wall in back of you, taken around the time I first knew him."

Griff turned to look at the portrait. It showed a middle-aged man with a thin face dominated by dark-rimmed glasses. A closer look revealed the tightness of the mouth. But no one would take a closer look, Griff thought. Henning was too ordinary-looking to attract notice.

He turned back to D'Amato who said, "What's this all about, anyway? I hope it's not going to make a big stink that will hurt the business. When I bought out Henning's widow the last thing I expected was that something he was mixed up in forty-odd years ago would come home to roost on my doorstep. Morton's is a solid old name. Henning kept it and so have I. I'd hate to think that skeleton in New Hampshire is going to hurt it. I'm just beginning to get my head above water here. It took every cent I could scrape together to make a down payment on the place."

"It's mostly Henning's name that's getting the publicity," Griff said. "I doubt that anyone will hold it against you, Mr. D'Amato."

"I sure as hell hope they don't." The funeral director's tone was moody. "There's no one I could come back on for the good will that went with the business. Mrs. Henning died two years ago and the daughters are married and living away. I don't even remember their married names—and here I am with all the grief dumped in my lap.

"I got out the 1918 book and looked up both the Scott funerals for the police," he said next. "Perfectly straightforward."

"Morton must have said something to him about

93

the similarity of names."

D'Amato gave a shrug. "If Henning said they were brothers or cousins or something Morton wouldn't question it particularly with so many people dying just then." He shook his head. "Imagine trying to get away with it today when we do all the embalming right here on the premises. Henning must have got paid plenty for taking a chance like that, patching up a bullet hole and combing the hair down nice and neat over it. He got away with it, but now it comes back on me."

D'Amato looked at Griff with an injured expression as if it were all his fault.

It was time to divert him from his wrongs, Griff thought. He had a one-track mind on the subject.

"We don't know yet that Henning was paid to do it," he said. "Did he ever reminisce to you about his early days and where he got the money to buy out Morton?"

"Oh, sure. I heard all about it. The poor boy who works hard, saves his money, and makes good. I figured it was a lot of crap. It would have taken him a lifetime to save enough to buy this place out of what he earned in those days."

"Where did you think he got the money?"

"Well, I knew it wasn't from his mother. We buried her a couple of years after I came here to work and you could tell she didn't have much. She lived in a bungalow over on Pine Street, everything very plain and old-fashioned." D'Amato paused for thought. "I guess I had it figured two ways; that he inherited it from some other relative or cut a few corners somewhere on a deal. I knew he wouldn't be

94

above anything like that, but God knows I never dreamed of a body with a bullet in it. Who would?''

He left it there. He had nothing to add except the name of Henning's bank.

Griff called Egan from the nearest pay phone. It was almost 12:30, though, and Egan had just left to go out to lunch. He had a stop to make after that and wasn't expected back much before two.

Griff had lunch in the restaurant of his motel and then went to his room. It would be another half hour before he could reach Egan to have him smooth the way at the bank.

Sprawled out in a deep lounge chair by the window he proceeded to go through the notes he had made since the start of the investigation.

He added one on D'Amato. He had known Henning for years and took it for granted that he had been well paid for what he had done and wasn't above cutting a few corners for money.

Pending what the bank records might offer, Griff had to keep in mind the alternate possibility that Henning had been Eliza Jane's lover and had got money to buy the funeral home from some other source; or from her, four years later, not as a bribe, but as a gift or a loan. In that case, she'd had money of her own; she would have had to wait seven years to have her husband declared dead.

Griff sat looking out the window, his dark face preoccupied. He was reminding himself of still another possibility; that Eliza Jane might have been single or widowed with a husband not entering the picture at all. Casciello's inquiries on Walnut Street had been made before the Scott identification was proved false and had been directed toward a married couple. Griff would ask about a widow or a single woman; his only criterion of status would be that she had lived alone, not with parents or others who would have acted as a brake on her activities.

It was long after two before he could reach Egan who said he would call the bank right away; not that there was any hurry about the closing hour, he added; it was Thursday and the bank would be open until nine o'clock.

It was within walking distance of the motel but a trip that turned out to be as fruitless as it was time-consuming. The record still extant of Henning's account was far too recent to be of interest to Griff. After much checking that eventually included card-board cartons in some remote basement—banks were not such infallible housekeepers as they liked to pretend, Griff reflected—the official he was dealing with said, "We just don't have any records on accounts as old as you're looking for. If we kept them that far back we'd have to move out ourselves to make room for our vaults."

Griff thanked him and left the bank, accepting the fact that Henning's finances in 1918 were lost in the mists of time—or rather, the limitations of vault space.

He went back to the motel for his car but gave his watch a doubtful glance on the way. It was almost 4:30. To get to Walnut Street he would have to go through the heart of the city with the late afternoon traffic slowing him down. He wanted people at leisure when he rang their doorbells; not starting to get their dinner ready.

96

Well, he could at least go and look the street over by daylight.

The traffic was what he expected. He crawled along with it, his map open on the seat beside him. The congestion thinned out when he reached South Main Street. At its midway point it began to take on a residential appearance with houses outnumbering places of business and trees shading it on either side. They were all maples, one of the few trees Griff could identify with confidence.

Ash Street came into view on his right and he glanced down it with the thought that it must have ash trees planted on it. Not necessarily, he corrected himself. Municipal authority was capable of infinite vagaries in naming streets.

He passed Beech, Cedar, Chestnut, and the rest and came to Walnut Street, noticing a sign not far beyond it that said CHATHAM CITY LINE. South Chatham, his map told him, lay on the other side of the line.

Within his range of vision it consisted of a few houses along the road, a gas station, and a snack bar.

He turned onto Walnut Street. It had an established look, a pleasant air of permanence enhanced by full-grown trees and shrubbery. The houses were of varying age and style, most of them dating back thirty or forty years. Middle-middle class, Griff thought, like the whole area. New houses in this bracket, deadly in their sameness, were built in developments and sold at ten to fifteen thousand. These, at least, were refreshingly individual with their diversities of age and architecture.

He drove slowly keeping track of numbers and

singling out the houses he would call at later.

The street was two miles long and at its far end still retained a faintly rural look with an occasional undeveloped lot scattered among the houses. It was easy to picture it as not much more than a country road in 1918.

Walnut Street ran into South End Avenue at a right angle that formed an inverted L. Griff made the turn visualizing the layout at city line as a ladder with South Main Street and South End Avenue as the uprights pointing north and south and the tree-named streets as the rungs.

Heading back toward downtown he passed Spruce Street and then turned right on Pine where Henning had once lived. He didn't know which house it was, but they were all similar to those on Walnut Street and fell into the same general bracket.

Pine Street brought him back to South Main where he turned left toward his motel. He would have an early dinner and then come back to start his calls.

Chapter 10

Griff was back on Walnut Street at seven o'clock that night, trying to erase from his mind what he heard of the people on the list so that he could make his own approach to them.

Mrs. Martha Snyder came first on it starting from South Main. According to Casciello's report she had been widowed about twenty years ago, had remarried, and was perhaps close to seventy but no older.

You could give or take five years from your estimate of most women's age, Griff reflected. He would make his own judgment on Mrs. Snyder's.

She lived in a square box of a house painted green, he remembered from his afternoon survey, and presently slowed to a stop in front of it. The September dusk was deepening but no light showed inside. Nevertheless, he went to the door and rang the bell. No one answered.

His next call was almost as profitless. Henry Reilly, still living in the house where he was born, had been only seven years old in 1918. His wife came from Delaware and had never been in Connecticut until she married him in 1940. Neither of them had known Henning.

Griff had heard all this from Egan but listened to it politely again in the Reilly living room. He asked if Reilly remembered any widow or single woman living alone on Walnut Street in 1918. Then, for good measure, he threw in single men.

Reilly shook his head. "The only people I remember much about from those days are the Amundsens. They had a son my age and we used to play together a lot. Like I told the detective who was here, how much attention does a kid pay to the grownups in his neighborhood unless he knows their children? I don't remember any single woman who lived alone or single man either. If the husband of some couple on the street dropped out of sight it might have stuck in my memory from hearing my mother and father talk about it. But I don't recall anything like that. It'd be different if they were still alive. They'd remember. They knew almost everybody on the street."

"Have they been dead long?" Griff inquired.

"My father died in 1946." Reilly grinned. "Not suddenly in 1918. My mother's gone six years. Thelma and I moved in with her. She was getting on and didn't like being alone. She'd married kind of late, you see. She was thirty-two when I was born."

She couldn't have been Eliza Jane. In 1918, when Reilly was seven, she would have been thirty-nine, too old by eight years.

Griff crossed the Reilly name off his list when he left; the late Mrs. Reilly could be eliminated from it; and, if the dead man were Eliza Jane's husband, he

100

could almost as positively eliminate children from her life. Reilly would have known them and remembered that something had happened to their father.

Miss Dunbar was next on his list. He regarded her with particular interest as a single woman living on the street in 1918.

Lights were turned on in her little white house. Neat was the adjective Griff had applied to it that afternoon; fresh paint, windows sparkling, grass newly cut, shrubbery carefully pruned. He had noticed a tool shed in the back yard but no garage or driveway. Apparently Miss Dunbar did not own a car.

She answered his ring at the door. She was as neat in person as her house, small and slight, with white hair drawn back into an old-fashioned bun on the nape of her neck.

Griff introduced himself.

"Oh yes," she said. "Another detective was here last week about the Scotts. Won't you come in?"

The front door opened into a narrow hall that ran back to the kitchen. Griff could look into it from the front door. A light turned on over the range was reflected off linoleum gleaming with wax.

The living room lay on the left. Miss Dunbar led the way into it and turned off the TV program she had been watching. The room was spotless, comfortably furnished but not at all modern. Some of the walnut pieces looked as if they might have belonged to her mother.

She invited Griff to sit down and seated herself opposite him, her feet placed together on the floor,

101

her back very straight. She was pretty in a prim sort of way. Her skin had healthy pink tones and her eyes were clear blue behind glasses with paler blue frames. Her crisp white blouse and plaid skirt gave her the look of an elderly schoolgirl, accenting some elusive quality of youthfulness about her that Griff couldn't quite pin down. He thought she was in her middle sixties, perhaps three or four years older; but not old enough to be Eliza Jane.

She smoothed down her skirt and said, "I told the detective who was here that I couldn't remember any Scotts on Walnut Street or any couple like them. Now the papers say their name wasn't Scott but I still don't remember them, Mr.—Hughes, did you say?"

"Yes. You lived here with your parents then, Miss Dunbar?"

"Oh no," she replied in her precise, ladylike voice, "both my parents were dead."

Well, Griff thought, and said aloud, "What a shame. You were young to be left alone."

"Not that young," she said with a smile. "I was twenty-five and working as a saleswoman at Gardiner's department store. I wasn't living in this house either. I lived beyond here where the street goes uphill a little. Just over the rise there's a big gray house on your right. Only it was painted red then."

Griff remembered it and nodded.

"It was Mrs. Saunders' house. I lived with her. It was all one house but she had a little apartment fixed up upstairs, a sitting room with an alcove for a bed and a tiny kitchenette and bath. It was after my mother died. I saw her ad and it said very reasonable, looking more for companionship, so I went out to see her. She was a lovely old lady, a widow all alone, her children married and living out of state . . ."

How people rambled, he thought.

"We took to each other right away. She had arthritis and was very deaf but a good, kind woman, always very good to me. We got along just fine. She treated me like her own daughter. I felt terrible when she had the cerebral hemorrhage. It was in the winter, January 1918. They took her to the hospital and her two sons came on from Chicago and Atlanta. She was a little better then and begged to go home and have me take care of her . . ."

Griff composed his face into a sympathetic expression.

"Well, finally I got a leave of absence from Gardiner's to take care of her. She had her bedroom and bath downstairs, anyway, and could help herself a little, so I knew I could manage. The poor thing wasn't much care, although her mind started to wander toward the end. She lived almost a year. Died the last day of December 1918. Then her sons put the house up for sale and I bought this place—they let me have some of her furniture—and I've been here ever since."

"Did you go back to work at Gardiner's?"

"Yes, indeed. I went to work there as a cash girl when I was sixteen and was promoted to silverware and except for the year Mrs. Saunders was sick, I worked there all my life until I retired four years ago."

She was sixty-nine, Griff thought. He had come close in estimating her age.

"You should go see it while you're in Chatham,

Mr. Hughes. It's a beautiful store. The nicest one we have." Miss Dunbar spoke on a note of modest pride. She had been part of it for almost half a century.

Griff tried to imagine it. Standing behind a counter selling silverware, helping radiant brides-to-be pick out their patterns, the years slipping by, their daughters turning up to select their own silverware, granddaughters, too, perhaps, by the time Miss Dunbar retired.

An onlooker's life. Hadn't anyone ever asked her to pick out a pattern of her own? He thought not. He looked at her again and found the word to describe the quality that contributed to her youthful look. It was innocence; virginal, faintly childlike innocence. He had met nuns who possessed it and it was Miss Dunbar's particular quality too.

Once and for all, he dismissed from his mind the least possibility that Miss Dunbar had ever had a lover, much less killed him. She was a born old maid.

She seemed to have run out of reminiscences.

"If you can't remember a couple like the Scotts," Griff said, "what about single women or widows living alone? Can you remember anyone like that, Miss Dunbar?" He smiled. "It's not an easy question, is it? The woman would probably have been dating the man and then he suddenly stopped coming around to see her."

"I can't say I do. But," she gave him a helpless look, "it was so long ago. A single woman or a widow living alone . . . ?"

"A single woman would include a divorcee."

She shook her neat white head. "There wasn't a soul like that, not that I can remember. There may

104

have been someone rooming or boarding on the street, though."

"What about single men?"

"I couldn't begin to name anyone. Wartime and all, there were people who had relatives living with them, working in the factories, and there were a few who rented rooms, I guess. But I'd be the last one who could tell you about them. I was busy taking care of Mrs. Saunders and never did mix much with my neighbors, anyway."

She came to a full stop. Then she said, "In those days, most of the houses were right off South Main Street. There was quite a little cluster of them on both sides, almost as many as there are today. But as soon as you got past them it was different. There weren't more than twenty-odd houses scattered along the rest of the street. It was after the war that a building boom started out this way. We were practically living in the country up until then."

"How did you get back and forth to work?" Griff asked.

"There was a trolley line on South Main Street."

"That was a good walk from here or from the other house. At least a mile, isn't it?"

"Just about. But people walked more than they do today and I never gave it much thought. Then they did away with the trolleys and put in buses. That was handier, of course. The bus comes down Pine Street and up Walnut right past my door, although I must say they don't run them as often as they used to. Everybody seems to have a car nowadays."

"Or two or three," Griff said. "Did you know Henning? He lived on Pine Street at the time."

"Yes, I knew him. His mother and Mrs. Saunders were friends."

"What was he like?"

"I never cared for him myself." Miss Dunbar's ladylike voice took on a severe note. "Not at all. He was a very selfish young man, one to look after Jim Henning and never mind the rest of the world."

Griff probed for details. Miss Dunbar simply repeated herself in different words. Henning was an opportunist who didn't much care what he did to get ahead. Then, when he bought Morton's and got married and moved away from Pine Street, his neglect of his widowed mother was the talk of the neighborhood. She, poor woman, thought the sun rose and set on him and had deserved a better son.

It crossed Griff's mind as he was leaving that some personal wound might lie behind Miss Dunbar's uncompromising attitude toward Henning. They were about the same age. Perhaps she'd been in love with him in her own sedate fashion and got nowhere. Sometimes such wounds never healed.

His next call was on the Amundsens who lived almost at the end of the street. They seated him in their living room, Mr. and Mrs. Amundsen and his sister, Mrs. Hadley, settling themselves in a semicircle around him.

Amundsen looked like a figure out of Norse mythology, an aging giant, his faded blue eyes still piercing, his great hulking body still showing strength, his voice booming with it although from what he said, he must be around eighty.

But he didn't live up to his appearance. He hadn't been a Viking seaman in his youth; he had been a farmer all his life, gradually selling off his land in later years—at considerable profit, Griff gathered—for building lots. He had four children, nineteen grandchildren, and six great-grandchildren, he said.

He did most of the talking. For the moment at least, his rolypoly wife and scrawny sister, widowed, Griff learned, since 1918 when her husband was killed on the Somme, were overshadowed by the strong personality of Nils Amundsen.

Griff, while he listened to him, took a careful look at the two women. Both were well into their seventies, he thought; Mrs. Hadley looked older than her sister-in-law, with her scrawniness emphasizing a network of wrinkles and a stringy throat, whereas Mrs. Amundsen's flesh served to pad out the marks of time. Either of them might have been born in 1887; but Mrs. Hadley, with a Norwegian background, didn't seem a likely candidate to have started life as Eliza Jane Upton.

Amundsen verified this. He and his sister, he said, had come from Norway with their parents when they were children. Their father had worked for a dairyman in northern Connecticut and he had worked for the same man as soon as he was old enough, eventually, with the help of his new father-in-law, getting together the money to buy land on Walnut Street running over into South Chatham.

"That was in 1905," he continued. "We laughed when we were building this house that it was supposed to be on a city street. It was real country around here then. I pastured my first herd where the second house up the street stands today. My wife's uncle used to own this land when there wasn't another house in sight. We worked hard in those days. Young people today don't know what hard work means. But we knew, didn't we, Mama?"

"Indeed we did."

"Were you born in Chatham, Mrs. Amundsen?" Griff inserted.

"No, I'm from Litchfield, Connecticut." Mrs. Amundsen's voice was as soft as her husband's was loud.

Griff looked at her. It was probably nothing more than a choice of words, but she hadn't said she was born in Litchfield.

Amundsen went on to inform Griff that they were following everything in the newspapers about the search for Eliza Jane Upton. "We've done a lot of thinking about it since the detective was here last week," he added. "First my wife would remember somebody who was living here in 1918, then my sister would mention somebody else and then I'd come up with a name. We've been up and down the street time and again and there was no one like that couple, whatever their name was, in the whole neighborhood. I'd be ready to go into court and swear ot it; wouldn't you, Mama?"

"I'd be scared to death to go to court," Mrs. Amundsen said.

"In a manner of speaking, I mean," Amundsen shouted impatiently. "Just a manner of speaking."

"Well, yes, if you want to put it that way," she said with a smile and slightly embarrassed glance at Griff.

As he smiled back he was trying to see her as Eliza Jane having an affair under her sister-in-law's nose and with a husband, four children, and a house to take care of. It seemed farfetched, but he would check it just to be on the safe side.

He asked about single women or widows living alone on Walnut Street and single men living alone or rooming with someone, and thereby precipitated a long discussion and much searching of memories.

It was all in vain. They could think of no one of the right age and situation to have been Eliza Jane or her lover.

"Did you know Henning?" Griff asked next.

"Oh yes, we knew him all right," Amundsen replied. "From the time he was a kid growing up over on Pine Street. Never took to him, though. As soon as I heard he was mixed up in this thing, I knew there was something crooked about it."

His tone was emphatic. Griff laughed. "Miss Dunbar feels the same way. With her, though, I thought it might be more personal. They ever date when they were young?"

"Miss Dunbar and Jim Henning?" Amundsen gave a roar of laughter. "She'd run a mile if a man ever looked at her twice."

"That's not very nice to say, Nils," his sister reproved him. "They were about the same age and she was rather a pretty girl. It's a wonder they never did go out together."

"Maybe Miss Dunbar had more sense," Mrs. Amundsen suggested. "Anyone who knew Jim Henning would soon find out that the only person he was really interested in was himself."

"I notice you still call her Miss Dunbar after all these years," Griff commented.

"She's a reserved little woman," Amundsen said.

"Very pleasant but inclined to keep to herself."

"I've always liked her," Mrs. Amundsen said.

"So have I," Mrs. Hadley agreed.

Griff brought up the question of Eliza Jane and the man living on some other street in the neighborhood.

They had thought of that themselves, Amundsen assured him. They hadn't known everyone on the streets nearby, of course, but among those they knew, there'd been no one who met the requirements.

It was a waste of time to ask the question, Griff thought. It had to be Walnut Street.

He turned the conversation to the Amundsens' children whose birth certificates would supply their mother's maiden name and date and place of birth and was regaled with their names and ages and many achievements.

Directing his attention to Mrs. Hadley, he learned that she had been married in 1917 only a few months before her husband, who belonged to a National Guard unit, was sent overseas.

"You had a lovely wedding, Mary," Mrs. Amundsen reminisced.

"June bride?" Griff queried.

"Yes. It was a beautiful summer day."

She was a bride past the first flush of youth, he speculated, or else much younger than she looked and much younger than her brother.

Mrs. Amundsen contributed the information that the wedding had taken place in the old Evangelical Lutheran church downtown. The church was gone now, she added with a sigh, and so was kind old Pastor Halvorsen.

Griff would confirm Mrs. Hadley's Norwegian

110

birth through her marriage certificate. Not that he doubted a word she said; he would just confirm it.

When he was back in his car he took out his notebook and put down the names and ages of the Amundsen children and appended June 1917 for Mrs. Hadley's marriage.

Going up Walnut Street he slowed down when he came to the Snyders'. There were lights on in the house but it was after ten, too late to pay them a visit tonight.

As he drove on his thoughts turned to what seemed to him a certainty; that whether or not the unknown man had been killed on Walnut Street some house on it was the center of all later activity involved in embalming his body and removing it for shipment to Collingswood.

Henning would have known from the start that he would need an assistant to help him carry the coffin in and out, put it in an outside box and take it to the railroad station. Griff couldn't see him permitting a discrepancy between the address on the death certificate and the address to which he took his assistant. The last thing he'd want would be to raise the least question about that particular corpse.

Therefore, the corpse had been connected in some way with a house on Walnut Street. If Eliza Jane hadn't lived in it herself, she had lived somewhere in the neighborhood and had known Henning well, either as her lover or as a potential hireling.

It was baffling that no one on the street seemed to remember her in any guise at all.

Chapter 11

He phoned Egan from his room the next morning and after he had informed him that the bank had turned out to be a dead end went on to the other inquiries he had made.

The lieutenant agreed that Mrs. Amundsen's background and her sister-in-law's should be verified and took down Griff's data on them. "I'll see if Casciello can't get over to the town clerk's office later today," he said. "Did you pick up anything else on Walnut Street?"

"Nothing much. I still have to see Mrs. Snyder but mostly I need to sort things out. Like the combinations I've been cooking up of Eliza Jane, the man, and Henning."

"What are they?"

Griff enumerated them and added, "But then I come up against the fact that no one on the street remembers a setup that would fit any of them, single woman, widow, single man, or what have you. I can't figure it out."

"There is the possibility that the address was as phony as everything else on the death certificate."

"How could it be? Henning had to bring in an assistant to help him move the body."

"Well, maybe the assistant got a cut too."

"Good lord, don't even suggest such a thing. It would stop us cold."

Egan gave it thought and then said, "I guess I'll withdraw it. Bringing in an assistant makes one too many. For that matter, we don't have any proof that Henning himself got into it for money."

"No, but from what I've heard, he was a money-grabber."

"Another possibility is that people on Walnut Street who could give us information are all dead or moved away," Egan said next. "Don't forget, we're dealing with only four families; not even that when you consider that Reilly was just a kid back then. I suppose you could get a list of the 1918 owners from the assessor's office. Renters, too, I think. But some of the houses must have changed hands several times since. It would be a hell of a job to track them all down. To say nothing of those that have died."

"Or were subletting at the time. Kee-rist, that's a new one I just thought up."

Egan grinned into the mouthpiece. "Skip it," he said. "You've thought up enough already."

"Okay. I'll go see Mrs. Snyder now."

"Why don't you drop by around noon? I'll let you know what Casciello finds out in Vital Statistics."

"Fine. That badge comes in handy, doesn't it? I've been in town clerk's offices where they guarded their records like the gold at Fort Knox."

"Join us and you'll have one."

"I don't want to spend my life in Vital Statistics,"

113

Griff said and on that note the conversation ended.

He found Mrs. Snyder home. At first sight she looked like a witch to him. Her gray hair hung in wisps around her wizened face and without her teeth in, her mouth was a sunken slit barely separating a pointed nose and chin. Although it was almost ten o'clock she appeared not to have been out of bed long. She had on a dingy housecoat and a boatlike pair of men's bedroom slippers.

From her first statement, however, it developed that she had been up for hours and had got her husband off fishing for the day.

"It's his great hobby," she said. "He's been retired for years. Excuse me a minute."

She disappeared up the stairs leaving Griff standing in the living room.

It was as messy as her person. What a slattern, he thought, glancing around him.

When she came back she looked less witchlike. She had put her teeth in.

"Sit down," she said waving to a chair. She sat down herself, lighted a cigarette and went on, "So you're following up that skeleton, too. Looks like Jim Henning had a crooked finger in the pie which don't surprise me in the least. He always was—" she broke off with a shrill laugh. "Well, I won't tell you what he was. You wouldn't think I was a lady if I did."

A lady? Griff looked at her. She puffed on her cigarette letting it hang from the corner of her mouth.

An old hag was more like it. How old? It was impossible to picture her young and alluring, bringing a man to his death.

Her cigarette wagged up and down as she continued, "Jim and I were in school together. Well, I was like in the fourth grade when he was in the first. A sneaky little brat. His mother had him rotten spoiled, my mother always said."

She knocked ash off her cigarette and put it back in her mouth squinting at him through the smoke. "After the detective was here I got to thinking about Jim and the girl friend he had in those days. Good-looking girl with black hair. They kept steady company for almost a year. She worked in some office downtown and boarded with the Bensons up the street. I was trying to remember her name. It's funny how those things slip your mind."

"About how old would you say she was?" Griff asked.

Mrs. Snyder shrugged. "Maybe around his age. Maybe a little younger or a little older. I only knew her by sight. All I remember about her is that she had beautiful black hair."

Mrs. Snyder lapsed into thought. "Seems to me it was kind of a common name. Not like Smith but something fairly common. Not Jones or Brown or Johnson or Anderson . . ."

She tried out several names but it was no use.

"What about the people she boarded with?" Griff said at last. "They might remember."

"The Bensons? They've been dead and gone for years," Mrs. Snyder replied cheerfully. She was a chain smoker. Yesterday's butts, overflowing un-emptied ash trays, bore testimony to it. She lighted a fresh cigarette and went on, "I don't know what

115

became of their children. The girls were a lot older than me. I was—let's see . . . twenty-eight, yes, that's right—at the time myself. So now you know how old I am, Mr. Hughes. I'm not like a lot of women, covering up my age. Born around the corner on South Main Street seventy-two years ago next month. The house has been torn down now. It was always called the old Stafford place. My maiden name was Stafford but," she smiled at him coyly, "I've changed it twice since."

She supplied a wealth of detail about herself; her children and grandchildren by her first husband, the progress of his fatal illness from his first pain to his last breath, and the set of coincidences, predestined, she felt, that had led to her meeting her second husband, a widower, nineteen years ago.

It all had the ring of truth, so much so, Griff thought, that it would be pointless to check her birth record.

He felt almost relieved when he left that Mrs. Snyder couldn't be Eliza Jane. He had formed his own image of that elusive lady, charming, well-bred, caught up in murder through some set of circumstances beyond her control. He had added hazel eyes and a sweet, infectious smile to his image of her. They came, of course, from Betsy Clarke. He laughed at himself.

Henning's girl should be followed up. He would try Miss Dunbar.

Her tidy person and house made a striking contrast to Mrs. Snyder's.

Yes, she said when they were seated, now that he mentioned it, she remembered Jim's girl friend. Her

116

name was Clara something. She had never met her but knew from his mother that she came from somewhere out of town.

No, she didn't recall that Mrs. Henning had ever mentioned the girl's age or why she and Jim had broken up.

Miss Dunbar, trying to remember her last name, asked no questions and gave no indication that she was equating the girl with Eliza Jane. Her manner impersonal, she left that to Griff.

He suggested the phone book as a memory aid. When she came to the Millers she said, "That was her name. Clara Miller."

A moment later she added, "But she's dead. It just came back to me. She boarded one year at Bensons' and two or three years afterward, I met Mrs. Benson one day on the trolley and she told me Clara Miller was dead, I forget from what. She'd gone back to her home town and died there."

"Was it in Connecticut?" Griff asked.

"Yes, it was a small town on the Housatonic River. Not too far away. Thirty or forty miles, maybe. Northford? No, that wasn't it."

"Well," Griff said, "we did all right with the phone book so now let's try a Connecticut road map. I've got one in my car."

He brought it in and suggested that she look through the index of towns. Almost immediately she found the name. It was North Grove.

He thanked her and left. By the time he was downtown it was quarter of twelve, close enough to noon to drop in on Egan.

The police lieutenant said that Casciello was due

117

back from the town clerk's office any minute. He said next that he'd just got a report on the skeleton from New Hampshire. It represented a member of the Caucasian race, six feet tall, weighing approximately 175, between thirty and thirty-five years old at the time of death, and suffering from no injuries or diseases of the bone. The New Hampshire police were not planning a reconstruction of the head and face from the skull.

"Neither am I," Egan said. "Costs money." He changed the subject. "How'd it go with Mrs. Snyder?"

"Well, I picked up something from her. What a hag, though. Be a pleasant change to interview some dish under seventy."

Egan chuckled. "Get yourself a case that's not out of the Ark. What'd she say?"

Griff told him about Clara Miller. He was disregarding the difference in name, he said. A stepfather adopting Eliza Jane could have had hers changed. While they were talking it over Casciello put in his appearance.

He was introduced to Griff, shook hands, and said, "We can forget Mrs. Amundsen. Like she said, she was born in Litchfield, Connecticut. She was twenty-one when their first child was born in 1906 so she's two years older than Eliza Jane. He was twenty-seven, born in Norway. Mrs. Hadley," he consulted his notes, "was married June 9, 1917, born in Norway in 1887. No chicken when she got married."

"And practically no married life before her husband went overseas and got killed," Griff remarked.

"I also looked up Mrs. Snyder while I was at it,"

118

Casciello continued. "She told me she married her first husband in 1911. She was twenty-one then, born in Chatham in 1890. That just leaves Miss Dunbar out of all those young Walnut Street chicks. I don't know where she was born but she said she retired from Gardiner's four years ago so I figured she's sixty-nine now."

"That's what I thought," Griff said. "Gardiner's would have it in their personnel files." He saw that Casciello looked pained and added, "I'll check with them if it seems necessary."

"Maybe we should take care of it now just for the record," Egan said. "Let's see if we can't do it over the phone."

He looked up Gardiner's number, dialed it on an outside line, and asked for the personnel department. He was put through channels to the personnel manager himself and told him that he was interested in whatever information Miss Dunbar had given on herself when she first applied for a job at Gardiner's.

The personnel manager said he would see what they had and call Egan back.

"Sometimes when you pull rank, Lieutenant, the other guy don't trust you," Casciello observed with some satisfaction. "He could of told you to hold the line but he wants to be sure it's really you he's talking to."

"It's okay by me if they want to guard their files," Egan said.

Presently his phone rang. It was the personnel manager calling him back. Egan reached for a pencil and pad and took down the information that Miss Dunbar had gone to work at Gardiner's in 1909. She was then sixteen years old, had attended high school

119

for one year, and had not been previously employed. Her mother, Mrs. Walter Dunbar, was listed as next of kin. Her address was the only other item on the original card. They hadn't kept detailed records on their employees in those days, the personnel manager explained.

Egan thanked him and hung up. "Now we can write off all your Walnut Street chicks," he said. "If she was sixteen in 1909, Miss Dunbar was born in 1893."

"I figured her for sixty-nine," Casciello said.

They went back to Clara Miller. When Griff had finished telling Casciello about her, Egan said to him, "If you want to go out to North Grove this afternoon, I'll try to fix you up with the town clerk. They don't have a police department; there's a resident state trooper. Let's see if I can get hold of him."

He reached for the phone and asked information for the trooper's number in North Grove.

He was home for lunch and answered the phone himself. Egan explained that he wanted clearance for a licensed private detective to look up a death certificate in the town clerk's office. It wasn't a recent one, he added. It went back to the early twenties.

The trooper, who knew Egan, raised no objections. It was arranged that he would meet Griff at the North Grove town hall at three o'clock.

Griff was prompt in arrival. The trooper drove up a few moments later and they shook hands outside the old brick building. It looked like a schoolhouse of an earlier day which it had once been, the trooper informed Griff as they went inside. Now there was a consolidated school on the edge of town, he added.

The town itself had a few stores on its main street, a village green with a Revolutionary War cannon in the middle aimed straight at the town hall, and two or three side streets that circled back to the center. Time had passed it by. It probably didn't look much different now, Griff thought, from the way it had looked half a century ago to the girl he had come to find out about.

They entered the town clerk's office on the first floor. He was an elderly man puttering around in solitary state. He examined Griff's license, took down the number and his name and address. The trooper departed with a nod for both of them.

Griff explained that he didn't know the exact year of death but would start with the 1920 volume.

"What's the name?" the town clerk inquired and when he heard it said, "Clara Miller. I remember her. Older than I was but a very good-looking girl. Never married. Makes you wonder why. I'm not sure myself what year she died. I'll get out two or three books and we'll see." He disappeared into the vault.

Clara Miller had died January 18, 1921, of lobar pneumonia. She was born October 5, 1894, the daughter of Clarence and Hilda Knight Miller.

The trip to North Grove had been made in vain.

It was after five when Griff got back to his motel. He had a bottle of rye in his suitcase. He rang for ice and soda, made himself a drink, and sat down at the telephone with it to call his father, catching him at the agency office just as he was about to leave.

The elder Hughes listened to his summary of the past two days, inserting a question now and then, and said at the end, "Well, let's face it, it doesn't look too promising. I must say I can't understand myself

121

why the people on Walnut Street have so little to offer. We're missing something, I'm afraid, although I've no idea what it is."

After a moment's thought, he added, "Why don't you try to locate some of Henning's old neighbors on Pine Street tomorrow? Perhaps you can pick up something from them."

"Well, I'll try it," Griff said. "For lack of a better lead."

His father continued, "Ryan phoned me from Boston this afternoon. He's had a couple of men working on it for nearly three days with nothing much to show for it. I asked him to get a preliminary report in the mail for me to take to Clarke tomorrow night. He called me today and I suggested that I'd have you come home over the weekend so we could talk it all over. He's invited us to dinner tomorrow night. We'll have a little conference and see where we stand."

"Do you think he's ready to drop the whole thing?"

"No, he didn't give me that impression at all. But unless we have some prospect of results soon, I'll recommend it to him. I didn't build up a good reputation by letting clients throw their money away on phantom cases."

"Well then, I'll be home about five tomorrow." Griff's thoughts turned to Betsy. "The whole family going to be there for the conference tomorrow night?"

"So I gathered. They show lots of togetherness on their problems, don't they?"

Was there a shade of wistfulness in his father's

voice as if he were thinking of Griff's mother, dead for twenty years?

Griff said warmly, "Like us, Dad? Hughes and son, togetherness all over the place."

"Yes, that's right." His tone told Griff that he was smiling. "See you tomorrow."

Griff made himself another drink and went back to the phone. Egan had given him his home number saying that he'd be interested to hear what came of the trip to North Grove.

Griff told him about it and that he was going home for the weekend. He had dinner and went to see a film on Africa.

He spent Saturday morning on Pine Street. A call to D'Amato supplied him with Henning's street number and Griff made it his starting point.

But the woman who came to the door had never heard of Henning until his name appeared in the papers. She had bought the house only three years ago, she said, and suggested that Griff try the old lady across the way; she had lived on Pine Street all her married life.

He went to see the old lady who had been a friend of Henning's mother and had known him from his early childhood. She said he had gone steady with three or four different girls before he was married but could recall no names. She sent him to another old lady up the street.

Shunted from one to another, Griff spent the morning in futile inquiries.

He checked out of the motel after lunch. But he expected to be back and made a reservation for Sunday night.

Chapter 12

The day had brought a renascence of summer that lingered into the evening. The Clarkes served drinks before dinner on the terrace. Beyond it a lily pool reflected the slanting rays of the sun. The lawn was shaded by oaks and maples while in the foreground a mountain ash, bright with berries, struck a different color note.

Griff, deep in a comfortable chair, looked about him with an appreciative eye. The two older men and Sam were talking about the coming state primary, discussion of Eliza Jane having been postponed until after dinner. Griff listened with half an ear and remarked to his hostess, "I can't think of a nicer spot for having a drink."

"We just about live out here all summer," Kitty Clarke replied. "I thought of serving dinner out here tonight but it starts to get chilly this time of year as soon as the sun goes down. After all, September's half over."

"Yes." Griff's glance went to Betsy stretched out on a chaise longue next to where her mother sat. "When do you leave for school?"

"The twenty-fifth, a week from Tuesday."

"Starting to get organized?"

"Well, not really." As a reminder of her adult status she added, "I'm a senior, you know, and each year I seem to take less with me. My freshman year, you should have seen the way the car was loaded down."

Sam drifted away from his elders and pushed her feet aside to make room for himself on the chaise longue. "Griff and I have forgotten all about packing for school, it's so far behind us," he said.

"You should talk," Betsy said. "The ink's hardly dry on your diploma from law school."

"That will do, infant."

It would be a pleasure to kill him, Betsy thought.

John Clarke said, "Sam, will you take care of refills all around?"

Sam collected glasses and took them over to the portable bar. Betsy carried around a tray of hors d'oeuvres and went back to her place on the chaise longue.

Sam sat down on the foot of it again and said to Griff, "Hey, you know Kip Massey, don't you? I ran into him in Worcester the other day and he told me he's getting married in December. Some girl from Buffalo."

"What d'you know," Griff said. "The ranks are thinning."

A sense of discouragement settled over Betsy as they went on talking about the marital status of their various acquaintances. Griff was Sam's age, almost five years older than she. He seemed aware of her, yes, but basically he probably still thought of her as

125

Sam's kid sister.

He had fabulous eyes, that light color against his dark skin. He didn't need to be handsome. Most handsome men were boring. She'd take Griff any time. If she could get him.

She fell into a daydream in which she invited him for fall weekend. She wore her new beige to the dance and he told her she looked beautiful. Everything was wild and cool and they had a marvelous time . . .

The talk eddied around her daydreaming head. She felt Griff's gaze on her and tried to look interestingly aloof. Then her sense of humor asserted itself. How hammy could she get? She gave him a warm smile.

He fell in step beside her when they went in to dinner.

They had coffee in the living room. The maid brought it in and withdrew. Kitty filled the cups and Betsy handed them around. Her father set his cup down on the mantel and remained standing with his elbow resting on it.

He had come to a first-name basis with Owen Hughes and said, "Well, where do we begin, Owen?"

"I think that before we hear from Griff, we might as well clear the decks by going over what Ryan picked up in Boston. He'll send in a full report later . . . No, thank you, Betsy." Declining cream and sugar, the elder Hughes took a cautious sip of his coffee. It was burning hot. He put the cup down on the table beside him, got out his notes and said, "It doesn't come to much but here it is: Harold Gridley Upton, Agnes Frances Williams married in Boston, August 10, 1886; she was twenty-seven, he was

126

twenty-six. Ryan includes the names of her parents and the witnesses but didn't attempt to follow them up in the kind of general investigation I asked him to make. Agnes's home address is now a part of Boston University. Harold was granted a divorce from her May 3, 1889, on the grounds of adultery.

"According to the testimony, Agnes left her husband on January 25, 1888—that would have been shortly before Eliza Jane had her first birthday—and set up housekeeping in her own flat. In the divorce suit Harold didn't ask for Eliza Jane's custody but was granted visitation rights."

Owen Hughes glanced up from his notes and said, "There's no way to tell after this lapse of time what private arrangements were made between them; but Ryan thought from reading between the lines that there might have been a certain amount of collusion in the divorce action."

He went on, "Joseph O'Neill was the name of the correspondent. He was listed in the Boston city directory for 1889 at the address given in the writ but not thereafter. Considering the Irish population of Boston, then as well as now, you can imagine how much help his name would be in tracing him. He was listed as a clerk for a firm long out of existence. There is no record of a marriage between him and Agnes—at least not in Boston—for three years after the divorce which is as far as Ryan carried the search; nor is there a record of Agnes's marriage to anyone else."

Owen Hughes paused to drink his coffee. Then he resumed, "The divorce got only routine mention in the newspapers."

"Oh." John Clarke raised an eyebrow. "I wish they

were giving Eliza Jane that kind of treatment now. Although it's at least moved off the first page."

"There's been nothing to keep it there," Owen Hughes said and went back to his notes. "Ryan could pick up no further trace of Agnes. It wasn't a thorough search, of course; it was confined to a check of city directories, phone books and tax records over a ten-year period. The 1890 city directory lists the same address for her that she had at the time of the divorce but from then on she dropped out of sight.

"Ryan then tried to trace Eliza Jane through her school attendance. There probably aren't many schools left that go back that far, but their records are still kept in the files of the administration building. Eliza Jane's name does not appear on them. They were checked from 1892 through 1906 which would be about the outside limit for her to graduate from high school. She had no listing in the phone or city directories through 1916."

Owen Hughes came to a halt. Then he said, "So there it is. As far as Ryan's investigation is concerned, Agnes left Boston, taking her daughter with her, not more than a year after the divorce. For all we know, of course, she may have married O'Neill in some suburban town the day after it was granted. If they left Boston, we don't know whether they went to the other side of the world or to some town that was just a stone's throw away."

"Or if they married at all," John Clarke appended.

"That's right. Or if she married someone else."

"It was over seventy years ago," Sam remarked. "What an undertaking to try to trace them now."

Owen Hughes smiled. "I would say this: anyone can be traced, even the flotsam of Skid Row, if enough time, money, and effort is put into it. Agnes Upton, for an example: Her parents, including her mother under her maiden name, left a record of themselves somewhere. So did the witnesses to her marriage; and O'Neill, who was named in the divorce suit. Vital Statistics, newspapers, obituaries, school and hospital records, in some cases, police records are all sources of information. It might take a small army of investigators to bring it to light but it can be done. But let's go on to Eliza Jane, who is the real object of our search, not her mother. She grew up and went to school somewhere. If not in Boston, the search could fan out to surrounding towns, to private schools, to—but I've made my point, haven't I?"

"Definitely." Sam grinned. "Give or take a few millions, and my Great-aunt Eliza Jane, living or dead, could be found."

"That's the general idea." Owen Hughes drank the rest of his coffee.

"Betsy, will you hand me Mr. Hughes's cup?" Kitty requested, picking up the coffee pot.

Betsy took the cup over to her mother to fill and brought it back to Owen Hughes.

"Thank you." He turned to his son. "Now, Griff, suppose you give us a rundown on your end of it."

As Griff recounted it, it seemed to him that he didn't have much to show for his efforts since Tuesday. But this was not the consensus of the others.

"You're making progress," John Clarke said, "particularly, when you consider how little there is to go on." He had finished his coffee. He picked up his cup and took it to his wife who was seated on a sofa with the coffee service on a low table in front of her. While she poured for him he sat down beside her and said thoughtfully, "You know, I'm inclined to think that the house on Walnut Street was the scene of the shooting as well as the embalming; if he were killed somewhere else, there might have been more of a problem in getting his body to the house than there would be today when almost everyone has a car. That kind of mobility didn't exist in 1918. The majority of people were still dependent on public transportation. A body couldn't very well be moved around on a trolley car."

"How about a wagon or buggy?" Sam inquired. "Weren't they still around?"

"Yes, but they wouldn't be a very fast method of getting a body under cover. Although I remember seeing plenty of them around when I was a kid."

"So do I." Owen Hughes laughed. "If I'd been born ten years sooner, I'd have been one of the small boys yelling 'Get a horse'!"

He added, "You're making a point I hadn't thought of, John. And I'm sure it wouldn't occur to our children, they're so used to having a car at their disposal."

"Well, I can recall a few arguments on that subject with you, Dad, before I got one of my own," Griff reminded his father with a smile. "But I see Mr. Clarke's point about lack of mobility. I don't think there'd have been much risk, anyway, in killing the man right in the house, unless it was in the little settlement off South Main Street where they were close together. A shot from a .22 pistol wouldn't be heard very far away."

He gave it further thought. "I suppose I should qualify that statement. We don't know what time of day or night the shooting took place; or if the weather were warm enough to have doors and windows open or cold enough to have the house shut up tight."

"Well, we can let that question rest for the time being," his father said. "But we can't postpone the question of how the victim's disappearance was explained away. All we know about him is that his name wasn't Melvin Scott; he had a name of his own, though, and some sort of a niche in life."

After a moment's thought Owen Hughes continued, "I can't find any way around your point, Griff, that even if the man were a drifter he had to have means of support and a place to live which gave someone the right to ask what had become of him. Perhaps the question was asked somewhere else, but not in Chatham."

"Or perhaps it indicates that the man was Eliza Jane's husband," Kitty suggested. "For instance, if I killed John, I'd fix up a story that he was called away suddenly on a new job and that I was planning to join him."

Sam, taking her literally, said, "With someone like Dad, you couldn't get away with it. The office would be on your trail and there'd be friends and relatives involved too."

"I'm thinking in terms of Eliza Jane's husband working for someone else. She couldn't get away with it, of course, if he had a profession or business of his own."

"You're still setting up a very special situation," John Clarke objected. "He was only about thirty, but both his parents would have to be dead and there could be no brothers or sisters."

"You're an only child," Kitty pointed out.

"Yes, but I have an uncle still living, a few cousins, and various friends who would want to know where I was, no matter what line of work I followed."

"I'll go along with you, John, on not liking special situations," Owen Hughes made comment. "Although, if the man really was a salesman as the death certificate says, I'd grant he had more freedom to get around than most of us have."

"Well, yes, but not in any responsible job. His company would know he was supposed to be in Chatham and would make inquiries for him there."

"What if he were a door-to-door salesman working on commission?" Griff put in. "With their high turnover, I should think they could drop out of sight without much attention being paid to it. Were there many of them back then?"

"Indeed yes," his father said. "A lot of them were still called peddlers."

"After the nutmeg boys?" Sam couldn't resist murmuring.

Griff looked mildly amused but Betsy wasn't. Why did her brother always have to say something corny at the wrong time and in the wrong place? Too bad he wasn't more like Griff . . .

Owen Hughes set aside his empty cup, folded his hands in his lap, and said, "I don't feel hopeful about it, but I wish Lieutenant Egan could turn up something on the gun. The German make does rather suggest someone in the armed services, although I wouldn't limit my thinking on it to the nearest camps. The man could have been on leave from almost anywhere; or in transit to a new assignment or even on his way overseas."

"And stopping off to pay Eliza Jane a visit?" John Clarke said.

"Yes, that's all it could have been. We know he didn't enter the service from Chatham or Lieutenant Egan would have found a missing report on him in the files."

"What if Eliza Jane put another obituary in the paper under his real name?" Sam contributed.

"Oh." The elder Hughes glanced at him. "You mean without having a genuine death certificate to go with it?"

"Yes." Sam continued, "If the man were in the Army we know she couldn't just send them an obituary notice as proof of his death or make use of it to settle his estate. But if he had any connections with Chatham it would at least serve the purpose of getting people off her back about what had become of him."

"That's quite an idea," Griff said. "As long as no one from Chatham was going to New Hampshire with her, I don't see how they'd find out that he was being buried up there under the name of Scott. Henning could take care of the whole thing for her."

"Using the name of a different town, though, in the second obituary notice," his father inserted. "Collingswood as the place of burial would be conspicuous appearing twice."

"Morton's would present a certain amount of risk too," John Clarke said. "They'd know they weren't handling a funeral under the man's real name and might ask the papers to correct it."

"If Henning waited to put it in until he'd shipped the body to New Hampshire, I think he'd eliminate

133

that risk," Owen Hughes replied. "By the time they saw it at Morton's the funeral would be over and there'd be no point in a correction. They'd just assume it was a mistake, wouldn't they? The papers must have made a lot of them during the epidemic."

"At least it's worth checking," Griff said. "I'll cover the whole week."

"Yes . . ." His father's tone was hesitant and his glance went to the elder Clarke. "That is, if you're sure you want to go on with this, John. We can leave it to the Chatham police, you know, passing on the ideas we've come up with tonight to do what they can with them."

John Clarke shook his head. "Don't forget it was Lieutenant Egan himself who suggested that I hire a private investigator. He made it very plain that the Chatham police could only give it routine attention."

"Well, you took his advice and hired us," Owen Hughes said. "Griff's put in the week on it, plus Ryan's time in Boston and the end is nowhere in sight. What we've been discussing tonight is just theories that may come to nothing. Meanwhile, the bills are running up."

"Let me worry about that. And the Collingswood bank. I've talked with them about it on the phone and in view of the present situation, they're in agreement that every effort should be made to find Eliza Jane. They feel that the trust fund has grown large enough for them to assume part of the expense."

"Well . . ." Owen Hughes gave him a quizzical smile. "Are you also keeping in mind what I said when we took the case—that only God knew what lay at the bottom of it that an investigation might bring to light?"

"Yes, I'm keeping it in mind, but I want to go ahead with it."

Owen Hughes said, "Then Griff will plan to go back to Chatham tomorrow night."

"Is there anything more that could be done in Boston?" John Clarke inquired.

"Not at the moment. If Eliza Jane's mother stayed on there after the divorce, the bank should have located her long ago. Or Ryan's search should have turned up some trace of her. I feel we'll do better to concentrate on Chatham for the time being."

They went on talking about the various possibilities Chatham offered.

"What if money were the motive?" Griff remarked presently. "We're more or less ignoring it just because the setup looks right for the man to have been Eliza Jane's husband or lover. But suppose they had another kind of relationship, such as his being a half-brother—if her mother remarried soon enough for his age to be right—or a cousin on her mother's side? All kinds of family quarrels grow out of money; the division of an inheritance, the settlement of an estate, an unrepaid loan or even the weekly grocery money."

"Well, leaving out the grocery money, we still come back to the lack of a death certificate in the man's real name," his father said. "Eliza Jane would have had to wait seven years to establish the fact of death and collect any inheritance."

"There are other motives too." Betsy was venturing an opinion. "You read them in the papers. Some of them sound just plain wacky."

"They sure are, but they exist." Griff smiled at her. "You might say we're only scratching the surface with ours, Betsy."

"Yes, that's right," Owen Hughes said. "But I think we've done enough of it for one session. If we keep on we'll end up in a state of total confusion."

He got to his feet. "Griff, shall we be on our way?"

"It's not late," Sam protested. "If your father wants to go home, Griff, why don't you let him take the car and I'll run you home later? Maybe we could go over to the lake and have a couple of beers at Kenmore's. I hear they've got a good band there this week."

"Fine," Griff said. "You mind driving my car home, Dad?" He reached into his pocket for the keys.

"Not at all." Owen Hughes took them from him.

Griff glanced at Betsy. "Why don't you come along too?"

"Okay with me," Sam said. "Come on along."

"Sure, why not." Betsy unfolded herself from her chair. "I'd better get a sweater, though. I'll be right down."

She said good night to the elder Hughes and left. She tried to make her exit from the room casual. She felt as if she floated out on air.

Chapter 13

Betsy broke a date she had already made when Griff called her Sunday afternoon and suggested that they go out to the lake again and have pizza. He picked her up at five and with the drive to Chatham ahead, took her home soon after nine.

It was the first time they had been alone together. Their attitude toward each other was even more tentative and exploratory than most relationships in the early stages, touched as it was with awareness on both sides that she was Sam's kid sister and that he was presently working on an investigation for her father.

Still, they made considerable progress in the few short hours that seemed to fly by. Betsy was happy over the warmth in his voice when he said good night to her at her door. Griff took away with him the memory of her last smile and a sense that she was a very attractive girl. He had enjoyed every minute of her company and was flattered, too, by the deference she gave his views on whatever subject came up.

His suitcase was in his car. He drove straight to Chatham from Betsy's house, arriving at the motel around midnight.

He began his working day the next morning at the office of the *Free Lance-Star* where he was soon settled in front of a viewer in the newspaper's library to look at October 1918 issues on microfilm.

He started with the October edition, giving himself five days' leeway on the recorded date of death, and scanning the news columns as well as the obituaries for an item that might be related to his quest.

The headlines brought home the scope of the flu epidemic. They ran: SHARP INCREASE IN INFLUENZA CASES IN CONNECTICUT; RED CROSS WILL BE MOBILIZED TO FIGHT EPIDEMIC; and on later dates: HEALTH BOARD ORDERS TROLLEY COMPANY TO AIR AND CLEAN CARS—PUTS BAN ON CARD PLAYING IN SALOONS: GRIP EPIDEMIC PASSES PEAK IN ARMY CAMPS; PUBLIC HEALTH SERVICE DIRECTING FIGHT AGAINST EPIDEMIC IN 30 STATES; SPANISH INFLUENZA SPREADING THROUGH ENTIRE COUNTRY. And later: EPIDEMIC PASSES PEAK; CONNECTICUT TOTAL ESTIMATED AT 110,000.

There were days early in the month when the obituaries, even in shortened form, filled a page or nearly, and on one day ran over onto another page.

But from peak to decline Griff found no death that met the three major requirements; a man in his early thirties whose funeral was in Morton's charge and whose burial would take place, if not in New Hampshire, then in some other state well removed from the immediate area.

138

There were obituaries that he paused over but in each case one of the requirements was lacking; the age was too far off or a different funeral home was in charge or the place of burial was not far enough removed from Chatham.

The October 12 obituaries were the last he read, but he continued to scan the news columns for the rest of the month without coming upon anything that suggested a link with the death of the unknown man.

The *Free Lance-Star* was Chatham's morning newspaper. He decided he'd better not overlook the afternoon paper; its obituary pages were bound to include some names that were different from those he had read. He went on to the *Globe*'s office.

When he had gone through the paper's October output without result he was ready to concede that no obituary had appeared under the man's real name. Either Henning and Eliza Jane hadn't thought of it or the man was so completely unknown in Chatham that there'd been no need of it.

The reason didn't matter; Sam's idea had fizzled out.

The morning was nearly gone when Griff emerged from the *Globe*'s office. He might as well drop by at police headquarters and see if Egan were available.

He had become a familiar figure at headquarters in the past week. The desk man gave him a friendly greeting but said that Lieutenant Egan wasn't in and that he didn't know just when he would be back.

"He's out on a murder case," the desk man added. "There was a fire in a house on Fisherman's Lane this morning and when they got it out they found a man's body in the bedroom with the head bashed in.

No telling how long the lieutenant will be over there but if you want to stop in late this afternoon you might catch him."

"If I have a chance," Griff said. "Was the fire started to cover up the murder?"

"Looks that way. It's not the first time it's been tried and it won't be the last. But it never works."

The desk man shook his head more in sorrow than in anger. "Wouldn't you think the dopes would know it by this time and try something else?"

Griff laughed. "Think how much easier it makes a policeman's lot that they never learn."

"Yeah, there's always that."

Griff said perhaps he would try to catch the lieutenant later.

On the way to his car he thought about how simple and clear-cut Egan's present task seemed. He was working on a murder just committed, gathering evidence and following up leads as fresh as the crime itself; he didn't have to burrow into ancient records and newspaper files. Witnesses would be right at hand or within easy reach, their stories vivid in their minds; they wouldn't be trying to remember events so far back in time that they were gone beyond recall; and none would be in their graves or lost sight of years ago.

There was more challenge, no doubt, in what he was doing, working mostly by himself without the facilities of a police organization at his disposal twenty-four hours a day. But—he smiled at the thought—his case had its fantastic side; such as asking about a door-to-door salesman—or peddler—six feet tall, weighing around 175 pounds, who had pushed his wares on Walnut Street forty-odd years ago and then, all at once, was seen no more.

His other questions might be less fantastic but would be directed toward the same remote past.

After lunch he repaired to the assessor's office in the Municipal Building.

The girl who came to the counter looked taken aback when he stated his errand. She'd have to ask someone else about their 1918 records, she said. Griff was moved up into higher echelons and eventually into the office of the assessor himself.

"Well," the assessor said, "so you're looking for the names of homeowners on Walnut Street in 1918."

"Renters, too, if you have them," Griff said.

"Assuming they owned taxable personal property, a car, a piano, something of that sort, they're in the rate book." He smiled cheerfully. "One way or another, we manage to catch most people. But there were no street books back then. The rate book was prepared for the tax collector in alphabetical order from the grand list. Quite a job to go through it looking for names on Walnut Street. I don't know what the population of Chatham was in those days, but it must have been at least ninety thousand."

"I guess I'll have to tackle it," Griff said.

"Well, let's see now . . ." The assessor rubbed his chin in thought. "We'll have to look for it in the back vaults. It may take a little while."

It took thirty-five minutes. Waiting in the outer office, Griff kept track of the time and wondered what the back vaults of banks and municipalities were really like. A clerk finally appeared with the rate book and Griff was given the use of a table at which

141

to work.

At quarter of five when the office began to take on the bustle of closing time he was three fourths of the way through the book and had compiled a list of thirty-six names. He turned it over to the girl at the counter and told her that he would like to have the use of it again in the morning.

Egan had got back to the police station and could spare a few minutes for Griff. He said the investigation of the Fisherman's Lane murder was moving along well. They had the murderer's identity and motive—a quarrel over a woman—established. He had been seen among the spectators at the fire and presumably had gone into hiding in the area. They had his known hangouts staked out and should get him soon.

Presently Egan asked about Griff's progress and shook his head over his afternoon in the assessor's office. "There must be an easier way to earn a living," he said.

"Can't afford to leave any stone unturned," Griff informed him and then came to the purpose of his visit. "The foreign-make gun bothers me," he said. "I wonder if we're paying enough attention to the possibility that the man was in service."

"I was giving that some thought myself over the weekend," Egan replied. "I had a letter Saturday from the Massachusetts state police that what records they have from 1918 on missing persons show no one who could have been our man. All our inquiries for a civilian seem to come to a dead end."

"I should think a serviceman who failed to return to his post would eventually get put on the deserters list," Griff said. "They must still have records on them buried somewhere in Washington. The Adjutant General's office. Or Archives, perhaps, for World War I."

Lieutenant Egan raised his eyebrows. "I'm to make the inquiry to give it official status?"

"Well, yes, now that you mention it."

"I can see the letter now," Egan said. "Man's name and rank? We don't know. Branch of service? We don't know; in fact, we don't know if he was ever in it at all. Post from which he vanished? We don't know; anywhere in the United States with special attention to the camps nearest Chatham."

Griff was laughing. "Well, we know a few things about him. His height, weight, race, and approximate age."

"Don't forget his bones," Egan said ironically. "No fractures or diseases. That should help a lot."

But he knew, and Griff knew, that with his interest captured from the start, he was now committed to seeing the case through. He went on protesting a little longer but finally agreed to write to the Adjutant General's office explaining the problem and asking what system of classification was used in the records kept on missing persons and deserters from World War I.

"It'll be a dilly of a letter," he said. "God knows what they'll think of it."

"But they must have some sort of a cross-index system," Griff countered. "Maybe it's the locality from which a man entered the service or his physical description or the date of his disappearance and the name of the camp he was stationed at; something

143

besides his name and rank and branch of service.''

"We'll see," said Egan.

Griff went back to the assessor's office in the morning soon after it opened but it was close to noon before he finished going through the rate book.

Counting married couples as one, he ended up with thirty-nine names. He had crossed off Mrs. Snyder's first husband, Henry Reilly's parents, and Mrs. Saunders.

Early in the afternoon he was ready to start his new round of inquiries on Walnut Street.

He went first to Mrs. Snyder's. Her husband came to the door. He had at least two days' growth of beard on his face and was dressed in a grimy T-shirt that bulged out over his fat belly and sagging trousers. His bare feet were encased in the bedroom slippers Mrs. Snyder had been wearing on Griff's last visit.

Her husband called to her and she trailed into the room as slatternly as before although fully dressed on this occasion. Griff looked at them with the thought that they fitted together, one suggesting the other as in word-association tests; table, chair; black, white; night, day; slob, slattern.

He brought out his list of names and asked Mrs. Snyder to study it to jog her memory. She exclaimed over one or two people on it whom she had completely forgotten. "Why, Mrs. Beaumont," she said. "She was the nicest little woman you'd ever want to meet. Lived up at the corner of Maple Street. But it must be thirty years ago that she moved away. Seems to me her husband lost his job and they couldn't keep up the payments on their house. I don't know what became of them. I haven't seen or heard of

144

them since.''

Mrs. Snyder could recall no woman on the list living with a brother or other male relative; but she was able to assure Griff that three of the people on it were dead.

He crossed off their names and brought up the question of a door-to-door salesman or peddler who had suddenly stopped making his calls.

Mrs. Snyder shook her head. "Heaven's sake," she said, "I couldn't begin to remember who came to my door away back then. Except my tea and coffee man. He came every week for years. But he wasn't a young man. He was at least sixty when I first knew him.''

That was all she had to offer. Griff went on to Miss Dunbar's.

He found her weeding a flower bed, looking her usual neat self in spite of the work she was doing. She took off her garden gloves and laid them on the front step with her tools.

"Shall we sit out here?" she said indicating lawn chairs under a tree.

She had an old-fashioned round straw hat set squarely on her head. Her cotton dress was two or three inches longer than fashion decreed. She wore lisle stockings and black oxfords. Griff smiled to himself, contrasting her with his next-door neighbor at home who must be almost Miss Dunbar's age but who did her gardening in shorts or sometimes in a swim suit to deepen her tan.

He produced his list. Miss Dunbar dutifully went through it and shook her head. She could remember no woman who had lived with a male relative on Walnut Street but could add two more to the three deaths Mrs. Snyder had mentioned.

Griff crossed off their names. His list was down to thirty-four.

Miss Dunbar was watching a robin on the lawn tugging at a worm.

"Poor worm," she said. "I can't help feeling sorry for them." She smiled apologetically. "I guess it's silly of me. I know robins have to eat and they're such useful birds. But worms are useful too."

Griff smiled back at her. "I'm afraid it's a problem without an answer, Miss Dunbar. May I ask another question?"

"Yes." She was still watching the robin.

"Do you remember a door-to-door salesman back in those days who suddenly stopped making his rounds? A tall man in his early thirties. Perhaps he was called a peddler."

She glanced at him in surprise. "You think the man whose skeleton they found was a peddler?"

"I don't know, Miss Dunbar. I'm ready to look into any theory at all."

She searched her memory and brought up Mrs. Snyder's tea and coffee man who had apparently been a neighborhood landmark, and added a peddler of housewares. But he had been short rather than tall and far from disappearing in 1918 had continued to make his rounds for years thereafter.

There had been others, a great many of them, who came and went, but none that stood out in her memory.

The robin, feet braced for a last powerful tug, captured the worm.

"Oh dear," Miss Dunbar said.

Griff went to see the Amundsens and Mrs. Hadley.

After much poring over his list it developed that they had no more to offer than Mrs. Snyder or Miss Dunbar on a woman living with a male relative on Walnut Street. They were the most helpful of all, though, in reducing the size of the list. They knew of five more who were dead and were able to supply the addresses of three others who still lived in Chatham.

When he asked about a peddler the debate that followed lasted longer than all that had gone before, but nothing of value to Griff came of it.

"To tell you the truth, Mr. Hughes," Amundsen boomed, accompanying him out to his car, "I think you're working the wrong street. Yessir, I do. Stands to reason, when we have to say no to whatever you ask us about. I think there was some hocus pocus mixed up in it to make it look as if the whole thing happened on our street."

Griff thought about Amundsen's comment as he drove away. It was all too true that he seemed to be getting nowhere on Walnut Street; but the fact remained that the unknown man's body had been embalmed in some house on the street and taken from it to begin that last journey to New Hampshire. Therefore, he must be at fault himself; either he was asking his questions of the wrong people or asking the right people the wrong questions.

He had his list to refer to next. Someone on it might give him a fresh start. It was too late in the afternoon to hunt up the three whose addresses he had; but after dinner tonight he would see what they could tell him. He had, at the moment, no other leads at all.

*   *   *

From that evening, then, until Friday afternoon Griff concentrated on his list. Here and there along the way he verified the deaths of seven more people on it. One of the first three he went to gave him the address of a fourth. City directories and phone books going back three decades led him to a few others who, in turn, were able to supply leads of their own. In some cases he found out through sons or daughters that the people he sought were deceased. One man, located in a town forty miles away, turned out to be completely senile. Another, tracked down in a town closer by, had just left on a weekend trip.

Griff's list was down to five names when he got back to Chatham late Friday afternoon. So far, no one on it had brought his case one step nearer solution.

He hadn't seen Egan since Monday and stopped at the police station to see if he was in. He might have a little free time right now, Griff thought. The arrest and confession of the Fisherman's Lane murderer had been featured in the *Free Lance-Star* that morning. He had been picked up through the stakeout of his known haunts, thereby revealing the lack of ordinary good sense that the desk man had deplored.

The lieutenant was just going off duty. He suggested that they adjourn to a nearby bar and have a couple of beers.

They walked over to it, Egan shrugging off Griff's comments on the Fisherman's Lane murder. "Just a routine affair," he said. "These dumb jerks who go around killing each other over nothing."

They went into the bar and sat down in a booth

that offered privacy. When their beer was served he asked Griff how things were going with him and was sympathetic over his lack of progress.

"It's damned discouraging," he said, and then, "I wish I could think of something to help you, a different approach to it, or something. Here you are with a whole list of Walnut Street people and you're not getting to first base with any of them. There has to be a reason for it but god only knows what it could be."

As they went on talking about it Griff's edgy mood lessened. Whatever the flaw in his approach, Egan, for all his experience, could not point it out to him.

"Take the weekend off," he said presently. "Go home and talk it over some more with your father and Clarke. You came back with some new ideas last weekend and maybe you'll do the same this time. Or maybe I'll get a report in that will give us a fresh lead. Let's just wait and see what Monday brings."

Griff took his advice. He checked out of his motel and went home to Worcester.

Chapter 14

It was Betsy who pointed the way to the truth for him although he didn't recognize it for what it was at the time.

Her father wasn't available that weekend. He had gone to Rhode Island to attend a conference on city planning and redevelopment.

Griff took Betsy out to dinner Saturday night. She would have no free time Sunday, she said. She and her mother were going to Fitchburg to have dinner with Grace and Mabel Clarke. "You know how old girls like that are," she added. "They'd be mortally offended if I left for school Tuesday without saying good-by to them."

They were having cocktails before dinner. "Will you get home any weekends this fall?" Griff asked.

"I don't really know. Perhaps once before Thanksgiving. I'm going to be loaded with reading courses. I'll be swamped with work."

"Well, if that's the way it's going to be," Griff said, "I'll have to see if I still know the way to Philadelphia. I used to weekend there occasionally a few years ago. Will the red carpet be out?"

"Yards of it," Betsy assured him, her light tone

150

covering up her glow of pleasure.

"You haven't told me what your major is," he continued.

French, she said, with Spanish as an elective. She had vague thoughts of the foreign service but hadn't made any real plans yet.

Presently she asked him how the search for Eliza Jane was progressing.

He talked about how little headway he'd made in the past week and then, in answer to her questions, more generally about his work.

While they were lingering over dessert Griff took out his notebook and said, "I guess I won't see you again before you leave so I'd better get your address and phone number now. By the way, are you Miss Elizabeth Clarke or is it just Betsy?"

"It's Elizabeth." She made a face. "I've never liked it. It always makes me think of portraits of stern maiden aunts looking down their noses at me."

Griff laughed as he looked at her round young face with its sweet mouth and faintly elfish expression. Candlelight on the table brought out flecks of gold he hadn't noticed before in her eyes. She had cat's eyes, he thought. No, they were warm and friendly, not at all inscrutable. He was smiling at the thought as he said, "I can't share that picture of you; I'll just go on calling you Betsy."

"Good. We've had enough Elizabeths in the family. A long line of them, from what Grandma Clarke used to say."

"With variants like Eliza Jane?"

"Yes. I suppose I should be thankful I didn't get that pinned on me."

The waiter brought the check. Griff wrote down

Betsy's school address and phone number and put his notebook away.

He played golf the next morning and sat down with his father after dinner to discuss what their next move should be if the people remaining on his list had no more to offer than those he had already seen. Owen Hughes was still reluctant to take up the search for Eliza Jane from the Boston end, reiterating his belief that it would be a very expensive, time-consuming approach. It was his thought that if Griff got nowhere in Chatham in the next few days they should talk it over with John Clarke again before they did anything else at all.

By seven o'clock that night Griff was on his way back to Chatham. During most of the drive his thoughts were centered on the lack of promising leads in the case at the start of his third week on it, but every so often Betsy came into his mind.

Practically overnight, she seemed to be occupying his thoughts more and more. The last time he could remember a girl becoming that important to him all at once was when he was seventeen and the wonders and woes of falling in love for the first time had burst into his life. There were tenderness and laughter, ruefulness, and touches of nostalgia in his memories of it. He had survived it, eventually recovered from it completely and gone on to other, lighter assays into love. Now there was Betsy, fitting into no particular niche and not to be considered lightly at all.

Her real name was Elizabeth. Eliza Jane was a variant of it; one variant. There were others . . .

*　　　*　　　*

The Amundsens greeted Griff as a friend when he appeared on their doorstep at 9:30 Monday morning. They were kindly people, he reflected. It wouldn't occur to them to say, What, are you back again?

Mrs. Hadley wasn't home. She had left early to spend the day with a friend, they told him.

Mrs. Amundsen announced that she had just made a fresh pot of coffee and invited Griff out to the kitchen to have a cup with them.

When they were seated at the table he made a tentative start. "I've been wondering if very many people on Walnut Street had a car in 1918," he said. "Did you have one, Mr. Amundsen?"

"I sure did." The old man nodded vigorously. "A tin Lizzie. Bought it in 1915 and drove it for six years. More people than you'd think had cars. Nothing like today, of course."

"Miss Dunbar doesn't have one now. Did she have one then?"

"Her?" Amundsen shook his head. "Never owned one in her life. She's such a timid little thing, she'd die of fright behind the wheel of a car, wouldn't she, Mama?"

"Well, I don't know about that." Mrs. Amundsen spoke in defense of her sex. "She doesn't go out a whole lot and I don't suppose she ever felt that she needed one. I doubt that she could have afforded one in 1918 when she was getting ready to buy her house."

"Was that when she bought it?" Amundsen put in. "I thought it was earlier."

"No, Nils." His wife was firm. "She came out here to board with Mrs. Saunders in 1914 before the war started and didn't buy her house until after Mrs. Saunders died. Our Thelma was born in February 1919 and I date Mrs. Saunders' death from that. It was about a month before. I remember I didn't go to her funeral because I felt self-conscious about how big I'd got and all. Nowadays," her aside was for Griff's benefit, "women don't think a thing of it, but in my day we were more inclined to stay home when we were expecting."

Griff hadn't listened too attentively when Miss Dunbar told him the same story herself. He sorted it out and said, "Miss Dunbar first appeared on Walnut Street in 1914 before the war started and boarded with Mrs. Saunders right up until her death. Soon afterward Miss Dunbar bought the house she lives in now. Have I got it straight?"

"Yes, you have," Mrs. Amundsen replied. "I remember meeting her soon after she came out here and thinking what a little slip of a thing she was to be left all alone in the world. Her mother had died just a few months before, Mrs. Saunders said, and she had no other close relatives. I don't know how long she'd been working at Gardiner's when I first met her. She was only about twenty or so at the time but she could have been there several years. Young folks could take out working papers at fourteen in those days."

"A good thing it was too," Amundsen inserted. "A lot of these juvenile delinquents we hear so much about would be better off going to work at fourteen. They don't amount to nothing in school."

"Now, Nils, you know that's not right." It was obviously an old bone of contention between them. "Young people need all the education they can get

154

nowadays if they want to amount to anything."

"I'm not talking about that kind. I'm talking about the kind that won't amount to anything no matter how much you do for them. It's like trying to make a silk purse out of a sow's ear."

"Mrs. Amundsen," Griff intervened, "when you look back on Miss Dunbar as you first knew her, could she have been older than you thought? Four or five years older, perhaps?"

Amundsen protested that it was foolish to try to guess a woman's age. His wife, pondering Griff's question, said she just didn't know. She had never had more than a neighborly association with Miss Dunbar or, for that matter, with Mrs. Saunders before her. She had based her assumption of Miss Dunbar's age on her appearance when she first came to Walnut Street. Looking back now, it was hard to say whether or not she might have been older than she looked at the time.

Griff asked next if Miss Dunbar had ever had a boy friend. The Amundsens were emphatic at first in declaring that in all the years, close to half a century, that Miss Dunbar had lived on Walnut Street, they had never seen her in the company of a man or heard of her going out with one.

Griff went on to her income. He was assured that she had always lived on her present modest scale, making no changes in it since her retirement. She probably had some savings to draw on, Amundsen pointed out. And Social Security to supplement whatever pension, if any, she received from Gardiner's. She couldn't be getting too much from either source, he added. Department stores weren't noted

155

for their high rate of pay, although they'd had to bring it up considerably in recent years.

"In other words, she spent most of her working life in the lower pay brackets," Griff said. "I don't see how she could ever have saved much. Where did you people think she got the money to buy a house?"

Mrs. Amundsen said, "Well, it seems to me we heard that her mother left her a little money. She'd been dead only a few years then, you know."

"Was the mother living in Chatham when she died?" Griff was thinking of probate court. Wills were a matter of public record. He could look up Mrs. Dunbar's and find out the total value of her estate.

"She must have been," Mrs. Amundsen replied. "I remember Mrs. Saunders saying that Miss Dunbar lived with her mother up until she died."

She spoke in an absent tone. Another memory was coming to life in her mind. "Nils," she said, "it seems to me we did see a young man we didn't recognize at Mrs. Saunders' a couple of times. He was wearing a soldier's uniform and we wondered who he was. It's coming back to me now—the first time we saw him we were on our way to church so it must have been a Sunday—and he was going into the shed in back of Mrs. Saunders' house."

"I think you're right, Mama," Amundsen agreed. "It wasn't a shed, though, it was a barn. Small, but a barn. Saunders always kept a horse when he was alive. You got all excited when you saw the fellow, Mama. You said Miss Dunbar must have a sweetheart in the Army. That's women for you." He winked at Griff. "Always trying to marry us poor devils off. But I don't remember that we ever saw him again."

156

"Yes, we did. One other time out in back of the house."

Griff thought that a Sunday visit from a soldier indicated a weekend pass from a camp nearby. "Do you remember when it was that you first saw him, Mrs. Amundsen?" he asked.

"Well, I know it was after Mrs. Saunders had the cerebral hemorrhage because I said to Nils at the time that I didn't see how Miss Dunbar could find time to visit with her soldier friend when she had the full care of Mrs. Saunders."

She paused in thought. "Mrs. Saunders was in bed a year before she died, so it must have been sometime in 1918."

"Spring, summer, fall?" Griff prompted her.

"Let me see . . ." Mrs. Amundsen closed her eyes trying to visualize the scene. "We didn't have the side curtains on; I wasn't looking through them when I saw the soldier going into the shed. I didn't see his face. He was tall, though, and had dark hair. He wasn't wearing a hat . . ." Her eyes flew open in triumph. "There was a rosebush near the shed and it was in full bloom. It must have been in June 1918 that I first saw him. The second time was about a month or so later. But I never got a look at his face."

"Did you mention him to Miss Dunbar?" Griff inquired.

Mrs. Amundsen chuckled. "Of course I did. After all, it was only human, wasn't it? I mentioned it the very next time I saw her. Not that it did me any good. She got a little flustered and then said something about how he was a distant relative and changed the subject."

157

Amundsen looked at Griff with thoughtful mien. "It was a tall man's skeleton they found in New Hampshire," he said. "A young man's. Now you're asking all these questions about Miss Dunbar, Mr. Hughes. Naturally, I'm putting two and two together and it adds up to the soldier being that man. Am I right?"

"I don't know, Mr. Amundsen, but I'm certainly going to try to find out. In the meantime," Griff got to his feet, "I hope you won't mind keeping this conversation to yourselves, just in case it doesn't come to anything." He added with a smile, "You've both been a tremendous help. I can't thank you enough."

Mrs. Amundsen, struck with belated doubts, said that perhaps she'd let her tongue run away with her. She wouldn't want to make trouble for Miss Dunbar; the poor little thing hadn't had much of a life and, nice as she was, couldn't possibly have had anything to do with the murder; she wouldn't hurt a fly.

Amundsen cut her soliloquy short. "Quiet, Mama," he said. "Mr. Hughes is just trying to find out the truth. If Miss Dunbar had nothing to do with it, the truth won't hurt her. If she was mixed up in it, well, she'll have to face the music. Murder is murder whether it happened yesterday or forty-odd years ago. That's right, ain't it, Mr. Hughes?"

"I guess it is," Griff said.

They stood in the doorway and watched him drive off. Mrs. Amundsen looked somewhat quelled but still doubtful about having said too much. It was a reaction not unfamiliar to Griff.

He went first to Gardiner's. Twelve stories high, it

158

was Chatham's oldest and largest department store; but Griff, looking around him as he rode the escalator to the personnel department on the sixth floor, thought that in its present state of elegance it was probably a very different place from what it had been when Miss Dunbar started to work there.

Producing his credentials, he was taken to the personnel manager who asked if his visit was related to Lieutenant Egan's call the other day and then sent for Miss Dunbar's file.

A thin folder was presently laid on his desk. It contained her original employment card, data on her work record and pay rate—she had started at twenty-five cents an hour in 1909 and was earning $1.50 an hour when she retired on March 1, 1958—and her Social Security number.

Gardiner's, it developed, had no pension plan. Long-time employees were given a lump-sum gift of money—a very modest gift, judging by what the help got paid, Griff thought—when they were put out to pasture.

The personnel manager pursed his lips as he looked at Miss Dunbar's address in 1909. "That was a run-down neighborhood as far back as I can remember. It's been completely torn down with redevelopment." He added with a smile, "I imagine that makes life rather difficult sometimes for detectives, doesn't it?"

"Yes, especially when you're looking for an old address."

They talked a minute or two on this subject and Griff then took his leave.

It was going on noon when he got down to the

159

main floor. He found a pay phone and called police headquarters. Egan wasn't in but would be back about three, he was told. After a moment's hesitation he asked for Casciello.

They met fifteen minutes later at the Municipal Building where the long-suffering town clerk groaned at the sight of Casciello. "What year do you want to look up now," he demanded, "1776?"

"Nineteen fourteen," Casciello replied, adding imperturbably, "I don't like ruining my eyesight hunting through your moth-eaten old records any better than you like lugging them up from the basement. On second thought, maybe you better bring 1913 too. We're not sure of the woman's date of death."

"You never are," the town clerk retorted.

Casciello grinned at him and turned to Griff. "If you don't mind, I'll run along and let you do the looking this time. I've got to see someone at one o'clock and I want to grab a bite of lunch first."

"Okay," Griff said. "Thanks for vouching for me."

Casciello left. He had asked no questions about Griff's interest in Mrs. Walter Dunbar. At the moment she was no more to him than another name in the ever-lengthening list he had looked up in Vital Statistics.

But his second thought on the 1913 book saved the town clerk an extra trip to the basement vaults. Agnes Williams Dunbar had died on December 2, 1913. Griff looked at her name almost unbelievingly. His search had come to an end.

She had died of cerebral edema with acute

alcoholism a secondary cause of death.

Acute alcoholism; poor Miss Dunbar, he thought, writing it in his notebook, and adding the rest of the information: Date of birth, January 18, 1859—she had been a little older than Harold Upton—place of birth, Boston, Massachusetts; color, white; marital status, widow; father and mother's names, address, the same one as at Gardiner's; the certifying physician's name, the undertaker's, and the name of the Chatham cemetery which was the place of burial.

It was just as well, Griff reflected as he left the town clerk's office, that Casciello hadn't waited to see the death certificate. There was no hurry about going to Egan with what he had just found out. He had to keep in mind his father's stricture regarding the role of the private investigator. His first duty was to his client; and though he must never withhold evidence of a crime from the police, his client had the right to be informed of it first except on the very rare occasions when even the slightest delay would involve obstructing the law.

This was far from being one of those occasions, Griff thought. With the case a long way from complete, John Clarke had the right to be told that he had found Eliza Jane Upton before he passed the information on to Egan.

Griff went next to probate court and asked to see Agnes Dunbar's will or the administrative record of her estate.

The clerk went to look it up and came back to inform him that there was no estate for Agnes Dunbar listed on the probate index.

"That means she had nothing of value to leave,

doesn't it?" Griff said.

"Yes, generally speaking."

"Would you mind seeing if you have a record of an estate for Walter Dunbar? I don't even know if he died in Chatham or when, except that it was probably before 1909."

The clerk went to look and came back again with a negative report. No estate for Walter Dunbar appeared on the probate index.

Griff had a late lunch and thought over the fruits of the morning, giving particular consideration to the fact that Miss Dunbar—Eliza Jane Upton—had inherited nothing from her mother or, it could be assumed, from her stepfather. She had acquired the money to buy a house and possibly pay a bribe to Henning from some other source.

He made a phone call to his father and a second call to police headquarters to leave a message for Egan that he was going back to Worcester and would get in touch with him on his return.

He didn't check out of his motel or go near it before he left. He expected to be back in Chatham tomorrow or perhaps even late tonight.

Chapter 15

Betsy went to the door that night to admit Griff and his father. She thought of it as an unexpected bonus to see Griff again before she left in the morning. They had only a minute or so to greet each other before he followed his father down the hall to John Clarke's study, but still it was a bonus to see him, a smile brightening the serious expression on his dark face as he spoke to her.

This was to be a private conference with John Clarke. Betsy watched Griff go into the study and close the door after him, reflecting that some sixth sense must have guided her last spring when she had refused to let Doug Raymond pin her. They had been writing all summer and she had been looking forward to seeing him again, but now he seemed callow compared to Griff. She smiled, as at something in the remote past, thinking of the silly things she and Doug had talked about doing in the future. Like the houseboat he was going to build for her, equipped with hi-fi, a bar, a ship-to-shore phone and wall-to-wall carpeting. Every morning she was to fry his eggs in butter as part of the Betsy Clarke New

163

England breakfast and every night they were to dine on steak and wine unless Doug wanted eggs fried in butter again.

How did Griff like his eggs cooked?

Still smiling, she went back upstairs to her room where her mother was helping her get packed. They were alone. Sam had left on a date right after dinner.

When they were settled in the quiet of the study Griff was prepared to let his father take the lead in bringing up the source of Miss Dunbar's money.

He disclaimed John Clarke's congratulations on having identified her as Eliza Jane Upton. "Maybe Betsy should get the credit because her name is Elizabeth," he said. "Or you and Mrs. Clarke should get it for giving her that name. When I started thinking about Betsy and Eliza as variants of it, it suddenly occurred to me that Bessie, the name Miss Dunbar uses, was another variant. Then I began to wonder if it couldn't be regarded as a nickname for Eliza Jane, perhaps going back to her childhood. After that, it was just a matter of routine investigation."

"Nevertheless, it's come off well. Although perhaps I shouldn't say that when it means turning my own aunt over to the police."

"I don't know that we're quite ready for that, sir," Griff said. "Not yet, at least." His glance went to his father. "Dad and I talked it over at dinner tonight and we feel there are a lot of things that need to be cleared up first. Such as where Miss Dunbar got the money to buy a house."

"Yes, there is that." John Clarke ran his hand over his thick crop of white hair. "And also, perhaps, the

164

question of bribe money."

"There was none in her immediate family," Owen Hughes pointed out. "Her mother died an alcoholic, leaving nothing behind her. The stepfather apparently left little or nothing, either, or they'd have been in better circumstances. As it was, they lived in a poor neighborhood and Eliza Jane, with no education beyond a year of high school, took a job at Gardiner's at twenty-five cents an hour. We can assume that she was given raises, but even so, it would have been impossible for her to save enough from her earnings to make a down payment on a house nine years later, to say nothing of paying off Henning too. He got money from some unexplained source to buy the funeral home with."

John Clarke stiffened as he became aware of the direction the conversation was taking. "Aren't you overlooking the possibility that she inherited money from her mother's side of the family?" he said. "For all we know, some maternal relative could have left it to her between 1913 and 1919 when she bought her house."

"Her personnel record gives her mother as next of kin," Griff said. "Her death apparently left Miss Dunbar completely alone in the world."

"Except for your mother, John," Owen Hughes inserted.

"But they never met or knew each other's whereabouts," John Clarke protested. "The fact that the trust fund was never paid to Eliza Jane is certainly proof of that."

Griff lit a cigarette and maintained silence. Let his father handle this touchy point.

165

The elder Hughes got to his feet, walked to the french doors opening on the terrace and stood looking out. There was nothing to see. The terrace and grounds were lost in darkness.

A moment later he turned around, eying John Clarke from under his shaggy brows. "I think we can forget about an inheritance from Eliza Jane's maternal relatives," he said. "We have the testimony of neighbors of fifty years' standing that she never mentioned any relatives and always appeared to be alone. If there were maternal relatives close enough to leave her money, I should think they would have seen to it that she had a better start in life than working as a cash girl in a department store and living in a tenement district with an alcoholic mother. Griff and I both feel that the only possible source she had of a fairly large sum of money was your mother.

"But—" he raised his hand to check the fresh protest John Clarke was about to make. "That doesn't mean that your mother cheated her out of the trust fund. The bank records will show what its value was in 1918, but I'm prepared to guess that it wasn't more than ten to fifteen thousand. It's quite possible that your mother gave her the equivalent sum with an agreement made between them to keep Eliza Jane's whereabouts from the bank. They may have had reasons we know nothing about; perhaps the choice was made by Eliza Jane herself."

John Clarke was slow to speak. He sat frowning into space. "I don't know," he said finally. "I just don't know. Let me get you a drink while I'm thinking about it. It's a brand-new idea to me."

He made drinks, handed them around, and sat

166

down again, his frown replaced by an expression of deep thought. Presently he said, "It so happens that we might be able to clear the point up, one way or the other. My mother was a methodical person. She kept ledgers of her income and expenditures as far back as I can remember. I'm sure none of them was ever thrown away so they must be somewhere in her attic. I've already come across the most recent ones in her desk."

Griff gave his father a faint smile as their glances met. His father had said earlier that in all likelihood Phoebe Clarke had kept some sort of financial records; that in his experience, rich people tended to keep track of where every penny of their money went.

It was a relief, nonetheless, that the proposal to examine the ledgers came without prompting from John Clarke.

They finished their drinks and he went upstairs for the keys to his mother's house. The couple who had worked for her and were staying on in a caretaker capacity were away, he said, on their vacation.

With Griff driving they went to the house, a few blocks away.

It stood dark against the sky, a big, rambling structure with a turret at one end that reminded Griff of a medieval watchtower.

"My lord," he said. "How many rooms are there, Mr. Clarke?"

"Twenty-one or two if you count the servants' quarters. I can't think why my mother didn't get rid of it long ago. The upkeep is tremendous. It'll be a white elephant to dispose of—if we can ever find a buyer at all. Stop under the portecochere, Griff. We'll go in that way."

"It could be made into a convalescent home," Owen Hughes remarked as they got out of the car.

"You'd never get a zoning exception in this neighborhood." John Clarke unlocked the side door and opened it. Reaching inside to turn on a light, he led the way into the house, through a side passage into a wide front hall, and on up to the third floor. Here the luxurious carpeting had given way to rubber tile, but there was brightly patterned wallpaper, and fresh starched curtains hung on the windows at each end of a long corridor.

John Clarke unlocked the first door at the head of the stairs. It opened into an unfinished attic that ran the whole length of the house, affording ample space for the furniture discards and miscellany of almost a century.

He went to an old walnut highboy, tried various keys, and finally found the one that unlocked the drawers. "It seems to me that this is where Mother used to put away her papers," he said over his shoulder.

They were still there, filling three drawers, stacks of clothbound ledgers in chronological order going back to 1915, the year that Phoebe Clarke became a widow.

He took out the 1918 ledger and laid it on a table where they could all look at it.

The neatly written entires for January and February produced nothing of interest to them but a March 5 entry read: "$12,000.00 withdrawal, Woodbridge Savings for B.D."

"Well, there it is." John Clarke's deep sigh of relief was a measure of the anxiety he had felt that his mother, for some inconceivable reason, might have cheated her half-sister out of her inheritance.

"There it is," he repeated. "We can assume that it represented the value of the trust fund at the time."

"Yes." Owen Hughes nodded with satisfaction that his theory had proved itself. "I wonder why they chose to handle it that way, though, instead of having Eliza Jane claim the trust fund. To say nothing of the fact that the Collingswood bank had every right to be notified of Eliza Jane's whereabouts."

John Clarke hesitated. "Well," he said, "Eliza Jane will have to answer that question herself. If I wanted to make a guess, though, I'd say it had some connection with my grandfather's divorce. Don't forget that in 1918 my mother still had contacts in Collingswood and there were plenty of people there who remembered his divorce and remarriage. We have no way of knowing what kind of a scandal it may have created at the time. It's possible that they decided not to bring it all back to life by having Eliza Jane show up to claim her inheritance."

"It could have been something like that, I suppose." Owen Hughes' tone lacked conviction. "On the other hand, banks don't go around broadcasting their business. I should think it could all have been handled very quietly."

"You don't know small towns. It would have got around. Someone in the bank was bound to talk."

Owen Hughes let the subject drop.

They went on turning the pages of the ledger finding nothing but routine expenditures from March to October. Then, on October 7, an entry read: "$500.00—B.D.—trip and fun. Expenses; $2000.00—H."

"Good God!" John Clarke shook his head in bewilderment. "My mother footed the bills for that man's funeral. Eliza Jane must have turned to her immediately for help. I can hardly believe it. She couldn't have unless they were keeping in fairly close touch with each other. Maybe it continued right up until my mother's death. And yet she never once let on to me that such a person existed. I don't understand it. I never will."

"Perhaps Eliza Jane will clear it all up for us," Owen Hughes suggested.

"I hope so. I certainly do."

As the first shock of the ledger entry lessened, John Clarke moved on to another point. "She couldn't have shot the man in that house where she was boarding. Not unless Mrs.—?"

"Saunders," Griff supplied.

"Well, not unless Mrs. Saunders was in collusion with her and God knows how that could be."

"She needn't have been," Griff said. "It was a big house and Mrs. Saunders was bedridden in a downstairs room. She was also very deaf and her mind was beginning to go. Unless the shooting took place right under her nose, I don't think she would have heard the shot or anything that went on afterward."

"H. is for Henning, of course," John Clarke said next. "I can't imagine his settling for two thousand, though."

"Neither can I," the elder Hughes put in. "He was taking the risk of prison and the loss of his means of livelihood. I think we'll find it was only a down payment, a stopgap, as it were, until your mother could arrange to get the balance together in cash for

170

him." He turned back to the ledger. "Let's see what else we find."

The next entry of note came on October 15. It read: "$3000.00—to B.D. for H."; and on November 4: "$3000.00—to B.D. for H." A December 6 entry read: "$2000.00—to B.D. for H.—final payment."

"Ten thousand in all," said Griff, who had been jotting down the dates and amounts.

The last entry of interest to them came on December 16. "$500.00—to B.D.—Xmas gift," it read.

John Clarke brought out the 1919 ledger. Skimming the pages they found an entry on December 11 that read: "$500.00—to B.D.—Xmas gift." There was no further record of payments to Henning.

"That ten thousand was it," Griff said. "I thought it would be a bigger bribe."

"It must have looked big enough to him," his father said. "And in terms of purchasing power it was equal to three or four times the same amount today."

John Clarke, making his choice at random, dipped into ledgers covering the next four decades. Each of them showed in the first half of December an entry that read: "$500.00—to B.D.—Xmas gift."

When he had put back the 1958 ledger, the last one kept in the highboy, he said, "A Christmas gift of five hundred a year for over forty years adds up to better than twenty thousand. That comes on top of twelve thousand to cover the trust fund and the ten thousand she paid to Henning. It seems to me that Eliza Jane has my mother to thank that she didn't have to stand trial for killing that man and is able to live in modest comfort today."

His glance challenged the elder Hughes and Griff.

171

"Whatever reasons my mother had for not notifying the bank of her half-sister's whereabouts, at least there was no question of cheating her out of any part of her inheritance. For that matter, it's doubled now because she'll get the trust fund too."

After a moment, he added, "Maybe she'll need it if she's charged with murder. Although where the state could get evidence against her after forty-four years is beyond me. If I were her lawyer I'd advise her to make no statements whatsoever. She couldn't even plead self-defense with the bullet wound in the back of the man's head."

"Well, all that can wait," Owen Hughes said. He and Griff listened noncommittally as John Clarke made further comments on the difficulties the state would face without witnesses or evidence. There was the ledger, of course . . .

"Which may have to be turned over to the police," Owen Hughes said.

"Yes . . ." John Clarke put the rest back in the highboy and locked it and tucked the 1918 ledger under his arm. "But as you said, we'll wait and see how this thing is going to develop."

They went back down the two flights of stairs, turning off lights, locking the side door and leaving the house dark and silent and empty behind them to await its uncertain future.

Griff had rather hoped he might see Betsy again but it was past 10:30 when they got back to the Clarkes' and her father did not invite them in. Instead, he sat in the car for a few minutes discussing what should be done next.

They were in agreement that whatever steps were to be taken would depend on Miss Dunbar's own

172

story. Griff would leave for Chatham very early in the morning to see her. He would then phone his father who would immediately get in touch with John Clarke.

The elder Hughes added, "No matter what Miss Dunbar has to say for herself, you realize, John, that Griff will have to pass it on to Lieutenant Egan that she's Eliza Jane Upton. What she chooses to tell him about the affair will, of course, remain confidential, at least until we've had a chance to talk it over with you."

"Yes, I know." John Clarke got out of the car and stood holding the door open. "It's really a hell of a situation," he said. "The woman's my aunt—half-aunt—she's lived only a hundred miles from me all my life and she's been wanted for questioning in a murder since the very moment I heard of her existence."

"Wanted for questioning in a suspected murder," Owen Hughes corrected him gently.

"That's Tweedledum, Tweedledee." He spoke sharply. He was on the defensive about his mother, groping for understanding of her lifelong secrecy over her half-sister, particularly as it applied to the bank and himself. When he thought of the part she had played in disposing of the body of a man presumably murdered, he knew he hadn't even begun to assess how he felt about it yet. He was shaken, too, by thoughts of unpleasant publicity lying ahead, worse than any that had gone before.

Owen Hughes, recognizing the state of mind he was in, reflected that he would be more shaken still if he knew the turn Owen Hughes's own thoughts, and possibly Griff's, had taken. He said, "We'll see what

173

develops tomorrow, John. But try to keep it in mind that no matter what the outcome is, none of this reflects on you personally."

"That's easier said than done." After a pause John Clarke added somberly. "Although I can't say I wasn't warned from the very beginning. You told me yourself, Owen, to think twice before I pushed the search for Eliza Jane, but I said I wanted it to go on regardless of what lay at the bottom of it. Now I have to admit that the closer I get to it, the less I like it. It would have been much better if that poor handful of bones had been left undisturbed in Hillside Cemetery until doomsday. I'm sure that's what my mother would have wanted too. After all, she made herself an accessory to the crime and—" he broke off. "Well, it's too late to cry over that now. Good night, Owen— Griff. I'll be waiting to hear from you."

Father and son said good night and watched him go up the front steps and let himself into the house. A lighted room upstairs was probably Betsy's, Griff thought. He wished he'd had a chance to say good-by to her again. No, not really. He'd already said it twice, Saturday night and again tonight. What he did want was to see her again, away from her family and continue to improve their acquaintance.

In Philadelphia, he thought, within the next couple of weeks.

As they drove home his father said, "Poor Clarke. I'm afraid the worst is still to come for him."

"So am I," Griff said.

They began to compare notes and discovered that their thinking tonight had been following parallel lines.

Chapter 16

The September sun shone brightly although not yet warmly on Miss Dunbar's little house when Griff got out of his car in front of it at 9:30 the next morning.

She was home. The slam of the car door brought her to a window to see who was arriving at this relatively early hour. Their glances met as he went up the walk. He smiled but she did not smile back. She moved away from the window and a moment later opened the front door.

"Good morning, Miss Dunbar," he said. "I'm sorry to come calling so early but there's something I'd like to talk to you about."

She hesitated, looking at him through the screen, this slight little woman who at seventy-five still retained some vestige, some fugitive, haunting look of youth on her face. Was it lack of the maturing experience of love or other lacks, Griff wondered, that had always made her look years younger than her age? She had faced poverty in her youth without the education or training to escape from it and probably much squalor and stress in coping with an alcoholic mother, but somehow these hardships had left her outwardly unmarked. She was past thirty when the violence of murder came into her life. Once it was behind her and apparently hidden for all time in the Collingswood cemetery, she had lapsed back into her ill-paid rut at Gardiner's, walled off in it from all love and hate and striving. Had she been afraid of life after the murder or somehow always excluded from trying to live it by the deprivations of her early years?

Whatever the reason, little Miss Dunbar had gone on rotating between her little house and her little job, perhaps welcoming the security of her rut and burrowing deeper into it as she let the years go past unchallenged.

Her face gave Griff no hint of her thoughts as she opened the screen door and said, "Come in, Mr. Hughes."

The living room, in perfect order, looked as if no one had entered it since Griff's last visit. Yesterday's newspapers had vanished, the sofa cushions stood up straight, two small glass ash trays were sparkling clean. Miss Dunbar herself did not smoke and seemed to leave no other traces of herself in the room.

Houses have their own characteristic odors but Miss Dunbar's had none, least of all the fragrance of coffee lingering on the air as at Amundsens'. She probably had a cup of instant and a bowl of dry cereal for breakfast, Griff thought.

They sat down, he on the sofa, she on a chair. He faced her squarely. "My first question is on your name," he said. "Is it legally Dunbar? Did your stepfather adopt you?"

"My stepfather—?" She gave him a startled look

and then bent over to pick up a leaf that had fallen from the plant on the table beside her. She put it in her apron pocket. Her hand shook.

"Yes, your stepfather. Your mother, Agnes Upton, and your father, Harold Upton, were divorced in 1889 and both of them remarried. That's why I'm asking if your stepfather adopted you." Griff's tone was uncompromising. "I know, you see, that you're Eliza Jane Upton and it seems as good a starting point as any to ask what your legal name is."

The faint natural pink of her cheeks drained away. She stared at him fixedly for an interval. She said, "My name is—" Her voice came with a squeaky sound. She swallowed hard and began again. "My name is Bessie Dunbar. It's the only name I've ever had and if that's what you've come to talk to me about, you can leave right now."

She stood up. She was trembling all over but held herself erect. "I've been very patient with you on your other visits but this is the limit. Now I just want you to leave."

Griff didn't move. He regarded her with compassion, the cornered mouse trying to behave like a lion. "Miss Dunbar—or shall I say Miss Upton?— this doesn't help at all. I know who you are, I know that the man whose skeleton was found was probably shot in Mrs. Saunders' house and that Henning was bribed to embalm the body and get hold of an extra death certificate to cover up the real cause of death. I also know what he was paid—two thousand down and eight thousand more within the next two months—and that your sister, Mrs. Clarke, gave you twelve thousand in 1918 and five hundred annually

177

thereafter as a Christmas gift. Your nephew, John Clarke, hired the Hughes agency to find you and that is what I've done."

"No," Miss Dunbar gasped. "No, no, you've mixed me up with someone else."

"This isn't any use," Griff said not letting his tone soften. "I know you're Eliza Jane Upton. I've seen your mother's death certificate. There's other documentary proof too."

Miss Dunbar's defiant pose, so alien to her, collapsed abruptly. She sank onto her chair and buried her face in her hands. She wasn't crying but her muffled voice held a note of hopeless despair as she exclaimed, "Oh, God, help me. I'm all alone with it now. I don't know what to do. I don't know—"

"You aren't all alone with it," Griff assured her with quick sympathy. "Your nephew wants to help you. My father and I, with the resources of our agency, are on your side. I'm to get in touch with them as soon as we've had a talk. But we'll need to hear the whole story before we can decide what is best to do."

She shook her head without lifting it from her hands. "It's no use. None at all. I knew it would all come out the minute I read in the paper that they'd found the skeleton. I always knew it, I guess. Forty-four years . . ."

Griff waited. At last she raised her head. The look of youth was gone from her face as if all at once her age had caught up with and even run ahead of her. She looked like an old, old woman and was so pale and shaken that Griff stood up quickly. "I'll get you a drink of water," he said.

He went out to the kitchen, found a glass, and filled it at the sink.

Miss Dunbar took it from him, holding it steady with both hands. After a few sips she gave it back to him. "Thank you," she said.

He set it down on the table beside her. Then he drew up a straight-backed chair and straddled it, eying her with concern. "Are you all right now?" he inquired. "Can I get you anything else?"

"No, thank you." She leaned back in her chair. "It's true what they say about how murder will out, isn't it?" she remarked in a faraway voice. "After forty-four years. And all because my sister Phoebe wouldn't face it that she was old enough to die and make plans about where she was to be buried. The last time she was here, I kind of looked ahead and tried to talk to her about it. But she wouldn't listen. Of course, neither one of us knew that the grave didn't get marked on the map or dreamed that it would ever get dug up again . . ."

She paused. "It was so long ago that sometimes it seems as if it never happened. But it did. There were two deaths in that house in my time there. First his and then Mrs. Saunders', three months later."

Her pause lasted so long this time that Griff asked, "What was his name?"

Miss Dunbar's blue eyes had the directness of a child's. "I never knew his name," she said.

"Oh." It was Griff's turn to pause. Then he said, "I think the best way to get everything straight is for you to tell me the whole story from the very beginning; your own early life, how you met your sister and so on."

"My early life?" She shook her head slowly. "The less said about it the better. It was just moving from one place to another. My stepfather would get a job in a town and we'd go there to live and the first thing you knew he'd lose it. He drank, you see." She came to a full stop. Then she added, "So did my poor, unfortunate mother."

From her detached tone she might have been talking about someone else's childhood. "He never legally adopted me. But I was only three or four when my mother married him and she thought it would be better, starting school and all, if I used his name. So I grew up as Bessie Dunbar and never thought of changing back. I was always called Bessie, anyway. My mother never liked the name Eliza Jane. She said it was my father's doing to name me after his mother. I don't remember him at all. Just my stepfather. I couldn't abide him but I got used to his name . . ."

Her gaze came back to Griff. She had been looking away from him as she conjured up the past. "It's funny about names, isn't it?" she said. "You're used to one, you wouldn't feel right with another."

Griff smiled. "No, you wouldn't. I guess we need our names to prove to ourselves that we exist; you, Bessie Dunbar, I, Griffith Hughes. Changing them would be like putting on a suit of clothes that couldn't be made to fit."

"That's right." For all her distress, she managed to smile back at him. "I was always Bessie Dunbar. Eliza Jane Upton, she was someone else, someone I didn't even know."

With a pensive sigh she continued, "My stepfather died not long after my fourteenth birthday. We were

180

living in Bridgeport at the time and so down and out that we hardly knew where our next meal was coming from. My mother's people were all dead and she didn't have anyone else to turn to. She got a job clerking in a store and when I finished my first year of high school in June I took out my working papers. But things seemed to be slack and there I was, a little, skinny kid nobody would hire all that summer. So then my mother began saying it was up to my real father to support me. Maybe he'd have me keep on in school or do something nice for me. She talked about how I was his flesh and blood and all that. Finally, she scraped up the train fare for us to go to Collingswood . . ."

Miss Dunbar hesitated, looked straight at Griff and said, "The truth is, she'd taken up with a man she met that summer and he gave her the money for the trip. I guess he thought it would get me off her hands."

Her tone became even more detached. "Perhaps I should tell you that my poor mother didn't have much of a life herself. Her parents died when she was very young and she grew up in an orphan asylum. But that's neither here nor there . . .

"We went to Collingswood early in October and had to change trains at the junction and didn't get there until late afternoon. We took a room for the night in a boarding house near the railroad station. My mother being Mrs. Dunbar, the Upton name didn't come into it at all. I still remember, though, how nervous she was. She said my father's store would close at six o'clock and maybe we'd better wait till morning to go see him. But when we took a walk over there after supper, his name wasn't on the sign out in front. It said WEAVER'S GENERAL STORE. My mother didn't know what do make of it. She stopped a man going by and asked him if the Uptons didn't still own it. He said my father and grandfather both died within a year of each other a few years back.

"My mother must have looked upset because then the man said Mrs. Harold Upton had sold the store but she and her daughter were still living in the old Upton place if my mother wanted to go see them. She asked if Mrs. Barney Upton—my grandmother—was still alive but he said she was dead too. Then my mother thanked him and we went on down the street. She said, well, that was the end of her hopes that my father or grandparents would do something for me. She said I wouldn't have any claim on my father's second wife. Then she said we might as well take a walk over to the house just to see what we could see. It was dark by that time . . ."

Griff pictured them walking over to the Upton house, passing other lighted houses on the way, with fallen leaves crisp under their feet and the smell of October in the air. The mother would have been dressed in what was probably her shabby best, sober for the occasion, but bearing the marks of dissipation on her face and perhaps looking stunned at the moment over the sudden stripping away of her daughter's prospects for a better life. Beside her walked the equally shabby, skinny girl who must have already learned to fend for herself, who had her working papers but hadn't yet found work. Since the trip was first proposed she had probably been building fantasies about the father she had never

182

known offering her an established home and the chance to go on in school.

Both had been robbed of their hopes by a sign on a store and a few words from a stranger. Now they were going to look at what they had lost, the mother long ago, the daughter that very hour.

"It's funny how some things stay with you," Miss Dunbar continued. "It's over sixty years ago but I still remember the house the way it looked that night. When I was back in Collingswood years later I went to look at it again. But it was daylight that time and the house was painted a different color and someone else owned it. It didn't look a bit the same to me. But the first time . . .

"It was a big white house with a porch across the front and trees and a nice lawn and everything. First we stood on the sidewalk but we couldn't see much because there were no lights on in front. Then we went around the side of the house under the trees where no one passing by could see us. We got up quite close where we could look right into the dining room. There was a lamp on a chain over the table and Phoebe was studying by it. It gave me the strangest feeling to see her sitting there, knowing she was my half-sister. She was ten years old then. She had on a blue plaid dress and blue bows to match on her pigtails. She was a beautiful child with nice rosy cheeks. She seemed to be making figures on a piece of paper. I guess it was arithmetic.

"Pretty soon her mother came in from the kitchen. She was rather tall and not nearly as pretty as my mother was when she fixed herself up. But she had a real sweet smile, one of the sweetest I ever saw . . ."

Genes, Griff thought. Perhaps Betsy had inherited her smile from her great-grandmother.

"She spoke to Phoebe and they both laughed. Then she pulled a rocking chair up by the table and sat down with a book. We just stood there watching them until Phoebe finished her homework and went out in the kitchen. We heard the back door open and she began calling her dog. He started barking up the street and we ran back to the sidewalk before he could get there and give us away. He was a black and white dog and he raced right by us to the house. We went back to the boarding house and the next morning we got on the train and went home to Bridgeport."

"Your mother didn't even mention going to probate court or the bank to find out if your father had made any provision for you?"

"No," Miss Dunbar said. "We just got on the train and left. The man who paid our way was mad at my mother over it. He said she should have asked, that maybe I could get something from my father's estate. But my mother said my father's second wife was the one who sold the store so he must have left everything to her and why should she give any of it up. Besides, she said, she didn't have any money to hire lawyers or go to court. So that was the end of it.

"A couple of weeks later I got a job as a mother's helper. Then I got a better job as errand girl in a store. I kept it until we came to Chatham. The reason we came was that a man my mother was keeping company with at the time got a job here. But they weren't getting along together and he just walked out one day and left. Mama kept getting sick—"

A long pause. Then Miss Dunbar said, "I want to tell the truth. Poor Mama couldn't stop drinking and

184

we had almost no money. I'd been looking for a job and when I saw Gardiner's ad for a cash girl I applied for it. Cash girls were usually a lot younger than I was, so my mother said maybe I'd have a better chance if I took a few years off my age; I was so little and skinny that I looked younger than I was. I told them I was sixteen and I got hired. After a few years I was promoted to silverware and there I stayed until I retired four years ago. I never told them my real age so I worked six years longer than I had to; but that was all right with me."

A headshake, a wry look. "I never dreamed the morning I went to apply at Gardiner's that I'd work there almost fifty years. Life's funny in a way, isn't it?"

"Yes, it certainly is." Griff kept his tone matter-of-fact, not letting the deep pity he felt for her come through in it.

When Miss Dunbar spoke again it was on an apologetic note. "I don't know what's come over me," she said. "Running on like this when you're almost a perfect stranger. I've never been one to talk about myself. All my life I've been that way, keeping to myself, not interfering in other people's business or wanting them to interfere in mine. When I was a little girl someone was always saying to me, 'What's the matter, cat got your tongue'?" She gave Griff a sad little smile. "They'd be surprised if they could hear me now."

"I don't know about that," he said gently. "Keeping things to yourself can become a way of life that you feel you've accepted as a part of you like the color of your eyes. But I don't think it ever really is for anyone. 'No man stands alone.'" He smiled at her. "I'm quoting a poet, Miss Dunbar. 'No man is an island. Each is part of the whole, the main continent.'"

"Part of the whole. That's true, I guess. What's the rest of it?"

"I can't quote it. Except the most famous line: 'For whom the bell tolls, it tolls for thee.'"

"Oh, that line's familiar," she said. "And it's true. Yes, it is." She was sitting forward. She leaned back and closed her eyes.

"Are you all right, Miss Dunbar?"

"Yes, I'm all right. It's a relief to let it out. Such a relief after all these years." Tears trickled down her face from under her closed eyelids.

After a moment she said, "That man. I didn't even know his name. And all these years—"

She couldn't go on. She began to cry as if her heart would break.

Chapter 17

Griff felt helpless. He made occasional soothing sounds and waited for Miss Dunbar to cry herself out.

It took a long time. Once she let down the barriers she had so much to cry about, he thought, that she might never stop. She had her whole life to cry about it.

But at last her wrenching sobs ended in gulps and hiccups. She wiped her eyes and blew her nose and gave an exhausted sigh.

Griff brought her a fresh drink of water and a handful of facial tissues from a container in the kitchen.

She drank and sat up straight saying shakily, "I'm sorry—going to pieces like that."

"You'll feel better for it," he said.

"It's been coming on ever since I read that they found the skeleton. It came as a double shock, you see. I didn't know until then that Phoebe was dead."

Her voice quavered, steadied. "Sometimes I bought the Woodbridge paper at the stand downtown just to see if any of them were written up in it. I guess you know how prominent the Clarkes are and

187

how often their name is in the paper. It happened, though, that I didn't get down to buy it the week Phoebe died. That's why I didn't know she was gone until it came out about the skeleton. I nearly died myself."

She reached for more tissues, blew her nose, and added them to the wad in her apron pocket.

Griff murmured sympathy. She gave him a wan smile and said, "The way I'm wound up, I just keep talking and you're waiting to hear about that man."

Griff smiled back at her reassuringly. "No hurry. I asked you to start with your early life and now we've got as far as your job at Gardiner's. What happened after that?"

Miss Dunbar's gaze seemed to turn inward reviewing that time. "Nothing," she replied in a bleak tone. "I just stayed on there. We had a hard time getting along. When I look back I don't know how we managed. My mother couldn't work much and didn't have men friends helping her out after the one that brought us to Chatham. Then she got very sick and was taken to the hospital. She died the year before the war. I sold what furniture we had to bury her. I didn't want to see her put in a pauper's grave.

"I rented a room downtown but I didn't like it. Then Mrs. Saunders put her ad in the paper and I went out to see her. That was another funny thing like getting the job at Gardiner's. Riding out on the trolley, I didn't dream I was going to live out here for the next fifty years. I'd never been out this way before. But like I told you, Mrs. Saunders and I took to each other right off . . ."

Miss Dunbar's voice gained warmth as she spoke of Mrs. Saunders. "She was so good to me. It was the nicest time of my whole life. It didn't last long enough, though. Less than four years later she had the cerebral hemorrhage. I told you how I got the leave of absence and took care of her. I was glad to do it. She'd made her house my home."

Griff mentally reviewed dates. They had reached the winter of 1918 with no mention yet of Phoebe Clarke.

As if she read his thought Miss Dunbar continued, "I've been trying to tell things in order but now I have to go back to 1915. There was a little piece in the paper one night about Phoebe's mother and husband being killed at a railroad crossing. Car accidents weren't so common back then and even though it happened in Massachusetts it got into the Chatham paper. It said that her mother, Mrs. Harold Upton of Collingswood, New Hampshire, had come to visit her and that her husband, Samuel Clarke, was a well-known lawyer and that they had a year-old son, John.

"I cut the piece out of the paper and put it away and every so often I'd think about how I had a half-sister and a nephew too. I wanted to write her a letter of sympathy but I felt funny about it. For all I knew, she'd never even heard of me and I thought it might make her more upset if I wrote to her at a time like that. I almost told Mrs. Saunders about it but then I didn't. There'd have been too much to explain.

"I'd thought about Phoebe lots of times, of course, before I saw the piece in the paper, wondering what she was like when she grew up and if she'd got married and things like that.

"Then, after Mrs. Saunders had the attack and I knew she wasn't going to live long, I got to thinking more and more about Phoebe. Mrs. Saunders slept a lot and I'd be sitting there alone and I'd think about her. One night in February I got feeling so lonesome that I sat down and wrote her a letter. I was so afraid I'd change my mind about sending it that I went right out and took it to South Main Street to the nearest mailbox.

"She wrote right back. She said she'd found out when her mother died that she had a half-sister somewhere and that she wanted to meet me right away. She said she'd drive down the following Saturday if I could get someone to take care of Mrs. Saunders—I'd explained about her in my letter—so that I'd be free to go out to dinner with her that night. I was to make a hotel reservation for her and she'd stay overnight and go home the next day.

"I was so excited I didn't know whether I was coming or going." Miss Dunbar's tone softened at the memory of how happy the prospect of meeting her sister had made her.

"There was a girl I knew at Gardiner's who was always glad to earn an extra dollar and she said she'd come out and stay with Mrs. Saunders Saturday night. I didn't even think of getting a hotel room for Phoebe. I spoke to Mrs. Saunders and she said to make up one of the spare bedrooms, although I doubt that she ever really understood who Phoebe was, what with her being so hard of hearing and her mind never quite clear again from the day she had the attack.

"I fixed the room up real nice for Phoebe and Friday night I hardly slept a wink thinking about her coming and all.

"Well, she got to the house about four o'clock driving a big Packard car. She was so beautiful I couldn't take my eyes off her. And the clothes she wore; a lovely brown suit that fitted her like a glove and a little brown turban to match with velvet roses on it. She had big brown eyes and just masses of hair, a rich, glossy brown like the color of ripe chestnuts.

"She had an air about her too. You'd know she was somebody as soon as you looked at her.

"I went outside to meet her and she laughed and kissed me and said, 'Well, sister . . .'

"She'd brought me presents, a handsome gold bracelet and perfume and a very pretty silk scarf; and linen handkerchiefs for Mrs. Saunders. I took her in to meet her and she was very friendly and patient trying to talk to her but it was hard all around.

"We had dinner at Sedgwick's, the nicest restaurant in Chatham in those days and stayed up half the night talking. She told me a lot about herself, growing up in Collingswood and how she met her husband when she was at boarding school in Boston and the big wedding they had and what a blow it had been to lose him and her mother both at once. She talked about her little boy John too. She'd brought snapshots of him and the big house they lived in to show me, but she didn't put on any airs about having so much money. She seemed real interested in me, asking all kinds of questions about my life. Of course, I glossed over a lot of things . . .

"Finally she asked me what would happen when Mrs. Saunders died. I said her children would sell the house and I'd start looking for another place to board. She said a couple of times that I should have a home of my own but I just smiled and let it pass.

"We were up so late that Sunday we didn't get to church at all. We didn't have breakfast until almost noon. She started home about one o'clock because she didn't want to be on the road after dark. The roads weren't like they are today and it would take her four or five hours to get home, she said.

"She wrote a couple of days later about how wonderful it was to meet me and that she'd be down again soon.

"The very next Sunday about 11:30 in the morning the doorbell rang and there she was, laughing because I was so surprised. I was just starting to fix Mrs. Saunders' dinner and Phoebe said to go right ahead, she had cooked ham and some other things for us in the car. She said not to even mention her being there to Mrs. Saunders, it was too hard to talk to her.

"Well, we had a nice meal of our own out in the kitchen. I couldn't take her upstairs to my apartment because it was on the other side of the house and I might not hear Mrs. Saunders if she wanted me. Phoebe left right after we ate on account of the drive home.

"The third time she came was on a Saturday and she stayed overnight again. I didn't feel right, not telling Mrs. Saunders she was there but Phoebe said no, not to bother her; as long as I had to sleep downstairs, anyway, on a cot in Mrs. Saunders' room, she'd just use my apartment. She was acting keyed up, I noticed, and before we went to bed she told me what was on her mind.

"She began by saying she was going to deposit twelve thousand dollars in a Chatham bank for me so I could buy a place of my own. I should be able to get a nice little house just big enough for me for four or five thousand, she thought, and I could leave the rest in the bank to pay taxes and insurance and have something extra put by for a rainy day.

"In return, all she wanted was for me to let her use my apartment, unknown to anyone, at least one weekend a month and sometimes two. She said she'd got married secretly three weeks before to a captain stationed at Camp Devens, and that her first husband's will had his estate so tied up for five years after his death that she might lose her share of it if word of her marriage got out. She was very much in love with her new husband but didn't dare spend what time they could manage to be together in a hotel for fear they might be seen by someone who knew her. What she wanted to do, she said, was meet him in Worcester and the two of them drive to Chatham and stay in my apartment. She said I wasn't using it anyway right then so it wouldn't really inconvenience me at all."

Miss Dunbar gave Griff a hesitant smile. "I guess I don't have to tell you that the whole thing took my breath away," she said.

"Well, at first I said I couldn't do it without Mrs. Saunders' permission. But Phoebe said no, it would be too complicated to make her understand, and that it was my apartment and I had a right to let my own sister use it if I wanted to.

"She said it would all be very quiet. They'd put the car away in the barn, come in through the back hall and go up the back stairs. Half the time I needn't even see them. I had a two-burner stove and they'd bring things from the delicatessen and take care of themselves. They'd arrive after dark on Saturday and leave after dark on Sunday and no one would be the wiser and there'd be no harm done.

"Well, finally I said yes, I'd be glad to help her out

but I couldn't think of taking money for it.

"She just laughed. Her eyes were bright as stars she was so excited. She said, 'What a good honest soul you are, Bessie.' Those were her very words. Then she said I was her sister and she was going to put the money in the bank for me whether I let her use the apartment or not. It would take a few days to arrange it, she said, and then the money would be mine to do what I pleased with. She talked so fast I couldn't get a word in edgewise . . ."

Miss Dunbar's voice fell away. She was lost in memories. Presently she continued, "In the end I couldn't refuse her. I wanted so much to have a home of my own and the rest of the money in the bank and I wanted to do her the favor she asked too. What a favor it turned out to be!" For the first time bitterness edged Miss Dunbar's voice.

"Didn't you ask what her new husband's name was?"

"Oh yes, I asked. She just laughed, though, to tease me and said she was keeping it a deep dark secret until they could announce their marriage. She said I could just think of him as the captain, that it would be fun for me to have a mystery man for a brother-in-law. Then she said she hoped I wouldn't mind, either, being a mystery woman, for the present. She wasn't going to tell her family or any of her friends about me until the marriage became public so that no one's attention would be directed to Chatham.

"Before the week was out the twelve thousand was deposited in a Chatham bank in my name.

"Phoebe called me that Friday night and I fixed up my apartment for them and took everything I'd need downstairs. I heard the car drive in while I was giving

194

Mrs. Saunders her supper. She didn't hear it at all and they went upstairs so quietly that I had to listen to hear them myself.

"About nine o'clock Phoebe came down and said she'd like me to meet the captain and have a glass of wine with them. Mrs. Saunders was asleep by that time so I went upstairs with her. Phoebe said, 'I'd like you to meet my husband, Bessie,' and then introduced me to him. He was real good-looking, tall and dark with lovely white teeth. He seemed pleasant but he didn't have much to say. Phoebe did most of the talking.

"That was the start of it and it went on that way, at least one weekend a month and sometimes two. Once in a while I'd see both of them but usually Phoebe would run down by herself to see me."

"I don't understand how the neighbors could have missed out on all this," Griff remarked.

"Well, for one thing, there was no one living very close by. Our nearest neighbors were an old Polish couple who could hardly speak a word of English. And it wasn't as if we had a lot of people dropping in. A couple of times someone came while they were there but they were private enough upstairs in my apartment. Then, too, for the first couple of months after they began to come it was dark when they arrived and when they left, and the car was in the barn with the door closed.

"When it got so that they came and went by daylight, it was different, of course. Occasionally they were seen, but if anyone mentioned it to me I just said they were distant relatives. Anyway, I don't suppose they were there more than six or seven weekends the whole summer and early fall. It wasn't easy, I guess, for both of them to arrange to get away at the same time. They came when they could, though, right up until the last weekend of all, the one that was like a nightmare . . ."

Miss Dunbar fell silent, her hands gripping each other in her lap.

Griff waited, letting her take her time.

At last she resumed, "Phoebe dropped me a note to let me know they were coming. I heard them drive in the yard a little after six but I was giving Mrs. Saunders her supper and didn't see them at all.

"I had my own dinner and cleaned up the kitchen after I fed her. Then I got her settled for the night and did a few little things. It was ten o'clock before I sat down to read the paper. I was in Mrs. Saunders' room. I had put an easy chair in there and a lamp to read by. I'd been sitting there about half an hour when I heard this sudden sharp sound from upstairs. I couldn't think what it was. The bedroom door was closed and the other doors beyond—I was careful about that when they were in the house—and I hadn't heard the sound too well. I thought maybe something like a lamp had got knocked over and broken.

"The next thing I knew, a knock came on the bedroom door and there stood Phoebe, white as a sheet, her eyes like saucers. She beckoned me out and shut the door after me.

"We went out in the kitchen. She was shaking like a leaf. I began to shake, myself, she scared me so. I made her sit down. Then she told me she'd shot the captain. He was lying dead on my floor upstairs."

Chapter 18

Griff felt no surprise or shadow of doubt that Miss Dunbar was telling the truth. Since he had found out that she was Eliza Jane and particularly since seeing the ledgers last night, what she had just told him was the very possibility that he and his father had been considering. It fitted the facts; it left no unanswered questions and no loose ends.

Most of all, it fitted Miss Dunbar herself. There was nothing in her makeup or background to suggest that she'd ever had a lover, let alone killed him.

Presently, in an empty voice, Miss Dunbar went on, "She was past trying to cover up anything with me. It all came out. They were lovers, not husband and wife, and that was what all the secrecy was about. He was married to someone else back home. They'd met almost a year before at a party friends of hers gave for some of the officers from the camp and fallen in love at first sight. He didn't tell her he was married at first and when he finally did he talked about getting a divorce. Early in January, she said, they spent the night together at some hotel and she went away with him again the first weekend of February. But it was too dangerous, she said. She was nervous the whole time thinking what a scandal it would make if someone saw them.

"Then she got my letter and came to visit me. The minute she saw my little apartment off by itself and the way the house was laid out and what Mrs. Saunders' condition was, she began to think of it as the answer to their problem. She talked it over with the captain and then came back to me offering the money in return for the use of my apartment. She said she'd had to lie to me about being secretly married because she knew from the start that unless she told me they were, I'd never get mixed up in it."

Miss Dunbar gave Griff an embarrassed glance. "You must be thinking what a simpleton I was to believe all that talk about keeping the marriage secret on account of her first husband's will."

"No, not at all," he replied. "A more worldly person would have questioned it, but I can understand that you wouldn't."

Miss Dunbar looked into the past with less lenient judgment on herself. "Time and again over the years I've asked myself if I wasn't so quick to believe her because I wanted to; because it meant I could have a home of my own and a nest egg in the bank."

"No one could blame you for that," Griff said. "You were alone and needed a sense of security. We all do."

She eyed him with a sad little smile. "That's what I mean. If there'd been no offer of money to sweeten the story would I have been so quick to believe it."

"Perhaps; or perhaps not. There's no way to tell now, Miss Dunbar."

She sighed. "You're right. It's too late. As soon as I let her give me the money it was too late. And what had come of it was the man dead on my floor and Phoebe ready to go out of her mind over it.

"The way she was crying and carrying on, it took a while to get it all straight from her. He'd been cooling off on her for the past couple of months; she couldn't pin him down at all about getting a divorce, she said. That afternoon he'd had very little to say on the way to Chatham. He'd been quiet from the time she picked him up at a trolley station outside of Worcester. She'd fixed dinner for them and he still didn't have much to say. But Phoebe had made up her mind there was going to be a showdown and she began talking about how the war was going to end pretty soon and it was time he did something about getting his divorce. One thing led to another and finally he told her right out that he wasn't going to get one at all but was going back home when the war was over. He couldn't hurt his wife that way, he said. She'd done nothing to deserve it. He had his job to think of, too, back in his home town and all kinds of things."

"Where was he from?"

"Somewhere in Indiana. She told me later, not that night, that he wasn't one of the regular officers at Camp Devens. He was an engineer and he'd been sent there to make some kind of survey of land or something. He was on—now what did she call it—"

"Temporary duty?"

"Yes, that was it. I've often thought since that if they'd just sent him back to where he was supposed to be it never would have happened. He'd have been alive and Phoebe would have got over how she felt about him and married someone else and not had to live with a thing like that the rest of her life. To say nothing of my part in it. It's hung over me from—" She stopped short, then said, "No use crying over spilt milk."

Griff smiled at her. "Sometimes it makes us feel better."

She shook her head. "It doesn't change anything. That man, for instance. He's been dead and gone for forty-four years. Although Phoebe never meant to kill him at all."

"There was a struggle over the gun and suddenly it just went off?"

Miss Dunbar looked at Griff in surprise. "Why, how did you know?"

"Let's say it was just a thought that came to me." His tone was neutral.

"They were in the bedroom. He was partly undressed. He wasn't wearing the gun, you understand."

"I wondered about that."

"It was a special little foreign gun he'd bought from another officer. It was in his suitcase which was open on the bed. There'd been a little stealing at the camp and he hadn't wanted to leave it in his locker."

"How did she say the gun got out of the suitcase?" Again Griff's tone was neutral.

"Well, she was lying on the bed crying while the captain was getting undressed. They weren't speaking by that time. Phoebe reached in the suitcase and threw his pajamas at him and said he could find some other room to sleep in. She said she was ready to die of grief and shame over the way their love affair was ending and hardly knew what she was doing when she grabbed the gun out of the suitcase and jumped up and told him she was going to kill herself with it.

"He tried to take it away from her and then there was this terrible noise and he fell against her and then slumped down on the floor with blood coming out the back of his head. He drew his last breath as she knelt down beside him. She was going to turn the gun on herself then, she said, but she got to thinking of her little boy and the disgrace to him and just dropped it on the floor. As soon as she was able to pull herself together she came down to get me."

"Did she explain how he got shot in the back of the head? I don't see how he could turn his back to her while they were struggling for the gun."

"She explained it to Jim Henning. I was too upset to think straight about it myself. She said she had the gun behind her back; he had hold of her by the shoulder with one hand and was reaching behind her with the other to take it away from her. It's not clear to me just what happened next. She had the gun in her left hand and shifted it to her right when he tried to get it and whipped it around in front of her and that was when it went off. I guess he must have had his head down to have the bullet strike him there. Maybe he was looking over her shoulder to see which hand she had the gun in."

"Did Henning question her about it?"

"Not much. He seemed to understand it better than I did."

Naturally, Griff thought. Ten thousand dollars had brightened his understanding.

201

Miss Dunbar returned to the mainstream of her story. "I went up to look at him myself to make sure he was dead. When I came down Phoebe started begging me to help her get rid of his body. She said we could remove all his clothes and identification, get him out to her car and take him somewhere. We could put him in the river or leave him in the woods or something. I was shocked at first but she kept saying it was an accidental death and she'd be acquitted if it went to court but just having it become known would ruin her life and her little boy's and why should she have to go through all that for nothing. So in the end I said I'd do what I could to help her.

"We went back upstairs to where he was. When I looked at him lying there, six feet tall and weighing about one hundred and eighty pounds, I began to wonder how we were going to move him around the way Phoebe was planning it. It didn't seem right, either, to take off all his clothes and just leave his poor body somewhere. Then I started to think about where we were going to leave him.

"Phoebe took off his watch and a ring and his identification tags. She said after we got him undressed we could roll him onto a blanket and drag him out to the car. But I said suppose we drove out in the country looking for woods and got stuck on some back road in the middle of the night. The Housatonic was the nearest river but I didn't know, and neither did she, where there was a road running right beside it so that we could just roll him down the bank and push him in. We could hardly stop on a bridge to do it. In fact, the more I considered her plans the less I liked them."

In spite of the seriousness of the occasion, Griff smiled to himself at the thought of the beautiful, guilt-ridden Phoebe, so frantic to escape the consequences of her own act that she was incapable of making any sort of sound plan; whereas mousy little Miss Dunbar, probably with not a hair on her neat head out of place, had brought order to bear on the problem.

"Then," she continued, "I began thinking about when the body was found as it would be sooner or later. I said there'd be some kind of fuss when he didn't show up at Camp Devens. He'd be reported missing and once the body was found they'd soon connect it with him.

"I asked her if many people knew they were acquainted. She said she'd been seeing him openly at quite a few dances and parties around Worcester and when they started investigating his death she might be questioned as someone who'd known him.

"Well, I thought about that and I couldn't see that her nerves were strong enough to stand up to the police or army people if they put her through any kind of questioning. I wondered, too, if Phoebe and the captain had always been as clever as they'd thought when they'd met in secret."

Miss Dunbar smiled diffidently at Griff. "After it was all over I was surprised, looking back on it, at the way my mind stayed so clear that night. I kept thinking about all the things that could go wrong if we did what Phoebe wanted to do and then, all of a sudden, I thought of Jim Henning. I told you before, Mr. Hughes, what kind of a person he was and I was sure we could get his help if he was paid enough for it. I mentioned him to Phoebe and asked her how much she'd be ready to spend to settle the whole thing for good and all. She said she didn't care what it cost if only it could be fixed up. She was afraid, though, that he might give us away but I knew better.

"I tried the funeral home first and got him there. I told him who I was and asked how soon he could come to the house on a private matter. He said he was on duty until midnight when someone else would take over. It was half-past eleven then. I told him to say nothing to anyone about my call but that it would be well worth his while to come to the house as soon as he could.

"While we were waiting for him we went back upstairs. The captain was in his underwear and we took away his uniform for fear Jim wouldn't want to get mixed up in it if he knew the Army came into the picture. We were going to tell him that I owned the gun as a protection against prowlers and that I'd brought it out to show it to them and left it on the dresser.

"We fixed up the whole story while we waited. Phoebe was to tell him that the captain was a salesman from out West, a casual acquaintance she'd just brought along for the weekend. She'd say they'd gone up to bed and I was out back in the barn and he'd suddenly come into her room in his underwear and tried to attack her. She'd grabbed up the gun and it went off accidentally and killed him.

"Not that it mattered much what she said to Jim Henning if she just backed up her story with enough money . . .

"He arrived soon after midnight, bursting with curiosity. Phoebe told him her story and I explained that we wanted the man to have a decent burial with no questions asked.

"Well, Jim talked about the risks we were asking him to take and asked Phoebe how much she'd pay him for it. They talked it over and finally he said he'd take care of it for ten thousand in cash. Phoebe said she'd give him two thousand Monday morning but would prefer to spread the rest over the next few weeks because she didn't often draw out large sums in cash from her bank.

"Jim was satisfied with that arrangement and began planning how everything could best be handled. He said he had a death certificate in his pocket for a man named Scott who'd died of the flu that afternoon—but I guess you know how he worked that out. It's been in the papers."

Griff nodded. "Yes, I know."

"He said he'd be alone at the funeral home for a couple of hours in the morning and he'd make a record of a call from Walnut Street on Melvin Scott. He asked where the man was to be buried and we said we hadn't settled it yet, that we'd let him know later.

"He wanted to see the body so we took him upstairs. He looked at the bullet wound and said he could cover it up all right. He had his embalming equipment in the car and went out to get it. After he spread a rubber sheet on the bed we helped him lift the body up on it and then we went downstairs.

"I looked in on Mrs. Saunders. She was sound asleep and hadn't heard a thing. Phoebe was crying. I went out in the kitchen and made us a cup of tea. We drank it at the kitchen table and Phoebe cried some more."

"But still didn't tell you the man's name," Griff put in.

"I didn't ask. I didn't want to know. I said we'd better decide where he was to be buried and what information about him Jim was to put down on the death certificate.

"But she'd gone all to pieces. She put her head down on the table and just cried and cried. We could hear Jim moving around upstairs and water running in the bathroom. It was awful. I never slept another night in that bed the rest of the time I lived there.

"Well, I finally got Phoebe quieted down a little but she said she just couldn't face any of the things I was asking her about. She wanted me to pretend to be the captain's widow or sister and buy a cemetery lot somewhere nearby and go to the funeral and all. But I put my foot down on that. I said I lived in Chatham and expected to go on living here; that there was no telling who I might run into while I was posing as the widow or the sister and I wasn't taking any chances on it, not within a hundred miles of Chatham.

"So then Phoebe brought up the family lot in Collingswood. She said the captain could be buried there as my husband, but not as hers, because everybody in the town knew her. It would be perfectly safe for me, though, because I wasn't known there at all. She said Jim would have to put down Eliza Jane Upton on the death certificate so the Collingswood undertaker would know it was someone who had the right to use the lot; but when I got there, she said, I could tell him I called myself Elizabeth and wanted it to read that way in the obituary for the Collingswood paper; it would protect me, she said, if anyone in the town tried to find out who I was."

Including the bank, Griff thought. For all her emotional stress, clever Phoebe Clarke had overlooked nothing that would serve her interests.

He was liking her less and less as the story unfolded. He saw her as a grossly selfish woman, who had bought her half-sister's love and loyalty with money that was already rightfully hers, involved her up to her neck in a murder that was none of her doing and then pushed onto her major risks and responsibilities in covering it up.

If Miss Dunbar had ever viewed the situation as Griff was viewing it, she gave no sign of it. She continued, "I knew it was safer than burying him around here so I finally said yes. Jim finished embalming the body and left before we got everything settled. It was going on toward four o'clock when we went to bed, Phoebe on the parlor couch with a blanket and I back on my cot in Mrs. Saunders' room. I don't think either of us closed an eye.

"Jim came back in the morning with a shroud—it was like a suit—and laid the captain out in it. We told him where the burial was to take place and he said he'd get in touch with the undertaker in Collingswood and make all the arrangements.

"Phoebe would have to take care of Mrs. Saunders while I was gone and we'd planned that she'd say she was a friend from Gardiner's to anyone who dropped in. We told Mrs. Saunders the same thing. She didn't even remember meeting her before when I took her into the bedroom.

"After Jim left Phoebe said she'd have to call her house and tell them she wouldn't be home until the middle of the week. She had such a thing about being connected with Chatham that she drove twenty miles away to make the call.

"We were there all day with the body in the bedroom. We shut the door and stayed downstairs except that I went up once and knelt down by the bed to say a prayer for the poor man.

"Monday morning Phoebe got a check cashed for the funeral expenses and Jim's first payment. I already had a black serge suit and black hat and Phoebe bought me a black shirtwaist and a widow's veil while she was downtown.

"Jim came by late that afternoon to collect from Phoebe and explain the arrangements he'd made. He was going to wait until dark to come with the hearse. He'd have a helper with him and they'd drive all the way into the yard to the back door. They'd put the body in the coffin and bring it down the back stairs. The shipping box would be in the hearse and they'd put the coffin in it and take it right to the railroad station. He already had the tickets. In those days all you had to do was buy two passenger tickets to ship a body anywhere. Perhaps it's different now."

"No, I think it's the same," Griff said.

"Well, anyway, he'd bought the two tickets and another ticket for me on the same train leaving Chatham a little after nine o'clock. We were to change trains in Springfield around midnight and he'd bought me a sleeper ticket on the connecting train that went right through to Collingswood

Junction. It got there at 9:30 the next morning and the Collingswood undertaker would meet the train with his hearse and take me to Collingswood in another car. We'd go straight to the cemetery and the minister would meet us there to conduct the burial service."

Miss Dunbar paused. "That was one of the things that struck me when it came out in the papers; that after all those years Phoebe's funeral was scheduled for the same time as the captain's and the same grave. Don't you think it was a queer kind of coincidence, Mr. Hughes?"

"Yes, it was."

"It gave me goose flesh when I read it. Well . . . everything went off like clockwork. I was a nervous wreck the whole time, of course, but there wasn't a hitch. Everyone was so nice to me, thinking I was a new-made widow. The minister invited me to his house for lunch but I said I'd go to the inn. I had my lunch there and took a walk over to the Upton house and then the undertaker drove me back to Collingswood Junction to catch the 2:30 train. I was so worn out I slept most of the way to Springfield. I had a wait there and it was three o'clock the next morning when I got home in a taxi from the Chatham railroad station. I was never so thankful in my whole life, before or since, to have anything over with. Phoebe said the waiting and worrying was almost as bad for her but I don't know about that."

Miss Dunbar fell silent and then said, "Well, I guess that's the whole story."

"Not quite," Griff said. "Once the man was safely buried, why was it still kept a secret that you were half-sisters?"

"It was Phoebe's doing. I'd have liked to visit her in Woodbridge and meet my nephew and all." Miss Dunbar spoke on a note of wistfulness. "But she was bound and determined never to be associated with Chatham in any way. Jim Henning lived here, for one thing, and she said she was always afraid he'd give her away or the duplicate death certificate would somehow come to light or something else would happen. You couldn't tell her that her fears made no sense. And in the end, of course, it turned out she was right.

"Not that she wasn't always very good to me," Miss Dunbar added a moment later. "She'd come and get me and take me on trips to New York to the theater and things like that. Two or three times she took me to Florida on my vacation. Other places too. And the check every Christmas. She did lots of nice things for me."

She had given the shadow but not the substance of a close sisterly relationship, Griff thought. She had never given that; she had left Miss Dunbar to her loneliness.

Miss Dunbar went on, "You'd have felt sorry for Phoebe if you'd known her as I did. She lived with the memory of that night for the rest of her days. She was a young, beautiful woman when it happened and would have married again and had more children and a full, happy life if it hadn't been for that grave in New Hampshire. She never really got over it. She pretended she had but I knew better."

Miss Dunbar smiled a little forlornly. "People are funny, though," she said next. "They can't stand being done a favor. I always wondered if it wasn't that, as much as her fears about Chatham, that made Phoebe want to keep me a secret. What I'd done for her was part of a terrible thing she was always trying to forget, and she knew she'd have to see more of me, a constant reminder of the past, if it became known we were half-sisters.

"She told me about the trust fund a few years after the captain's death. She didn't spare herself about buying my help and gratitude with money that rightfully belonged to me, anyway. She felt very bad about it but I told her it didn't matter, she'd more than made it up to me and I'd never think of going to Collingswood to claim it. What I said was perfectly true. She couldn't change how she felt about having it come out that we were sisters and in everything else she was always good to me. It's hard to believe I'll never see her again." Miss Dunbar's voice wavered. She was close to tears.

Griff, to divert her, asked, "What did you do with the man's belongings and the gun?"

"We burned his clothes in the furnace. Phoebe took the gun and whatever wouldn't burn with her when she left the day after the man was buried. She said she stopped on a bridge going home and threw everything into the Connecticut River. So there's no way now to tell who he was."

Griff said nothing but didn't agree with her. A captain in the engineers, reported missing while assigned to temporary duty at Camp Devens should be traceable even at this late date.

"I often thought of his poor wife, never knowing what became of him," Miss Dunbar continued. "I

211

spoke to Phoebe about it more than once. Years later when she was visiting friends in Indiana she drove to his home town and inquired about his wife pretending she was an old friend of hers. She found out that the wife had the captain declared dead and remarried and moved away. I was glad she wasn't still waiting for him to come back but I always felt sorry for her just the same."

Miss Dunbar stood up. "I think I'd like a cup of tea. How about you, Mr. Hughes? Or would you prefer instant?"

"Yes, I'd prefer that," Griff said.

Her phone was in the kitchen. He followed her out and asked if he could make a collect call on it to his father in Worcester, explaining that his father would pass on the information he gave him to John Clarke. They would undoubtedly come to Chatham sometime today but in the meantime, Griff himself would have to let Lieutenant Egan know that he had found Eliza Jane Upton.

She would be within her rights, Griff emphasized, if she refused to make any statement to the police and would be well advised not to make one until they had a better idea of where she stood in the case.

She listened attentively to this and with equal attentiveness to what Griff said to his father during their long telephone conversation.

When he hung up he told her his father would get in touch with John Clarke and they would set out for Chatham immediately.

His coffee was ready. Miss Dunbar handed it to him and said, "I've been thinking it over while you were on the phone, Mr. Hughes, and I'm going to tell the police the whole story just as I told it to you—that is, the part that has to do with the captain's death. The truth can't hurt Phoebe now and whatever is coming to me I brought on myself. I'm afraid it will hurt John and his children but that can't be helped."

Griff protested her decision, telling her he felt a sense of responsibility toward her and urging her to wait at least until John Clarke arrived. He was a lawyer and she should have a talk with him first.

But whatever he said, Miss Dunbar shook her head. "It's gone on long enough," she said. "I'm going to tell the truth without worrying about my legal rights. Go ahead and call the police, Mr. Hughes."

She stood by the phone while he made the call. He was connected with Egan and said, "Griff Hughes, Lieutenant. I'm at Miss Dunbar's on Walnut Street. She's Eliza Jane Upton. Can you come and have a talk with her?"

"I sure can," Egan replied. "I'll be right out."

Griff hung up and looked at Miss Dunbar, the bystander who had become an accessory to her sister's crime and lived thereafter on crumbs from her sister's table. Her youthful look, her strangely innocent look had come back to her face and a new serenity with it.

She said softly, more to herself than to him, "Phoebe used to bring me snapshots of John so I could watch him grow up. And just think, in another few hours I'm actually going to meet him."

Chapter 19

"You haven't got a thing to go on," Starkey, chief prosecutor of Circuit Court 22, said. He lay back in his desk chair, propped his feet up on the waste basket and repeated, "Not a damn solitary thing."

Egan and Griff, expecting that kind of a pronouncement, glanced at each other. They were in the chief prosecutor's office in the Circuit Court building next door to the Chatham police station. They had left Miss Dunbar at home in Casciello's custody or, as Egan put it, keeping her company until they returned.

"Let me just run through it for you again," Starkey continued. "To issue a warrant for the woman's arrest she has to be charged with a crime. Accessory to murder?" He shook his head. "That's like trying to prove a donkey has a tail when you haven't got a donkey to start with. Before you can prove she was an accessory to murder, you've first got to prove that the murder took place and for that you produce no evidence at all. The woman didn't even witness the actual shooting. What she told you is hearsay, inadmissible in court. And according to her account

214

of the man's death, as told to her by her sister, it wasn't murder, anyway. It occurred during a struggle for possession of the gun which itself has vanished."

"The man was shot in the back of the head." Egan's tone was mild.

"I know. But we won't go into the gymnastics involved because we have no case. Everyone connected with it, except for this woman, Miss Dunbar, is dead and whether it was an accident or murder is water over the dam now. We don't even know the victim's name or much of anything else about him."

Starkey paused to light a cigar after offering them to Griff and Egan who declined. He puffed, blew out smoke, and continued, "So what else could we charge her with? Concealing a crime—obstructing justice? We've already conceded that we can't prove a crime was committed. All we know is that a man, shot through the head, was buried in New Hampshire with a faked death certificate that said he died of Spanish influenza. This woman admits she was in collusion with her sister and the undertaker to cover up the true cause of death but her admission isn't worth a damn in the legal sense."

Starkey tapped his cigar against the ash tray although no ash had yet accumulated on it and fixed an accusing glance on the police lieutenant as if, somehow, this were all his fault. "You've been a cop long enough, Egan; you know we need substantiating evidence extraneous and independent of the woman's confession before we can make a move. Unless we're going to charge her with attending the victim's funeral. No, we can't even do that; we can't prove she was there."

215

"Chrissake, why put the blame on me?" Egan's tone remained mild. "I'm just passing on information brought to my attention by Mr. Hughes who was hired to dig it up."

"Yes." The chief prosecutor looked at Griff with no particular enthusiasm as the source of this preposterous affair. He was a man who disliked complicated cases and carried on a running feud with the Chatham police force demanding that the evidence they presented to him should be complete, tidy, and irrefutable. Egan detested him.

"It's too bad, Mr. Hughes," he said, "that you couldn't dig up some independent evidence while you were at it."

"Well, I don't want to see Miss Dunbar under arrest," Griff stated. "In fact, for her sake, I'd like to ask a few questions just to be sure, once and for all, that there'll be no charge against her. You don't consider the altered death certificate evidence?"

"No. The doctor who signed it is dead. All we know of the circumstances is what Miss Dunbar tells us."

"There's Mrs. Clarke's ledger indicating payment of ten thousand to Henning."

"Payable to Miss Dunbar for H., I believe you said. H. could be anyone."

"What about Henning?" Griff persisted. "If his purchase of the funeral home could be checked and it showed he paid ten thousand down, that wouldn't be evidence either?"

"If Henning were alive and wanted to say he won it on the horses or his grandfather kept it under his mattress and made him a gift of it, who's to prove otherwise? No, Mr. Hughes, none of this story you've brought me means a thing. The rule of guilt says that guilt must be established through facts consistent with a conclusion of guilt and not compatible with a conclusion of innocence. We have no such facts here on which I could issue a warrant for Miss Dunbar's arrest."

Starkey's glance shifted to the lieutenant. "Of course, if you feel it's possible to go out and get the evidence we'd need—and in the meantime, ask the woman to remain within our jurisdiction—"

"I don't know where the hell I'd get any evidence after forty-four years," Egan said.

"Neither do I. The vintage of the alleged crime, the woman's present age—seventy-five, you said?"

"Yes."

"White hair, I suppose?"

"Yes."

"A white-haired old lady whose only motive was to help her sister and whose life has otherwise been blameless—" The chief prosecutor shook his head. "If we had anything to charge her with we'd never get a conviction. Of course, it's your duty, Egan, to look for independent evidence, but—"

He was still shaking his head when they left his office.

Griff felt a double sense of relief. Miss Dunbar wouldn't have to face any charge and the Clarkes would emerge relatively unscathed from the affair. It had died out of the newspapers and would soon be forgotten.

"I'll buy you a drink," he said lightheartedly to Egan as they came out of the Circuit Court building.

217

"Thanks, but I'll have to take a rain check on it. I've got to get back to work."

"Well, later then." Griff gave him a broad grin. "We'll drink to Anglo-Saxon law, that marvelous heritage of ours, that marvelous body of jurisprudence, coming down through the ages, collecting the rule of guilt on the way, putting the burden of proof on the prosecution."

Egan reacted predictably. "I don't know that I want to drink to it," he said. "Considering some of the characters I've seen taking shelter under that marvelous body of Anglo-Saxon law and walking out of a courtroom scot-free. Ask any cop. Burns you up plenty of times."

"But by and large—"

Egan grinned back at him suddenly. "All right, by and large, which includes Miss Dunbar, maybe I'll drink to it with you one of these days."

It was midafternoon when they got back to her house. Egan explained that no charges would be brought against her. He went through the formality of asking her to remain within the jurisdiction of the Chatham Circuit Court and then left with Casciello.

Miss Dunbar saw them go with mixed feelings. She was astonished; enormously relieved; but she felt somewhat belittled and let down too. She had confessed her crime of long ago and been prepared to face whatever came of it; but it was to be nothing, it seemed; nothing at all.

She turned to Griff and said shakily, "I don't imagine you ever found time for lunch today, did you?"

"No, as a matter of fact, I didn't."

218

"I'll fix you something. I'm so fidgety I can't sit still, anyway." She looked out the front door. "I wonder how soon they'll get here from Woodbridge."

John Clarke was outraged when he first heard Miss Dunbar's story. He was in his office where Owen Hughes had sought him out. He said he wouldn't believe a word of it in a million years. Eliza Jane was throwing mud at his mother, dead and beyond defending herself, to cover up her own guilt. When he got to Chatham he'd get the truth out of her, by God, if it was the last thing he ever did.

There was much of this. It was Sam who finally quieted him down.

"I know how you must feel, Dad, but blowing your top won't do any good. Eliza Jane is your aunt and—"

"Half-aunt!"

"All right, half-aunt or whatever, she's still entitled to a fair hearing which you can't give her storming around your office. Let's get going and find out what it's all about."

During the three-hour drive John Clarke began to face the bitter truth he had been evading since they had looked at his mother's ledgers last night; she had had a lover, a married man, and she had killed him. He brushed aside the story that it was an accident. The man had declared his intention to break off with her and go back to his wife; she had picked up the gun and shot him.

For the most part during the drive John Clarke

219

maintained a heavy silence. Occasionally he roused himself to remind Sam, who was at the wheel, that he was exceeding the speed limit.

Miss Dunbar was in the kitchen when they arrived, keeping Griff company while he ate. The doorbell brought her instantly to her feet. She gave him a terrified glance and hurried to answer it.

Owen Hughes took the lead, introducing himself and the Clarkes. Then he removed himself from the family scene and asking, "Is my son here?" quite as if he hadn't seen Griff's car out in front.

"Yes, he's in the kitchen."

"Well, I'll just speak to him." Owen Hughes vanished into the kitchen.

John Clarke's pride was in the dust. He had suffered many wounds that day. The aunt he was now meeting for the first time had been the instrument that had inflicted them upon him; not the cause—his sense of fairness had come into play— but the instrument. His mother had been the cause; his lifelong concept of her was shattered; the pieces would have to be put back together in some other form, but not yet. Meanwhile, here was the aunt his mother had deeply wronged. It was up to him, her son, to do what he could to right it.

Miss Dunbar stood in the hall looking at him eagerly yet apologetically, small, humble, and very frightened. Her hand had trembled when she offered it to him and then to Sam.

"I recognized both of you right away from snapshots Phoebe brought me," she said.

She took them into the living room. "Won't you sit down?" She sat down quickly herself before her knees buckled under her.

Sam sat down near her. "I like your house," he said. "It looks very comfortable."

"Yes, it is. I'll show it to you later." She was grateful for his small talk but her gaze went to John Clarke.

"Your wife didn't come with you," she said.

"She drove Betsy back to school today. I'll call her when she's had time to get home."

"This is Betsy's last year at William Penn, isn't it? Your mother told me how well she was doing there."

John Clarke found her effort to be counted as one of the family almost unbearably pathetic. Embarrassment over it made his voice a little stiff as he replied, "She usually makes the dean's list."

"That's wonderful."

The conversation, under the circumstances, was becoming grotesque; it was up to him to give it reality.

"Have you talked to the police yet?" he asked.

"Yes, they've been and gone. They're not going to do anything about it. It was too long ago, they said. Mr. Hughes went with the lieutenant to see the prosecutor. He'll tell you what went on. It seems funny, doesn't it? But I'm glad for all our sakes, especially your mother's. She was always afraid it would come out and I'd hate to see her name spread all over the newspapers. Now there'll be nothing more said about it, nothing anywhere."

At least that much was salvaged, John Clarke told himself thankfully. His mother's crime wouldn't become public knowledge, a disgrace to her memory and to him and his family. He felt a little better and sat up straighter in his chair.

After a brief silence Miss Dunbar added, "I'm sorry

it had to come out at all. I never meant it to."

"I know you didn't," John Clarke said. "It was my own doing, getting Griff to search for you."

"And he found you for us," Sam put in cheerfully. "An aunt we didn't know we had. By the way, would you rather be called Aunt Bessie or Aunt Eliza?"

Miss Dunbar looked at him with her heart in her eyes. Her lips began to quiver. "Aunt Bessie would be—just fine," she said and then broke down utterly.

John Clarke found himself out of his chair bending over her with his arm around her shoulders saying, "There now, everything's going to be all right. There, there . . ."

He had taken the first long step toward forgiving her for not being guilty of his mother's crime.

Sam, another generation removed from it, had nothing to forgive her for. Nor did Betsy, he thought. Betsy, in fact, would probably fall in love with this little new-found aunt who was in far more need of love than their imperious, self-contained grandmother had ever been.

He smiled and yet was touched by his father's awkward efforts to check Miss Dunbar's flow of tears.

He was still smiling when he went out into the kitchen to look for Griff. "We seem to be enlarging the family circle," he said.

Presently, when Miss Dunbar's composure was restored, and they were all gathered in the living room, Griff told them what the prosecutor had said.

"So it's all over," John Clarke said.

"Except for the victim's name," Griff reminded him. "Egan's going to try to find out who he was."

*   *   *

Betsy met her great-aunt when she came home for the weekend the middle of October and took her under her wing as Sam had known she would.

Miss Dunbar was invited for Thanksgiving. The weekend before Betsy's Christmas vacation began she got an unexpected ride home and Griff and she drove to Chatham and took her out to dinner.

When they brought her home they stayed for a few minutes and Griff gave her the news he had withheld during dinner.

"They've identified the captain," he said. "His name was Kenneth Spencer. He trained in the engineering section at Camp Lee, Virginia, went from there to Camp Humphries—Fort Belvoir nowadays—and was assigned to Camp Devens in September 1917 to make a topographical survey. When he disappeared in October 1918 a board of officers was convened to look into his absence. The available evidence—that would be his state of mind, I suppose, his general attitude, his personal belongings still in his locker—indicated that his absence wasn't intentional and the assumption was made that he was the victim of some sort of accident. The records show that his wife was contacted but could supply no information—"

"Poor woman," Miss Dunbar said.

"Yes, but she remarried and made a new life for herself. She's been traced too. It was easy enough. She only moved about thirty miles away to Evansville, Indiana. She died there a few years ago and left several children and grandchildren."

"All her life, though, she must have wondered what became of her first husband. It's too bad she died without finding out."

Griff shook his head. "I doubt that it would have brought much joy into her declining days to have found out that he had taken on a mistress, led her to think he was going to get a divorce and marry her and got himself killed when he tried to break off their affair."

"Well, yes, there's that." Miss Dunbar glanced at Betsy who wore a faint frown of distaste. It was, after all, her grandmother who had been the mistress, the other woman in the classic triangle.

Miss Dunbar, who had adored her great-niece from the moment she met her, made haste to change the subject.

Betsy gave her a hug and a kiss when they left. "Don't forget now, I'll come down to pick you up the day before Christmas. I'm thinking of giving you a new hairdo for the occasion. Something real sharp. Okay?"

"Okay." Miss Dunbar looked ready to melt with delight on the spot.

She stood in the doorway as they went out to the car. Griff was pleased by the fuss Betsy made over her. He was glad she had a warm, loving heart with plenty of room in it for lame ducks. It would be a nuisance at times, he knew, but still he was glad.

Before he started the motor he leaned over and kissed her.

The Last Ride
of Her Life . . .

"I know how scared you are of the Ferris wheel," Robin told Dierdre. "And I know why. But once you get on it, and you have a safe ride, all your awful memories will disappear."

"You really think so?" Dierdre asked.

"I'm positive," Robin insisted.

Except your ride *won't* be safe, Robin thought. I'll make sure of it.

Because I'll be up on the Ferris wheel with you, Dierdre. Way up in the sky, in that little, swaying car.

And I'll send you right off the top.

You'll make a lovely puddle when you land, Dierdre.

Books by R. L. Stine

FEAR STREET®
R·L·STINE

FEAR PARK #2

The Loudest Scream

A Parachute Press Book

AN ARCHWAY PAPERBACK
Published by POCKET BOOKS
New York   London   Toronto   Sydney   Tokyo   Singapore

AN ARCHWAY PAPERBACK *Original*

An Archway Paperback published by
POCKET BOOKS, a division of Simon & Schuster Inc.
1230 Avenue of the Americas, New York, NY 10020

ISBN: 0-671-52956-0

First Archway Paperback printing September 1996

10 9 8 7 6 5 4 3 2

FEAR STREET is a registered trademark of
Parachute Press, Inc.

AN ARCHWAY PAPERBACK and colophon are
registered trademarks of Simon & Schuster Inc.

Cover art by Bill Schmidt

Printed in the U.S.A.

IL 7+

The Loudest Scream

chapter
1

"**D**ierdre, look out!" Robin Fear grabbed Dierdre Bradley's arm and pulled her to a stop.

She gasped, startled.

"Sorry, I didn't mean to scare you," Robin told her. "You were about to step in that mud puddle."

Dierdre glanced down at the deep pool of muddy water inches from her feet. "Thanks, Rob. I didn't even notice it."

"No wonder." Robin patted her arm tenderly. Dierdre's green eyes didn't sparkle the way they usually did. Her long, straight, dark brown hair hung limply. Her face sagged with sadness.

Robin followed her gaze. The two of them stood in the middle of Shadyside Cemetery where Paul Malone, Dierdre's boyfriend, had just been buried.

The graveside service was over. Almost everyone had left.

1

Fog drifted through the trees and slithered around the headstones like smoke. A drop of water splashed onto Robin's head, and he glanced up. Thick gray clouds covered the sky. The rain had let up for the moment. But the ground was a swamp, and moisture dripped from the trees.

"I feel as if I'm in a horrible nightmare," Dierdre declared. "I still can't believe Paul is dead."

Robin felt her trembling. He slid his arm around her shoulders and turned her away from the sight of the fresh grave. "Come on, let's get out of here," he urged. "The sky looks ready to open up on us again."

"I don't know what I'd do without you, Rob." Dierdre leaned against him as they slowly made their way along the cemetery path.

"Hey, I haven't done anything special," he protested.

"Yes you have. Just being with me helps." Dierdre's lips trembled. "I still can't believe he's gone. And the way he died!" She shuddered.

Robin squeezed her shoulder, but didn't respond. In his mind, he pictured Paul Malone as he'd last seen him.

Crushed beneath a giant Ferris wheel.

His head—sliced off. His legs splayed out, wiggling and jerking each time the cars of the giant wheel passed over his broken, lifeless body.

Robin sighed. He would never forget that sight.

"I know how you feel," he murmured to Dierdre. "But try to force it out of your mind."

"I can't help it!" Dierdre cried. "Every time I shut my eyes, I see him lying there." She shivered and leaned closer to Robin. "I don't know if I'll ever be able to enjoy Fear Park."

"I don't blame you," Robin said softly.

"So many horrible things have happened ever since my family decided to build an amusement park here," Dierdre declared. "My grandfather was killed. Then those kids who were clearing the land went totally crazy and chopped each other to pieces with their hatchets. That freak accident with the scaffold that killed all those painters. Now Paul is dead, and I can't help wondering what's going to happen next!"

"I've been wondering the same thing," Robin admitted. "You know, there's an old story that Nicholas Fear put a curse on the land."

"A curse?"

Robin shook his head. "I know it sounds crazy, but maybe it's true. Maybe all the tragedies are some kind of warning that the curse is real."

He glanced at her out of the corner of his eye. Did she believe the story of the curse? He couldn't tell. "It makes me wonder if Fear Park should open," he added.

Dierdre stopped walking and stared at him. "You mean not open at all? Not ever?"

"I guess that's what I mean," he admitted. "What do you think?"

"I'm not sure. But it doesn't matter what I think," she said. "My father is the one in charge."

Robin frowned. "And he's going ahead with the opening, even after what happened to Paul?"

Dierdre nodded. "He feels awful, naturally. But he's definitely going to open the park."

Robin's hands curled into fists. The park was actually going to open! He couldn't believe it!

More than sixty years before, a Bradley had come up with the idea of Fear Park—a huge amusement park to be built in the Fear Street Woods.

But a Fear—Nicholas Fear—claimed that the Fear Street Woods belonged to the Fears. He had opposed the park.

Violently.

The town had ruled in Bradley's favor.

And now, sixty years later, Jason Bradley— Dierdre's father—planned to open Fear Park in a few days.

Robin's hands shook with fury. But he forced them to relax. He took several deep breaths, until he was sure Dierdre wouldn't hear the anger in his voice.

"Maybe you could talk to your father," he suggested to her. "Tell him how you feel. Get him to change his mind."

"Forget it," Dierdre told him. "Daddy won't let anything stop him from opening the park. And I don't blame him. I mean, he's worked so long for it. It's his dream, Rob."

Yes, Robin thought. Fear Park is Jason Bradley's dream.

Too bad.

Because that dream will become a nightmare if the park doesn't shut down forever.

I'll make sure of it.

I'll do whatever it takes to ruin things for Jason Bradley. To make his life miserable. I'll kill again if I have to.

After all, I already killed Paul. And all those kids back in the '30s. Why not someone else?

Robin's lips curled in a small, satisfied smile. He'd killed Paul to make trouble for the Bradleys. He'd kill again. Again and again and again.

Whatever it takes, he thought to himself.

He turned to Dierdre. She leaned against him, her head pressing against his arm.

She's so trusting, Robin thought scornfully. She has no idea I was responsible for Paul's hideous death. She thinks I'm her friend. She thinks I'm more than a friend.

As they passed through the cemetery gate, Dierdre sighed again. "I guess you're right, Rob. I really have to try to forget the way Paul looked when he . . . died. That's not the way I want to remember him."

"Right," Robin agreed. "Try to blot it out of your mind." He squeezed her shoulder, thinking. Maybe he'd wasted his time on Paul. After all, Paul Malone didn't mean much to Dierdre's father.

But Dierdre was another story. Dierdre was the apple of her father's eye.

Maybe he should kill Dierdre. It would be so much fun to watch Jason Bradley suffer over the death of his precious daughter. He'd have to think about that.

"Paul was so full of life." Dierdre sighed, interrupting Robin's thoughts. "He had his bad points. He bragged a lot. But he had a ton of energy."

Not anymore, Robin thought.

"And he was so athletic," Dierdre continued with a sad smile. "Basketball, swimming, track. He was good at all of them."

"Mmm," Robin murmured. He wished she'd shut up. Paul Malone was history. He was sick of hearing about him.

"I can just see him now, finishing the cross-country race last year against Waynesbridge High." Dierdre's voice became more lively. "A bunch of us were waiting at the finish line. Then we heard a loud shout. I looked up and there was Paul. Way ahead of the pack."

He still is, Robin thought with a sneer. Nobody else in his group has died.

Not yet, anyway.

"And he didn't even look tired," Dierdre said. "He had a big grin on his face and . . ."

Dierdre broke off. Robin felt her body tense. "There he is!" she cried. "It—it's Paul! Here he comes! It's Paul!"

Robin's head snapped up. His body went cold as he followed Dierdre's gaze.

A guy strode quickly toward them down the sidewalk. Tall, with broad shoulders. Wavy dark blond hair. A silver ring glinting in his ear.

Paul Malone.

chapter
2

Robin's heart pounded. He fought to keep himself from screaming.

It can't be! his mind shrieked. It's impossible! Paul is dead. I know it. I killed him!

Something must have gone wrong. Horribly wrong!

Robin felt Dierdre's cold hand grasp his.

He watched as Paul Malone advanced on them, his dark tie whipping back in the breeze. His eyes narrowed to slits.

Coming closer.

Closer.

"Oh!" Dierdre gasped again. She squeezed Robin's hand.

Robin closed his eyes. Braced himself.

And then Dierdre let out a startled laugh.

Robin turned and stared at her. How could she laugh? Had she gone totally crazy?

"Oh, wow!" Dierdre exclaimed. "It's not Paul. It's Jared!"

Robin licked his lips. "Who's Jared?"

"Paul's brother," Dierdre explained. "He's a year younger. I can't believe how much they look alike. They could be twins, couldn't they?"

A younger brother. A younger, look-alike brother. Robin felt a flood of relief wash over him. "Definitely," he replied. "They could definitely be twins."

But they're not.

Paul is dead.

Calm again, Robin peered through the fog at Jared Malone.

"Jared is kind of wild," Dierdre murmured. "He's always getting into trouble. Paul told me he has a terrible temper. And see those three guys behind him?"

Robin nodded. Three guys, uncomfortable in their dark-colored funeral suits, leaned against the wrought-iron fence of the cemetery, watching Jared.

"Those are his buddies. Joey is the short one. Steve has the ponytail, and Kevin is the one with the muscles. They're even wilder than he is." Dierdre squeezed Robin's hand again. "Paul tried to get him to drop these guys. But Jared wouldn't. I guess he's kind of stubborn."

At the moment, Jared looked furious as well as

9

stubborn. His square jaw jutted angrily. And as he drew to a stop in front of them, his blue eyes glared menacingly at Dierdre.

"Jared, what is it?" Dierdre asked. "Why are you staring at me like that?"

"Why do you think?" Jared snarled. "My brother's dead. We just buried him. And whose fault do you think it is?"

Dierdre shook her head. "It wasn't anybody's fault. It was a terrible accident."

"Yeah, right." Jared's lips curled in a sneer. "I should have guessed you'd say that. I should have guessed you'd stick up for your dad!"

"What are you talking about?" Dierdre cried.

"Oh, come off it!" Jared snapped. "I'm talking about how Paul wouldn't be dead if your father didn't care so much about his stupid amusement park!"

Robin felt a surge of pleasure. So Jared blamed the Bradleys for Paul's death. Great! A few more deaths and disasters, and everybody would be screaming at Bradley to close the park.

"That park is the only thing on his mind," Jared went on. "He just has to get it open. And if somebody dies because your father is too lazy or cheap to make sure the equipment's running right . . . well, too bad! I mean, what does one dead body matter? We'll still have Fear Park!"

"That's not true!" Dierdre shrieked. "My father

feels *terrible* about Paul. He had that Ferris wheel checked over and over. It *was* running right! Paul was the one he hired to operate it. And Paul would have told him if something was wrong!"

Jared's eyes flashed angrily. "Oh, so now it's *Paul's* fault, huh?"

"I didn't mean that and you know it!" Dierdre shot back. "It was nobody's fault."

"Wrong." Jared stubbornly shook his head back and forth. "It's somebody's fault, all right. You know what I think? I think maybe I should talk to *him* about it."

"To . . . to Daddy?"

"Yeah. Somebody has to tell him he's a killer!" Jared shouted. He spun away from her and sprinted down the sidewalk toward his buddies.

Dierdre turned to Robin. "I can't *believe* this!" she cried, her expression worried and frightened. "If he really says those things to Dad's face, there's going to be major trouble."

Good, Robin thought. The more trouble for Bradley, the better.

"Jared was upset," he told Dierdre, his voice smooth and comforting. "I think he just had a lot of steam to blow off, and he did it with you. He'll cool down now."

"Maybe. But he scares me, Rob." Dierdre shuddered as they began walking. "I'm afraid he's so angry he might do something terrible."

"I think he's just talk," Robin assured her. "Come on, I'll walk you home. You'll feel better once you're warm and dry."

Robin slid his arm around Dierdre's shoulder, and she leaned against him. He smiled, thinking how much power he had over her.

As they passed a parked car, Robin's smile suddenly froze.

That face! That face reflected in the car window!

One half of it was his. Robin Fear's pale, young face. Straight brown hair. Intense, dark eyes.

The other half was his, too. But the sight of it sent a shiver of horror down his spine.

Wrinkles like cracked, dried-up gullies twisted through the sagging flesh of his cheek.

Deep lines at the corners of his eye and mouth looked as if they'd been gouged with a knife.

His cheekbone jutted out from under the skin. His eye was sunk deep behind a ridge of bone.

And his skin! The deep, bluish-purple of a bruise, his skin sagged and rippled and seemed ready to slide off his skull.

Staring into the car window, Robin could almost smell the stench of decay.

Robin gasped.

Had Dierdre seen it? Has she seen the decayed half of my face?

Do I have to kill her *now*?

chapter
3

Robin quickly turned partway to Dierdre.

She stared straight ahead, frowning.

Probably still thinking about Paul, Robin decided. Or worried about Jared. It didn't matter.

All that mattered was that she hadn't seen his face.

But he had to get away from her now. Before she *did* see the decaying half of his head.

Dropping his arm from Dierdre's shoulders, Robin came to a sudden stop. He turned away, covering the rotting half of his face with a hand.

"Rob, what is it?" Dierdre asked. "What's wrong?"

He let out a low moan. "My head," he mumbled. "I get these migraines sometimes. They can be pretty bad."

13

"I think I have some aspirin in my bag," Dierdre told him. "Let me look . . ."

"Don't bother!" Robin sucked air in through his teeth. "Aspirin doesn't do any good. The only thing that helps is to lie down in a dark room. Listen, Dierdre, I'd better get home fast. Will you be okay? I mean, I wanted to walk you home, but . . ." Robin let his voice trail off and moaned again.

"Don't be ridiculous," Dierdre told him. "I don't feel like going home yet, anyway. I want to walk a little and think about Paul by myself."

She put her hand on his shoulder and gently rubbed it. "You go ahead, Rob. And thanks for everything."

Robin nodded, as if he hurt too much to speak. He groaned softly and shuffled away. When he reached the end of the block, he took a chance and glanced behind him.

Dierdre was nowhere in sight.

Robin raced around the corner. Down another block. The rain started up again, the cold drops pelting his head and face.

His face! Robin reached up to feel it. The decay was worse now. His fingers slid deep into the slimy, rotting flesh, as if he were poking at a slug. He shuddered and yanked his hand away. What had gone wrong?

At last he came to Fear Street. His father's huge stone house loomed out of the mist. Behind it rose the dark, twisted trees of the Fear Street Woods. And way beyond that—but still too close—Robin could see the top of Fear Park's giant Ferris wheel.

Don't think about that now! You'll take care of the park soon enough. First, take care of yourself!

He hurtled across the sweeping lawn. Then burst in through a side door into the pantry.

Taking great gulps of the mansion's musty air, Robin pounded down the dimly lit hall and into the library. Gray light seeped through gaps in the thick velvet drapes. An enormous stone fireplace took up one wall. Floor-to-ceiling bookcases lined the other three.

Robin hurried across the Oriental rug to the far wall and climbed the ladder up to the second level of books.

A collection of ancient, leather-bound volumes stood between two marble bookends. Books on the occult and the dark arts. Robin's fingers raced over their gold-lettered spines as he searched for the right volume.

Where was it? *Where was it?*

There! Robin grasped the slender book of chants and spells with shaking fingers and tugged it out. He clambered down the ladder and strode to the fireplace.

A silver urn studded with precious stones stood on the center of the mantel. Slender handles widened at the top to become the open jaws of snarling lions. Robin tucked the book under one arm and carried it and the urn to the claw-footed library table on the far side of the room.

He lifted the lid from the urn. A bittersweet odor drifted up as he paged rapidly through the book.

There it was—the immortality spell. The spell Robin had been using since 1935 to keep himself seventeen forever.

The spell that kept him alive and young and strong.

Robin closed his eyes and began to chant.

Purple smoke began to drift around the room. Thin at first, it grew denser and denser until it became a swirling, purple mass that filled the entire room.

The spell was working its magic.

Robin dipped his fingers into the urn.

Slowly, he spread the thick, bittersweet-smelling cream onto his hands.

As he continued the chant, he scooped up more of the cream and began rubbing it onto his face. It burned when it hit the rotting flesh. But Robin ignored the pain. Pain was a small price to pay for immortality.

Gradually, Robin felt his skin begin to tighten. The grooves and wrinkles smoothed out. The jutting bones sank back behind the youthful flesh of a teenager.

Robin finished the ancient chant and took a deep

breath. The smell of decay disappeared. He opened his eyes. The purple smoke was thinning now. A few lavender curls drifted lazily through the room, then vanished.

The immortality spell had worked its magic again.

Robin smiled to himself.

Then he froze. What was that? A noise that didn't belong.

He heard it again! A shuffling sound at the library door.

Robin's heartbeat thudded loudly in his ears. He'd left the door open. He'd been in such a hurry to work the spell that he'd forgotten to shut himself in here.

Someone had witnessed him working the immortality spell. Seen the purple smoke and heard the chant. Watched his face magically transform from the decay of death to the firm flesh of youth.

He wasn't alone.

Someone had sneaked into the house.

Slowly, he turned to the door.

chapter
4

A girl stood in the doorway.

Long, wavy red hair framed the young, smiling face of Meghan Fairwood.

"Don't sneak up on me like that!" Robin snapped. "I didn't even know you were there. You scared me!"

"Sorry. I didn't mean to, Robin." Meghan's smile faltered a little. But then she tossed her coppery hair back and stepped into the room. Her glance fell on the urn and the book of spells. "How come you've been working the spell? I thought you were supposed to do it last week."

"I was, but I forgot," Robin admitted. "Half my face started to go. I almost didn't make it home in time!"

"Oh, Robin! I wish you wouldn't wait so long between your treatments!" she cried. "What if you

18

didn't use the spell in time? What would I do then?"

Meghan's eyes filled with tears. She ran across the room into Robin's arms. Her silky hair brushed his cheek. Her hair smelled of flowers. It was her shampoo, Robin knew. The shampoo Meghan had used ever since he'd known her.

Ever since they'd been teenagers together—back in 1935.

Meghan was the one person I brought with me into immortality, Robin thought. After all this time, we're still together. I can't believe it.

Tightening her arms around his neck, Meghan snuggled close to him, planting little kisses on his neck. Then she leaned back and gazed at him with love in her eyes.

"I'm glad you're back," she told him. "I get so lonely when you're gone."

"I had things to do, Meghan. You know that."

"Oh, sure . . . I know!" Meghan leaned against the table and watched as Robin put away the book and the urn. "So how did it go? Were you able to protect the Bradleys and Fear Park for one more day?"

Robin forced an exhausted sigh. "Battling the curse my father put on the park is incredibly hard," he told her as he climbed the bookshelf ladder. "But I managed to do it again today. The Bradleys and their park are still safe."

Robin wanted to laugh. Meghan was so easy to fool!

"That's really great," Meghan told him. "I started to get worried when you didn't come home sooner. I kept thinking something horrible had happened. Something as bad as the hatchet murders." She shuddered. "I can still see it, Robin. All of my friends, chopping themselves to death. Such horror. I can see it as if it was yesterday, can't you?"

"Yes." Of course I remember the hatchet murders, Robin thought. How could I forget?

How could I forget something so totally perfect?

As Robin stared at the bookshelf, the row of books blurred and he pictured the grisly scene.

Dozens of kids—laughing, joking, singing—had gathered in the woods. All wore work shirts and jeans and boots.

And all carried hatchets.

Jack Bradley had hired them, at a dollar a day, to chop up the tree stumps left when part of the woods had been cut down. Cut down to make way for Fear Park.

Meghan was there with her friends. Including her boyfriend at that time, Richard Bradley. Richard Bradley, whose father, Jack, had ordered the clearing of the Fear land.

Robin was there, too, pretending to help. He told

Meghan that he'd sneaked away from his father to be with her.

Meghan had been worried. "Are you sure you want to be here, Robin?" she asked. "I have a bad feeling about it. A very bad feeling."

"Everything will be fine," Robin assured her. "I can take care of myself."

And I can take care of Fear Park, too, he thought. Just wait. You think you have a bad feeling now. Wait until you see what's coming!

The youth crew began swinging their hatchets, chopping at the tree stumps. It was the Great Depression, and a dollar a day was a lot of money. The kids laughed and joked as they worked.

And then Richard Bradley spotted Robin. Jealous because Meghan liked Robin, Richard picked a fight. Robin didn't have to do a thing. He just stood by as Richard's anger built into a wild rage.

Out of control, Richard swung his hatchet—and just missed Robin's head.

Richard swung the hatchet again. The glistening silver blade whistled as he swept it through the air—and sliced into another boy's throat.

Screams and cries of horror broke out.

Richard's next swing finished the job. The boy's head flew off.

Blood spurted like a fountain from the boy's ragged neck. His head rolled into the leaves and wood chips.

Screams filled the woods.

Thick purple smoke began to swirl through the air.

Another hatchet sliced through the air. Then another, and another.

The kids shrieked in a murderous frenzy as they whipped their deadly blades at one another.

Blood and hunks of flesh flew through the air, spattering the tree stumps, the ground, the faces and arms of everyone in the clearing.

One of the shining blades sank deep into Richard Bradley's back. With a groan, he sank to the ground. Crimson blood poured from his wound and seeped into the forest floor.

The strange purple smoke rose and twisted and surged through the clearing.

Meghan screamed as a blade flashed close to her head. Robin grabbed her hand and pulled her to safety at the edge of the clearing. "Robin, how can this be happening?" she cried.

"I don't know. They've all gone crazy!" He put his hands on her shoulders and gave her a shove. "Run, Meghan! Run home and call the police! Hurry!"

Meghan raced off through the trees, and Robin turned back to the clearing.

The slaughter continued.

As Robin gazed on the scene of horror, a smile of triumph crossed his face.

I did this! he thought proudly. I caused this massacre! The kids will chop one another to bits. The park will never be built now! Never!

That's what he had thought then, sixty years ago.

But now, standing on the library ladder, Robin gritted his teeth and sighed in frustration.

"Robin, are you okay?" Meghan's voice broke into his thoughts. "I'm sorry I said anything about the hatcheting. I didn't mean to make you remember something so awful."

"It's all right." Robin rearranged his expression so he looked serious and concerned, then climbed down the ladder. "I think about it all the time anyway," he told her with another sigh. "And I'm like you. I can't stop worrying that something like it might happen again."

"Then let me help you!" Meghan cried. "There must be something I can do! I mean, you made us *both* immortal so we could prevent another tragedy from happening. But you've been trying to do it alone, and it's not fair. Please let me help you fight your father's curse!"

Robin shook his head firmly. "No, Meghan. I know you want to help, but I can't let you. I don't want you to be hurt."

"But . . ."

"No!" he repeated. "You've already lost too much because of this park. Your home. All your friends. Everything. I can't let you take a risk after what you've been through."

"I just wish there was something I could do for you," she insisted.

Striding to her side, Robin slid his arms around her. "You already are," he told her softly, resting his chin on top of her head. "It's enough that I find you here waiting for me when I come home. It's more than enough. It keeps me going."

As Meghan leaned against him, Robin smiled grimly. Meghan never found out that I was responsible for the deaths of all her friends so many years ago, he thought. And she must never learn the truth—that I learned the Fear magic to protect my father's land.

She thinks I learned it so I could protect the Bradleys. But she's wrong. So wrong. I'm going to destroy all their plans. No matter what I have to do. No matter who I have to kill.

Thinking about what he would do, how he would get even, Robin squeezed Meghan tightly.

"You're so wonderful, Robin," Meghan murmured. "I haven't had a normal life since you made us immortal. No friends. Hiding from the neighbors so they won't realize we never age. But I don't regret it. We're together, and that's what matters."

As she spoke, Meghan stretched her hand up and caressed Robin's face. Her fingers softly stroked his

24

cheek, then came to a sudden stop. She pulled away with a jerk.

"What's wrong?" Robin asked.

"Nothing, really." Meghan kissed his cheek. "You just missed a little spot, that's all."

With a gasp, Robin pulled away from her and raced to the mirror. Meghan was right. A purple, decaying spot of flesh still remained just above the left corner of his mouth.

Robin hurried up the ladder and pulled out the book of spells again. He grabbed the urn and set it on the library table. Opening the book, he began the chant of immortality.

Meghan left the library, shutting the door softly behind her.

Robin closed his eyes and continued the chant.

The purple smoke swirled and billowed around the room.

Dierdre climbed the three steps into her father's office—a blue trailer at Fear Park's front gate. The trailer was empty.

She sat in the leather chair and frowned at the desktop. Stacks of folders and contracts covered its surface. All of them were labeled FEAR PARK.

Dad won't stop, she thought with a sigh.

Paul's funeral was yesterday. But not even that will stop Dad from going ahead with the park.

Dierdre knew how much the park meant to her father. And she was on his side, she really was. But maybe Rob had been right. Should her father forget the whole thing, and find some other project? A safer project?

It wasn't just Paul's death that made her wonder. It was the history of the place. A history of hate. Of blood. Of violent death.

Dierdre shuddered. That history was so strong, she was afraid it would overpower all the good her father wanted to do.

She decided to talk to him about it. She owed it to Paul.

Dierdre glanced at her watch. Twelve noon. Rising from the desk, she strode to the tiny refrigerator and pulled it open. A tuna sandwich wrapped in plastic sat on the shelf next to an apple and a small carton of milk.

Daddy's lunch, she thought. And he'll be here to get it any minute. Should I try to talk to him when he comes in?

As Dierdre shut the refrigerator, the office door flew open. Expecting her father, she turned around, smiling.

Jared Malone stood in the doorway.

Dierdre's smile faded. "What are *you* doing here?" she demanded.

Jared's eyes shifted nervously around the office.

Without replying, he burst across the floor and grabbed Dierdre's arm.

Dierdre tried to pull away, but Jared tightened his grip. His fingers squeezed tighter and tighter.

"Jared!" she gasped. "What are you doing? What are you *doing?*"

chapter
5

"What's your problem? Think I'm going to hurt you?" Jared asked. He dropped her arm and smiled. "I just want to talk to you."

Dierdre drew back, her heart pounding. "How did you get into the park anyway?"

"A guy who knew Paul let me in. All I want to do is talk," he repeated. "I . . . I need a favor. From your father."

"Are you kidding?" Dierdre replied. "After what you said yesterday, isn't he the *last* person on earth you'd ask for a favor?"

Jared shook his head. "Look, I said some things I didn't mean, okay? I was upset about Paul. You can't blame me for that, right?"

He tried to sound sad and apologetic. If he could just get Dierdre on his side, then everything would work out the way he'd planned.

Dierdre gazed at him for a moment. "No, I guess

28

I can't blame you," she said. "What kind of favor do you want? Maybe I can help."

All right! Jared thought, nodding eagerly. "Yeah, I think you *can* help," he told her. "I think you can smooth the way for me."

"Smooth the way for what?"

Okay, Jared told himself. Here goes. He took a deep breath. "I need a job, Dierdre. I came to ask your father for a job."

Dierdre blinked in surprise. "You mean a job at Fear Park?" she asked.

"Yeah, that's right," Jared replied. "See, I figured I could take Paul's place. Run the Ferris wheel, do whatever else he was going to do."

Not that anybody can take Paul's place, he thought to himself. But if I can just get a job here, I'll be on the inside. The perfect place to cause trouble. Major trouble for Jason Bradley.

"Listen, Jared—" Dierdre started to say.

"I know I can do it," he interrupted. "I'm good with mechanical stuff. Cars, lawn mowers, VCRs, all kinds of machines. Why not a Ferris wheel?"

Dierdre kept quiet.

Jared couldn't tell what she was thinking. He lowered his eyes and spoke softly. "It'll really mean a lot to me, knowing I'd be carrying on in Paul's place."

If that doesn't get her, nothing will, he thought.

He studied her face. Her lips shook as if she were about to cry. Great! She's definitely buying my sob story!

"Please, Dierdre," Jared pleaded. "All I want is a chance. Couldn't you ask your dad for me?"

"Why don't you ask me yourself?" a voice demanded.

"Daddy!" Dierdre cried. Sidestepping Jared, she sped across the office to her father.

Jared stayed where he was, gazing at the short, overweight man with bushy black hair. The man he blamed for Paul's death. No, not death—murder.

Jason Bradley glanced at Dierdre, then Jared, then back at Dierdre. "What's going on, Dee? You look upset."

"No, I'm okay," Dierdre told him. "Dad, you know Jared Malone. Paul's brother."

Mr. Bradley's expression softened. "Of course. Jared, I want to tell you again how terribly sorry I am about Paul."

Jared didn't respond. Just the sight of Bradley made him want to bash something. He clenched his jaw to keep from shouting.

Keep cool, he told himself. Don't blow it now.

"We'll all miss him," Mr. Bradley continued. "He was—"

"Okay, thanks," Jared cut him off. "But I didn't

come here to talk about my brother. I came to get work."

"He wants to take Paul's place," Dierdre explained.

"Right," Jared agreed. "I was telling Dierdre I'm good with machines and stuff. I can run the Ferris wheel and anything else, just as good as Paul."

"Oh, too bad," Bradley replied. "I've already hired a replacement for Paul. Rob Fear. Do you know him?"

"No." He probably hired the guy before Paul's body was even cold, Jared thought angrily. "But that's okay. How about some other job?" he suggested quickly. "I could sell tickets, maybe, or run an ice-cream stand. Anything!"

Mr. Bradley kept shaking his head. "All the jobs are filled right now. I have a waiting list. Maybe next summer."

"But that'll be too late!" Jared blurted out.

"I'm sorry, truly," Bradley said.

Jared finally lost control. "Yeah, right!" he snapped. "If you're so sorry, how come you replaced Paul so fast, huh? I know why. Because you didn't care about him. All you care about is the lousy park!"

"Now just a minute!" Bradley cried.

"Forget it!" Jared shouted. "Don't even bother making any excuses. They'd all be lies!"

Jason Bradley's eyes narrowed. "I think you'd better leave, son."

"Good idea! I can't stand the smell in this place, anyway!" Furious, Jared strode across the office. He shoved Bradley roughly aside as he bolted out the door.

Behind him, he heard Bradley shout. But he didn't turn back.

His anger built as he raced down the steps and onto the path where his friends waited for him.

"Hey, man," Steve called, "what happened?"

"Forget it!" Jared snapped.

"I guess Bradley didn't go for it, huh?" Kevin asked.

"I told you to forget it!" Jared grabbed a rock from the path and squeezed it in his hands. "It was a dumb idea, okay?"

Joey frowned. "So what are you going to do now, Jared?"

Jared marched quickly along the path, shaking his head, too angry to speak.

Jason Bradley! he thought. The guy practically murders Paul and won't even give me the time of day! Says he's *so* sorry, but he can't do a thing for me. Can't even find me a job selling ice-cream cones!

Jared's anger boiled up inside him until he could hardly see straight. He wanted to hit something! To bash something to pieces!

THE LOUDEST SCREAM

In a rage, he cocked his arm back and hurled the rock through the air as hard as he could.

"Hey, man, watch it!" Joey cried out.

Too late.

A high-pitched shriek of pain split the air.

chapter 6

The shriek spiraled up through the empty park. Jared shut his eyes.

What did I hit? A child?

His eyes snapped open.

At the end of the path stood a sign—THE MONKEY PRESERVE.

The rock rested at the base of a tree just inside the fence. On one of the tree limbs sat a small squirrel monkey. A trickle of bright red blood ran down one side of its face, matting down the fur. Its eyes were bright with fear, as if it expected another rock to come hurtling out of nowhere any second.

A monkey, Jared thought. Not a kid. Still, he felt bad. He hadn't meant to hit the little guy. He hadn't meant to hit anything.

As Jared moved closer to the edge of the preserve to get a better look, a tall, muscular man wearing a brown-and-gold Fear Park uniform raced from an adjoining path. Two more uniformed men ran behind him.

"Hey, you!" the man shouted angrily. As he drew closer, Jared saw the words S. GUNTHER, PRESERVE MANAGER, on his name tag. "Did you throw that rock? Get away from there!"

Before Jared could say a word, Gunther ran up and shoved him roughly away from the edge of the preserve.

Jared stumbled back, falling against Steve. He held his hands out, palms up. "Hey, man, I'm sorry!" he exclaimed to Gunther. "I didn't mean to hit him. It was an accident!"

"Tell that to the monkey!" Gunther's hard brown eyes were hot with anger. He gave Jared another shove.

"Hey!" Jared's own temper flared. "I *said* I was sorry!"

"Yeah, give him a break!" Kevin shouted. He flexed the muscles under his tight T-shirt.

"The only break you get is not being arrested— not this time, anyway," Gunther declared. He waved to the two workers, who stepped forward. "Get these four thugs out of the park," he ordered.

"You can't do that!" Jared cried.

"Oh, yes I can." Gunther gave him an icy smile. "I'm giving you a two-man escort out of here. We do that with all our VIPs—Very Important Punks!"

One of Gunther's men put a hand on Jared's arm. Jared stiffened. A fight would feel great right about now, he thought.

Four of us and three of them? Gunther looks pretty solid, but the other two are mostly flab. We could take them, easy.

"Don't even think about it, punk," Gunther warned, as if he could read Jared's mind. "One swing from you or your buddies, and my men will have the entire park security crew in your faces in a minute flat."

Jared felt his face heat up with anger and embarrassment. He hated being pushed around. But Gunther was obviously ready to call in the cavalry. "Don't bother," he told the preserve manager. "We can't get out of this lousy park fast enough!"

He glared at Gunther, then shook off the worker's hand and strode away.

From a bend in the path, Robin Fear watched as Jared and his friends hustled toward the park exit. Gunther's men stayed a few feet behind them, making sure they really left.

Robin stepped out and began to follow. As he passed Gunther he gave the preserve manager a friendly smile. "Hey, Mr. Gunther, how's it going?"

Gunther nodded briefly, then turned toward the monkey preserve.

Robin chuckled to himself as he hurried along. He wasn't surprised to see Gunther kick Jared and his buddies out. The preserve manager liked being King of the Mountain. Always had to be on top and in control.

Jared Malone is another story, Robin thought. Talk about being out of control. The guy is a walking time bomb!

And I just might be able to use that temper of his to help me mess things up around here.

Jared and his friends were out of the park now, heading down the street. Robin picked up his pace to a jog. "Jared!" he called. "Hey, Jared, wait up a sec!"

Jared stopped and turned around, frowning when he saw who had called his name. "What do *you* want?" he demanded. "Gonna get on my case for yelling at Dierdre yesterday?"

Robin shook his head. "No way, man. That's between you and her," he said. "I wanted to talk to you about something else."

"Yeah? What?"

"Gunther," Robin replied. "I saw what happened back there at the preserve."

Jared scowled. "So what? You want to make something of it?"

"No!" Robin widened his eyes in fake surprise. "Are you kidding? I'm on your side. Gunther is a prime jerk."

Steve chuckled. "You got that right."

Jared's scowl deepened. "I shouldn't have let him push me around like that."

Kevin nodded. "Yeah. You want to go back and get him now, Jared? Jump him before he can call in his guys?"

"I've got a better idea," Robin said quickly. "A much better idea."

"What's better than jumping the guy?" Kevin demanded.

"Scaring him," Robin replied. "And I mean *really* scaring him—so bad he'll cry for his mommy."

Jared's buddies laughed at the thought.

"So what's your idea?" Jared asked.

"Come on. I'll show you." Robin took off down the sidewalk, which wound around the outside of Fear Park. Jared and his friends followed. Like mice sniffing at a trap, Robin thought. If only I can get them to go for the bait.

The sidewalk sloped steeply upward, leading them to the top of a hill. From there, they could look down on the trees and rolling hills of Fear Park's wild animal preserve.

"See that cliff over there?" Robin asked.

"Yeah." Steve shrugged. "Big deal."

Robin ignored him and spoke to Jared. "That cliff juts out over the lion pasture. And every night at nine-thirty—like clockwork—Gunther goes up there and drops meat down to feed the lions." He licked his lips. "Those lions are *hungry,* too. They're just waiting down there with their jaws wide open!"

"Okay, I get the picture. So what's your idea?" Jared asked again, staring at the cliff.

"The park opens tomorrow," Robin told him. "There'll be a few people around tonight, checking things out. But not many. So you guys come here tonight."

He lowered his voice. "Then, the four of you sneak up on Gunther, surprise him from behind. Get it? You let him think you're going to push him off that cliff—straight into the lions' jaws!"

Steve and Kevin laughed and slapped each other high-fives. "That'll make him wish he never messed with us!" Joey exclaimed. "Right, Jared?"

"Yeah," Jared agreed. "But we're not supposed to be here. What if we get caught?"

"You won't," Robin assured him. "I'll make sure one gate is unlocked and I'll show you the service road that runs behind the park. You can use it without being spotted. Anyway, if somebody *does* see you, just say you're part of a work crew, checking the grounds."

"And then we sneak up on Gunther, right?" Joey asked eagerly. "And freak him out!"

"Yeah," Jared repeated thoughtfully. "Except Gunther doesn't look like the kind of guy who freaks so easy."

Robin smiled. "Believe it or not, Gunther is terrified of those lions. Why do you think he feeds them from the top of a cliff? You pretend you're going to shove him off, he'll go down on his knees and beg you not to!"

Kevin's lips curled in a sneer. "We gotta do it!"

Jared laughed. But then he stared at the cliff again, frowning and chewing his lip.

Don't let him think too long or he might not go for it, Robin told himself. "It's a chance for revenge—big time," he murmured, stepping close to Jared. "Just picture Gunther—his knees shaking, his face all white and scared, his eyes bugging out."

Jared glanced at Robin, then back at the cliff.

"What do you say?" Robin asked. "Will you do it?"

chapter
7

Jared let his eyes wander along the winding trail. The full moon cast spooky shadows over the ground. And the night breeze made weird rustling noises in the trees and bushes.

Jared's heart thudded as he crept cautiously up the trail with his buddies. A twig snapped close by, sounding like a firecracker going off in his ear. "What was that?" he whispered. "Anybody see anything?"

"Nothing," Steve murmured. "Probably a bird or a squirrel or something."

Jared narrowed his eyes and peered down the path. All he could see were shadows. The path seemed empty.

"Think a night watchman spotted us?" Joey asked, gazing around anxiously.

"Nah. Remember? Rob Fear told us they won't

patrol this part of the park until it's open," Kevin replied. "Maybe it was a raccoon. Come on. Let's get going."

As they moved on, Jared lagged behind, thinking. He was almost positive the noise had been a footstep. *What if Rob Fear is wrong and a night watchman catches us? After that scene I made in his office this afternoon, Jason Bradley will probably have me thrown in jail.*

The wind picked up, noisily blowing the leaves and branches. Jared tensed with every creak and rustle. *It's not too late to turn back,* he thought. *Gunther is not going anywhere. I can get to him some other time.*

But it wouldn't be so easy once the park had its grand opening tomorrow. Then the place would be packed all night. Not much chance of catching Gunther feeding the lions by himself.

Thinking of Gunther, Jared gritted his teeth. *The guy has to pay for the way he treated me,* he thought. *And Rob Fear had the right idea—catch the preserve manager alone and scare the pants off him! Teach him a lesson he'll never forget!*

Jared picked up his pace and hurried after his friends. The path wound through the trees for another fifty yards. Then it began to steepen, just as Rob had described.

"This is it!" Jared whispered. "About twenty

more yards and we'll be at the top. We've got to be real quiet from now on."

"Yeah." Kevin snickered. "We don't want to spoil Gunther's surprise!"

The path grew more narrow. With Jared in the lead again, the boys walked single file.

Almost at the top of the incline, Jared came to a halt and held his hand up. The others stopped behind him. Together, they listened.

Jared heard a night bird warble two notes. Then . . . silence.

Jared inched the rest of the way up the incline. At the top, the ground flattened out. He could see the waist-high rail running along the edge of the cliff.

No sign of Gunther.

Jared checked his watch. Twenty-seven minutes after nine. If Rob Fear was right, Gunther should be coming up the other path any minute now.

Jared rejoined the others. And the group quietly crept into a small grove of trees to wait.

The wait didn't last long.

Jared almost gasped aloud as a rattling, clanking sound broke the quiet of the park. Faint and distant at first, it grew closer and louder. Soon Jared could hear footsteps, and the shrill sound of someone whistling through his teeth.

The rattling noise and the footsteps stopped abruptly, but the whistling continued.

Jared relaxed and exchanged grins with the others. He waved his arm and motioned them out of the grove. "Let's do it!" he whispered.

Cautiously, the four boys crept to the top of the incline and peered across the clearing.

Gunther stood near the rail, whistling as he pulled on a pair of plastic gloves. Two large metal buckets sat on the ground beside him.

With the gloves on, Gunther reached into one of the buckets and pulled out a huge slab of raw meat. The gristle and fat ran through it like thick veins, glistening white in the moonlight. Dark red juice oozed from Gunther's plastic-covered fingers and dripped onto the tops of his boots. He didn't stop whistling.

Probably eats the stuff himself, Jared thought. And then his skin prickled as a deep rumbling sound echoed up from the base of the cliff.

The lions, hungry for their dinner.

Waving his arm again, Jared led the others into the clearing. As planned, Joey and Steve crossed to the right side to block Gunther's escape to the other path. Kevin moved to the left.

Keeping to the middle, Jared strode quickly across the clearing until he was only a couple of feet behind the preserve manager. He watched Gunther bend over the bucket again.

"Hey, Gunther!" Jared's voice rang out loudly. "Having a little snack?"

Gunther straightened up with a jerk. The startled expression changed to anger when he saw Jared. "What do you think you're doing here?" he demanded.

"You threw me out of the park today, remember?" Jared replied. "You shouldn't have done that."

Gunther's lip curled scornfully. "Get lost, kid, or I'll throw you out again. And this time, I'll make sure you're *never* allowed back in."

Joey giggled from the right side of the clearing. "I don't think so!"

"Yeah," Kevin called from the left side. "You don't have any backup this time."

"Can't call in your troops tonight," Steve declared.

Gunther's head swiveled from side to side as he located the other boys. Then he turned back to Jared. "What do you want?"

Jared smiled coldly and stepped closer to Gunther. "We thought we'd help you feed the lions."

"Get lost," Gunther repeated.

At the bottom of the cliff, the low growls grew louder. More urgent.

"They want fresh meat. Not that stinking stuff!" Steve called.

Jared took another step toward Gunther.

His friends edged in closer.

Jared grinned. "So what we thought we'd do is give them a meal they'll never forget—*you!*"

"You're lion meat!" Steve threatened.

Gunther stood his ground. But his cheek twitched.

Jared's smile widened. The jerk is getting nervous now, he thought. Good. Make him think we're really going to throw him off that cliff. Wait until he gets on his knees and begs us not to. Then we'll split.

Gunther turned back to Jared. "Don't take another step," he ordered. But his voice shook. "You and the other thugs get out of here now, before I—"

"Before you *what?*" Jared interrupted.

Jared edged closer. His friends moved up until the four of them formed a tight semicircle around the preserve manager.

Down below, the lions roared.

Gunther glanced nervously over his shoulder.

"They're waiting, Gunther," Jared told him. "And they sound real hungry!"

Slowly, the four boys edged toward Gunther.

Gunther took one step back. Then another. Now he stood with his back pressed against the railing.

"Okay, Gunther," Jared began. But he stopped as Kevin poked him in the ribs.

"What's that stuff?" Kevin asked, pointing to the edge of the clearing.

Jared gazed over and frowned. A cloud of smoke drifted along the ground toward them.

A fire? Jared wondered. No. He couldn't smell anything burning. Besides, this smoke was a weird color—a pale purple. He'd never seen smoke like that.

"It's getting higher!" Joey cried.

Jared gasped. Joey was right. The smoke thickened until it blocked out the trees behind it. It twisted and writhed as if it were alive, churning along the ground and billowing into the sky. Its color deepened to a dark, rich purple.

"Let's get out of here!" Joey urged. "That stuff gives me the creeps!"

Jared nodded and was about to leave when a sound stopped him. He turned around.

In front of him, Gunther dropped the two slabs of meat to the ground. His face had gone slack. His eyes glazed over, blank.

"What's his problem?" Kevin asked. "He looks like a zombie."

"Who cares?" Joey replied. "Come on—let's go!"

"Yeah," Jared agreed. "Hey, Gunther, this is your lucky day. We're outta here."

Gunther didn't reply. He turned his back on the boys and climbed onto the railing.

"Wrong way, Gunther!" Kevin shouted.

Gunther kept moving.

"Hey!" Jared cried. "Gunther! What's the matter with you, man? You're going to—" He broke off and dove toward Gunther.

Too late.

Gunther swung himself over the railing—and over the edge of the cliff.

chapter 8

"No!" Jared wailed. He scrambled to his feet and stared down the cliff. "Nooo!"

The crack of bones breaking against rocks rose up through the billowing purple smoke.

A brief silence followed.

Then a lion snarled. A ferocious roar.

Jared dropped to his knees and covered his ears.

But he couldn't block it out. Beneath the snarling, he could hear the sickening, wet sound of flesh being ripped from bones as the lions tore into their dinner.

"Jared!" Kevin grabbed Jared's arm. "What are you doing? We have to get out of here!"

Jared didn't move. "Did you see him? He climbed that rail like a robot or something."

"Yeah, I saw it." Kevin tugged Jared's arm again. "Come on, man! We gotta go!"

The night had grown quiet again.

The growls and snarls from below had stopped.

Jared rose shakily to his feet. As he did, he peered over the edge of the cliff.

"No!" he moaned. "Oh, man! Oh, no!"

In the moonlight, the rocks at the bottom of the cliff glistened with what looked like thick, dark paint.

It's not paint, Jared thought.

It's blood.

Gunther's blood. Spattered all over the rocks.

And Gunther's body, or what was left of it. It didn't look human anymore. The flesh was torn and twisted, like hunks of raw, bloody meat.

One eye stared sightlessly toward the sky.

Jared's stomach heaved.

He bent over, braced his hands against his thighs, and vomited in the dirt.

Wave after wave of nausea hit him, until his muscles ached and nothing remained in his stomach.

"Jared, are you okay?" Joey whispered, sounding very frightened. "We have to go. Can you make it?"

Jared wiped his mouth on the back of his hand and nodded. He tried to walk. But his knees turned to jelly again, and he started to sink.

Kevin and Steve grabbed him before he fell. "Come on. We'll help you," Steve said. With Joey leading the way, the four boys left the cliff and started back down the path.

"How did it happen?" Jared murmured, shaking his head. "We never touched him!"

"I don't know," Kevin replied. "Don't think about it, okay?"

But Jared couldn't stop thinking about it. Couldn't stop seeing that glazed look in Gunther's eyes. The way he had turned and threw himself over the cliff to his death.

"How?" he muttered again. "We didn't touch him. Nobody laid a finger on him!"

Steve shrugged. "The guy was crazy, that's all."

"He wasn't like that before," Jared argued. "What happened? We didn't touch him. We never touched him!"

"Yeah, it wasn't our fault," Joey agreed.

"Right. We're in the clear on this." Tightening his grip on Jared's arm, Kevin helped steer him around the last bend in the path.

"How could something like that happen?" Jared repeated as they stepped onto one of the main walkways of the park. "How?"

No one answered.

"We didn't touch him," Jared chanted to himself. "We didn't! We didn't!"

Jared stopped suddenly. He had to go back up there. He didn't know why. Maybe if he did, he'd

find out the whole thing had been a nightmare.

He turned around.

And froze.

Two security guards came hurtling toward them,
grim expressions locked on their faces.

Too late to run.

chapter 9

"**O**h, no," Joey groaned.

"Come on, Jared!" Kevin tugged hard on Jared's arm. "Come on! We can outrun them!"

Jared numbly shook his head. Can't run, he thought. Besides, it's too late.

The security guards ran breathlessly toward them. The man was short and thick, with a beefy face. The woman was tall and strong-looking.

Both had their eyes on Jared. "Hold on there!" the man called out.

Jared tried to brace himself. But his legs were like jelly. If his friends hadn't been holding him, he would have fallen to the ground.

"What'll we do?" Kevin whispered. His fingers dug painfully into Jared's arm. "What'll we say?"

Jared just shook his head. He didn't have the answers.

The guards drew to a stop in front of them.

53

Putting her hands on her hips, the woman bent forward slightly and peered into Jared's face. "Are you okay, son?"

Jared blinked, confused at her tone. She sounded worried. "What?" he asked, not sure he'd heard right.

"I asked if you're okay." The woman frowned, but it was a frown of concern, not anger or suspicion.

Her partner nodded. "We saw your friends helping you. What's wrong?"

"Are you ill?" his partner asked.

Jared felt a flood of relief. The security guards hadn't found Gunther. They didn't suspect him of anything. They were actually worried about him!

"Yeah, I am a little sick," he told them. His voice came out shaky and weak. "I . . . I ate too much cotton candy, I guess."

"Yeah, we were working on one of the food stands." Joey quickly picked up on the story. "Getting it set up, you know? We kept telling him to stop pigging out. But he kept stuffing it in his mouth!"

"I can't resist that junk, either." The man said with a chuckle, and patted his belly.

Jared managed a smile.

"You still look awfully shaky," the woman said. "Can we give you some help getting home?"

"No, thanks," Jared replied. "Really. My friends will get me back okay."

"All right. But take it easy," she told him. "And next time, lay off the candy."

"You bet. Thanks." Jared smiled again. Then he turned away, leaning on the arms of his friends. He wanted to run, but he didn't dare. He could still sense the security guards behind him, watching.

"Can you believe that?" Kevin whispered as soon as they were out of earshot. "Luck is definitely on our side tonight!"

Yeah, Jared thought. But not on Gunther's.

Dierdre squeezed Rob's hand as they walked along the path leading around the wild animal preserve. "It's such a beautiful night," she murmured, gazing at the full moon. "And so quiet. It's hard to believe that tomorrow night this place will be a total madhouse. All the rides and booths and crowds and lights. It'll be wild."

Robin squeezed her hand back, but didn't say anything. She glanced at him. "You're awfully quiet, too, Rob. What are you thinking about?"

Robin flashed her a quick smile. "I'm just hoping that everything goes all right tomorrow night," he replied.

"Me too." Dierdre sighed. For her father's sake, she really did want everything to be okay. But for herself? I'm just not sure, she thought. So much has gone wrong. She shivered and felt Rob's arm slide around her shoulders.

"Cold?" he asked.

She started to shake her head, then changed her mind. "Well, maybe a little," she replied. Actually, the night was warm. Her shiver didn't have anything to do with the weather.

But she liked the feel of Rob's arm around her.

She enjoyed being so close to him.

She enjoyed it even when Paul was alive.

She loved Paul. But there was something about Rob Fear. Something so attractive.

Not his looks or his brains or anything she could name.

I don't know what it is, Dierdre thought.

I only know that it's powerful.

And I can't resist it.

Sighing again, Dierdre snuggled closer to Rob. He tightened his arm and she felt his cheek against the top of her head. But he still didn't speak.

He must really be worried about the park, too, she thought. Maybe that's what I like about him— that he cares about me and Dad so much.

Dierdre smiled to herself, then stopped suddenly. "Did you hear that?" she asked.

"What?"

"Listen!" She pulled free of Rob's arm and stood

rigid, waiting. "There!" she cried. "Can't you hear it?"

Rob frowned. "All I hear is some growling. Probably the lions."

"I know. But they sound strange," Dierdre replied. She listened again. "Can't you hear it? They sound as if they've gone crazy or something."

"They *are* wild animals," Rob reminded her.

Dierdre jumped as a fierce roar cut through the silence. "Do you think they're fighting?"

"They're probably just playing," Rob suggested. "Come on, Dierdre. Let's go get something to eat."

Another roar broke through the stillness of the park. Dierdre shook her head. "It just doesn't sound right," she declared. "Let's go see."

"I'm sure nothing's wrong," Rob assured her. "And I'm getting awfully hungry, aren't you?"

"Please, Rob." Dierdre held out her hand. "You're probably right. But I want to see for myself."

Rob took her hand and smiled again. The smile that lit up his dark eyes and made Dierdre shiver with pleasure. "I'll do anything for you," he told her softly.

As they walked toward the cliff overlooking the lion preserve, Dierdre laughed softly. "Tell you what. Since you let me drag you all the way up here, I'll buy the ice cream . . ." She broke off suddenly.

"Rob, look—there's Daddy! What's he doing up here?"

Without waiting for his reply, she pulled her hand free and ran across the clearing.

Jason Bradley had been staring over the edge of the cliff. But when he heard Dierdre's footsteps, he turned sharply.

Something's wrong! Dierdre thought. Something's terribly wrong!

Her father held up his hand. "Stop, Dierdre!" he shouted. "Don't come any closer!"

Dierdre kept running. "What's wrong, Dad? What's the matter with the lions?"

"Just stop!" Bradley yelled. "You don't want to see it, believe me!"

"See what? Daddy, what *is* it?" Dodging her father's outstretched arm, Dierdre raced past him and peered over the edge of the cliff.

At first, all she saw were some uniformed park workers, standing in a clump at the base of the cliffs. They shifted their weight from foot to foot and glanced around tensely.

Then Dierdre saw a round object covered with a stained piece of cloth. Nearby sat a huge chunk of meat.

"You're right, Dad," she murmured. "I wish I hadn't seen that meat—it's pretty disgusting. But how come the workers are down there? And why are you so upset?"

"Because that isn't meat, Dierdre. It's . . ." Bradley swallowed hard. "It's what's left of Gunther!"

"Gunther? But . . ." She stopped as her father's words sank in. "No!" she whispered. "Oh, no!"

As she stepped away from the cliff edge, she felt the blood drain from her face. A fuzzy blackness closed in and she stumbled. Then she felt Rob's arm around her waist. Rob's strong arm, holding her up.

"Come on, Dierdre," he murmured. "I'll take you home."

"No." Dierdre took a deep breath and shook away the image of that hideous sight at the bottom of the cliff. "I want to know what happened. Tell me, Dad."

Bradley shook his head. "We're not sure, honey. Obviously, it was an accident."

"What do you mean?" Dierdre asked.

"Well, he probably stood on the rail so he could throw the meat way out in the pasture. He must have lost his balance—and toppled over."

"First Paul, and now Gunther," Dierdre murmured.

Bradley nodded grimly. "It's terrible . . . just terrible."

Dierdre gazed sadly at her father. He looked so pale and shaken. And no wonder! He'd been working so hard on the park, and horrible things just kept happening. "I feel so bad for you, Daddy," she told him. "Is there anything I can do?"

"Don't worry about me, honey." He patted her shoulder. "I have you. And I have my work."

"Then you're going ahead with the opening?" she asked.

"Of course," he declared. "Why wouldn't I?"

"I just thought because of all the accidents . . . all the people getting hurt, you might change your mind." Dierdre hesitated. "So you still think it's worth it, even after everything that's happened?"

"It's my dream, Dierdre," Bradley told her. "I can't give it up because things go wrong."

"But aren't you worried?" Dierdre asked. "I mean, what if something else happens? Something much worse?"

"What could be worse than these two horrible deaths?" her father replied.

"I don't know!" Dierdre cried. "I just have a horrible feeling that the park is jinxed or something." She turned to Rob. "What do you think, Rob?"

Bradley interrupted before Rob could reply. "Nonsense, Dee. These deaths were both accidents. They have nothing to do with the park. There's no jinx on this place. Or on *any* place! You're much too levelheaded to be superstitious, honey."

"I guess you're right," Dierdre admitted. She

reached out and hugged him. "I'm sorry, Daddy. I'm just upset."

"Of course you are. I am, too." He hugged her tightly. "Just remember, this place is my dream," he repeated in a fierce voice. "I'll never give it up. Never. They'll have to shoot me and carry me out of here before I'd give up on Fear Park!"

Bradley hugged Dierdre for a moment longer, then strode away toward the cliff.

Dierdre turned to Rob.

As she did, a sharp crack ricocheted through the night.

Dierdre screamed. She recognized that sound.

A gunshot.

chapter

10

Another shot rang out. Dierdre screamed. Dad! she thought.

Another crack of the rifle.

"Dad!" Dierdre shrieked.

She spun around. He stood as before, staring over the edge of the cliff.

"What's going on?" Dierdre shrieked. "Dad! What's happening? Why is somebody shooting?"

"I called the wildlife officials," Bradley called back. "The lions are in a frenzy. So they're shooting them with tranquilizer darts to calm them down!"

"Why are the lions in a frenzy?" Dierdre asked. Her father didn't seem to hear her.

Rob touched her arm. "It's the meat," he told her. "The *human* meat. Now that they've had a taste of it, they want more."

"Oh!" Dierdre shuddered as the image of Gunther's ripped and shredded body flashed into her mind. "Come on, Rob. Let's get out of here!"

"Do you think it was an accident?" Robin asked as they walked down the employee service road.

"What do you mean?" Dierdre replied. "You don't think someone threw Gunther over the rail, do you?"

"I don't know what to think," Robin told her. "But I can't help wondering about the Fear curse."

"I know. That's what I was thinking about when I told Dad the park might be jinxed," Dierdre admitted.

"After what happened to Gunther, I got a weird feeling, as if there really *is* a curse on the park," Robin continued. "I always laughed it off as a family rumor. But now I'm starting to believe it."

"Don't," Dierdre told him. "Really, Rob. There isn't any curse."

"How can you be so sure?" he asked. "You said yourself that's what you thought when you saw Gunther."

Dierdre shook her head. "I won't let myself get all superstitious and start believing in curses. Dad is right," she told him. "Everything that happened has been an accident."

Robin nodded and gritted his teeth in frustration.

So much for scaring her with the curse.

Well, at least I caused Bradley some grief. I got that weak-brained Jared and his buddies to do exactly what I wanted. Without even realizing it, they've been acting in my own little drama. And they played their parts perfectly.

Everyone had.

Except Jason Bradley.

Bradley's reaction surprised Robin. He expected the man to be much more upset. What does it take to break him? Robin wondered.

Well, it doesn't matter. I have plenty more tricks up my sleeve.

Plenty more "accidents."

Robin tightened his arm around Dierdre's shoulder.

She gazed up at him, a concerned expression on her face. "You're not still thinking about the curse, are you?"

Robin shrugged. Actually, he was thinking about what other damage he could cause. "A little, I guess," he lied.

"Look at it this way," Dierdre suggested. "If there *is* a curse, we can't do anything about it. Right?"

"I suppose not."

"Right, so we just have to forget it." Dierdre wrapped her arm around his waist. "Anyway, there isn't one. And I have a feeling everything's going to be all right from now on."

"I hope you're right."

"I am," Dierdre declared. "I'm sure of it."

Robin nodded and glanced around.

They were on one of the main paths now, but the area was deserted. The workers had either left for the night or were up in the wild animal preserve, calming the lions.

A few feet ahead stood a workstation, a small shed where work crews stored their tools. A single light shone above the station.

On a bench in front of the shed, Robin could see a hammer.

Someone left out a nice big hammer with a gleaming steel head.

Robin grinned. The hammer was perfect for bashing skulls.

As he and Dierdre strolled by the workstation, he casually reached out his free arm. He slipped his fingers around the hammer and silently lifted it from the bench.

Good, he thought, holding the hammer against his thigh. A leather grip on the handle. No chance of it slipping. Wouldn't want to swing and miss!

He glanced at Dierdre. She hadn't noticed.

Pretty soon, she wouldn't notice anything.

Anything at all.

A few more steps, and they had passed the workstation. The path became dark and shadowy again.

To gain some distance, Robin took his arm from around Dierdre's shoulders. He faked a yawn and raised both arms in the air, as if he were stretching.

Dierdre walked a step ahead of him now.

Do it before she turns around!

Robin stopped. Gripping the hammer tightly, he brought his arm back.

And then he swung it as hard as he could at her head.

chapter 11

The hammer sliced the air with a singing, whistling sound.

Dierdre's head is going to split like a ripe watermelon! Robin thought.

His lips twisted in a fierce smile.

He braced himself for the impact.

Dierdre cried out.

Too late, Dierdre! Robin thought. He waited for the crack of the hammer against her skull.

The hammer completed its arc.

And hit nothing but air.

Robin stumbled, thrown off balance.

Completely unaware, Dierdre had run across the path.

"Look, Rob!" she called. "Look at that poor little thing!"

Gasping, Robin quickly hid the hammer behind his back and straightened up.

Dierdre had dropped to her knees by the fence that ran along the outside of the park. "Oh, you poor thing!" she murmured softly.

Rob shook his head, trying to clear it. Who was she talking to?

"Look, Rob!" she repeated. Dierdre sat back on her heels and pointed.

A small, ginger-colored dog was stuck halfway under the fence, whimpering.

A dog! Robin thought in disgust. Everything was going fine, and then a stupid mutt has to ruin it!

Dierdre reached through the wires and petted the dog's head. "We'll help you out, cutie," she cooed.

The dog licked her hand.

Dierdre laughed.

I'll kill them both, right now, Robin decided. Dierdre first. Then the mutt. That will teach it to wreck my plans.

"Give me a hand, will you, Rob?" Dierdre asked. She kept cooing at the dog. Trying to free it.

"Sure." Robin hefted the hammer again and took a quick glance around.

And froze.

Three workers strode along the path toward the workstation.

Dierdre saw them, too. "Robin, ask those guys if they have some wirecutters or something."

"Sure." Robin knew he had no choice. He hurried to the workstation and replaced the hammer. By the time the workers reached him, he was able to smile as he told them about the dog.

But inside, he seethed with frustration.

He'd come so close.

Still, things weren't totally ruined. He'd have other chances at Dierdre.

And the park opened tomorrow. The place would be packed with people.

Robin grinned.

He could have a lot of "fun" in a crowded amusement park.

Alone in the mansion on Fear Street, Meghan paced tensely back and forth across the library floor. Every few seconds, she glanced at the ornate black clock on the mantel.

Almost seven-thirty now. Robin had left for Fear Park an hour ago. She'd pleaded with him not to go.

"It's the grand opening, Meghan," he said as he kissed her good-bye. "I have such a strong feeling that something might go wrong tonight. I have to be there to protect the Bradleys and the park from the Fear curse. I'm the only one who can."

Meghan knew he was right. But that didn't stop her from worrying. Robin had been protecting the Bradleys for so long. How much longer could he do it?

He was wonderful, the most incredible guy Meghan had ever known. But he was all alone in this fight. He wouldn't let Meghan help him. He wanted to protect her, too.

Meghan rubbed her arms against the chill air and glanced at the clock again. The feeling of dread grew stronger as the seconds ticked by.

The Fear curse is so strong! she thought. Robin *can't* fight it by himself. He can't go on trying to protect the Bradleys and the park without help!

As the clock chimed the half hour, Meghan raced from the library and down the long hall toward the side door. Terror washed over her as she yanked the door open. She'd been outside the mansion only a few times since Robin made her immortal. And never by herself. What if something went wrong?

You have to go, Meghan told herself. You have to be with Robin tonight!

Forcing the terror down, Meghan left the mansion grounds and walked quickly along Fear Street, toward the park.

People on foot and in cars crowded the sidewalk and the street. Teenagers, families with little kids, older people walking hand in hand.

Meghan gazed around. Everything had changed so much. The cars were sleek and fast. And so many girls wore jeans, or dresses with hems way above their knees. Some boys actually wore pony-tails and . . . earrings! And everyone seemed to wear sneakers—even the older people!

They all look so happy, Meghan thought as she hurried down the sidewalk. So excited about going to Fear Park. They don't know about the Fear curse. They have no idea that something might go terribly wrong tonight.

The line at the admissions booth seemed to stretch for miles. As Meghan waited, she scanned the crowds inside the park, hoping to spot Robin.

No sign of him. But no sign of any trouble yet, either, thank goodness.

At last she reached the head of the line and bought a ticket. Her mouth felt dry and her heart beat painfully as she hurried through the entrance gate.

The place was magical!

Meghan couldn't help wishing she were here to have fun like everyone else. Clowns roamed the walkways, giving out free balloons. The aroma of hot dogs and hamburgers and cotton candy filled the air.

A carousel with the most beautiful wooden horses spun around and around. Meghan stopped for just a moment and watched it. Its flashing lights and bouncy music actually made her smile. She loved carousels.

A sudden wild shriek rose above all the other noises, and Meghan jumped, her heart pounding.

But it was only a group of kids, climbing in for a ride through the Tunnel of Love.

Meghan quickly turned away from the carousel. She couldn't waste time. She had to find Robin.

Threading her way quickly through the crowd, Meghan hurried toward the Ferris wheel, where Robin worked. It soared high above the park, making it easy to find.

Let Robin be all right, Meghan thought. Let *everything* be all right!

A long line of people stood near the base of the giant wheel, waiting to board one of the little cars. Meghan rose up on tiptoe, craning her neck to see the little booth where Robin worked the controls.

But someone else was at the controls. Not Robin. Meghan scanned the crowd carefully, trying to find him. He had to be here. He wouldn't leave.

An icy pinprick shot up Meghan's spine.

Robin wouldn't leave the Ferris wheel.

Unless something had gone very wrong.

That must be it, she thought in panic. Something is wrong. Robin is in trouble! I have to find him!

Meghan's hands began to shake. She shoved them into the pockets of her skirt and turned away from the Ferris wheel.

To her surprise, Robin stood across the walk from her.

Meghan opened her mouth to call him.

But his name died on her lips.

And all that came out was a cry of shock and horror.

chapter
12

"**H**ey, are you okay?" a man asked, hearing Meghan's cry.

"I'm fine. Too many rides on the merry-go-round," Meghan lied. She brushed quickly past the man. She kept her eyes on Robin, but she didn't run to him.

Robin was busy.

Busy kissing a girl.

Smoothing down the girl's dark hair with his hands. Holding her close against him.

Hot anger boiled up inside her as Meghan stared at the romantic scene. Her hands began to shake again, this time from anger. Tears spilled over her eyes and dripped from her chin.

Robin kissed the girl again.

Meghan couldn't watch anymore.

Shaking with rage, she shoved her way through the crowd and began to run home.

Home! she thought bitterly as she ran. It's not my home—it's my prison!

And Robin Fear is the prison keeper.

I'm the only one who can fight the curse on the park, he had told her over and over. I'm the only one who can protect the Bradleys.

That liar! No wonder he didn't want Meghan's help. He had a big romance going. The last thing he needed was his old girlfriend tagging along.

His *old* girlfriend.

Meghan sobbed as she ran out the park entrance. He made me immortal so we could be together forever. But he betrayed me! He's been out having fun, kissing some other girl, and I've been stuck inside that cold stone mansion.

A ghost, that's what I've been!

And what about the curse, anyway? she wondered. Was it true? Or had Robin made it up?

He wasn't worried about the curse tonight. The whole park could have blown up while he was kissing that girl. And he wouldn't have noticed!

Had he been lying to her about the curse? About protecting the park and the Bradleys?

Had Robin lied to her about everything?

If he has, I'll teach him a lesson, Meghan vowed. He has made me live a life that isn't a life at all.

But I'll find a way to pay him back!

* * *

75

"You look great tonight, Dierdre," Robin murmured. His lips grazed her ear as he spoke. "I wish we could stay like this forever."

"Me, too." She tilted her head back and gazed at him. Her short, green dress matched her eyes. "When you kiss me, I forget all the bad stuff that's happened." She laughed. "Maybe you should just kiss me all night."

"That's not a bad idea." Robin grinned and kissed her again.

Then he rested his chin on the top of Dierdre's head and gazed around the crowded park. At the laughing couples. The excited little kids. The clowns with their giant, painted-on smiles.

The sight of it all turned Robin's stomach.

The park should never even have been built. And now it was actually open!

He wished he could kill every person in it!

Anger pulsed through him. But Dierdre didn't even feel his fury. "You know what?" she asked. "I haven't been able to eat for days, but now I'm actually hungry! Must be all the food smells floating through the air. Let's get a hot dog, okay? And a sno-cone!"

"Excellent!" Robin agreed, even though the thought of eating anything at this park made him gag. As he took Dierdre's hand, he checked his watch. "Uh-oh."

"What?" she asked. "Don't tell me your break is over already!"

Robin nodded. "Almost. And I really have to finish out my shift at the Ferris wheel. The guy who's running it now is new. If it breaks down or something, he won't have a clue how to fix it."

Dierdre gazed up at the brightly lighted wheel circling the sky. "Don't talk about it breaking down," she pleaded. "It reminds me of Paul."

"Hey." Robin squeezed her hand. "Nothing bad is going to happen to the Ferris wheel."

But something terrible is about to happen to *you,* he thought as an idea suddenly popped into his head.

And I know exactly what it is!

I've decided what the next "tragedy" will be.

Robin tugged Dierdre's hand. "I just had a great idea," he told her. "I still have a few minutes on my break. So how about a free ride?"

"On the Ferris wheel?" she asked as he pulled her through the crowd. "Oh, Rob, I'm not sure. I keep thinking . . ." Her voice trailed off.

"Look at it this way," Robin urged. "You know how everybody says when you fall off a horse you have to climb right back on, or you'll never do it?"

"Yes, but . . ."

"Well, think of the Ferris wheel as your horse," he told her. "I know how scared you are of it. And I know why. But once you get on it, and you have a safe ride, all your awful memories will disappear."

"You really think so?" Dierdre asked.

"I'm positive," Robin insisted.

Except your ride *won't* be safe, Robin thought to himself. You'll climb on that horse, but you'll fall right off again.

I'll make sure of it.

Because I'll be up on the Ferris wheel with you, Dierdre. Way up in the sky, in that little, swaying car.

And I'll send you flying right off the top.

You'll make a lovely puddle when you land, Dierdre. A lovely puddle at the doorstep of your father's office!

The big wheel had stopped to reload passengers. Giving her a confident smile, Robin pulled her toward the waiting car.

"How about it?" he asked, holding the seat.

Dierdre gazed at the car for a moment, biting her lip. Then she took a deep breath. "Okay!" she agreed. "I'm ready to get rid of all those awful memories!"

Good, Robin thought. Because I'm ready to get rid of *you*.

chapter
13

Robin tipped the car down to make it easier for Dierdre to climb in. He held out his other hand to her. "This is going to be great," he told her enthusiastically. "You won't believe how beautiful the park looks from so far up. All the lights spread out below, and everybody looks so small. And there we'll be—on top of the world. Together."

Dierdre grinned. "Sounds awesome."

"Definitely," Robin agreed.

But not for you, Dierdre.

Not for long, anyway.

Oh, you might get a couple of spins. A few glances down at your father's monstrosity. But the second our car stops up there at the top, you'll be on your way to the very *bottom* of the world!

As Dierdre took his hand, Robin's heart began to

beat in anticipation. This is it, he told himself. This is the beginning of the end of Fear Park!

A deafening explosion shook the air.

Dierdre dropped Robin's hand and jumped away from him, terror in her eyes. "What's that?" she gasped.

Another explosion erupted, followed by voices shouting and screaming in panic.

"Rob, what *is* it?" Dierdre cried. "What's happening?"

"It's just the Inferno. Look." Robin pointed across the midway.

The Inferno was Fear Park's most exciting roller coaster. It looped the loop at top speed, sending its riders upside down six times. And its terrifying run ended in an explosion of shattered tracks and cars consumed by flames.

The flames and broken tracks were all an illusion. A special effect. But a very *real*-looking illusion.

The fake flames still roared as the line of roller-coaster cars coasted to a stop. But the riders had stopped screaming, and they laughed and chattered in amazement as they climbed off.

"Look at those people. They had a great time," Robin assured Dierdre.

"Yeah." Dierdre took a shaky breath. "I guess I'm still nervous. I should know the sound of the Inferno by now."

"It surprised you, that's all." Just the way I'm about to surprise you, Robin thought. "Come on, let's get on the Ferris wheel. We're holding up the line."

Robin reached for her hand again, but Dierdre pulled back.

"I can't, Rob." She stepped away from the car to make room for the next people in line. "Maybe I'm being silly, but I'm just too nervous to go on a ride right now."

So close, he thought. I was so close!

"Oh, Rob, I'm sorry! I can tell you're disappointed." Dierdre stood on tiptoe and kissed his cheek. "We'll go on it together later, okay?"

"You mean it?" Robin asked. "I don't want to force you to . . ."

"No, I'm going to do it. I really am," Dierdre insisted. "Finish your shift, and I'll walk around for a while. But I promise I'll come back and we'll ride to the top of the world together."

And I'll hold you to that promise, Robin thought. "That's great," he said. "And don't worry, Dierdre."

"I won't." Dierdre kissed him again. "I know everything's going to be great."

No you don't, Robin thought as he watched her walk away. You have absolutely no idea how horrible everything's going to be.

* * *

"Up next—tragedy at Fear Park," the newscaster announced. "Stay tuned."

As the television went to a commercial, Jared grabbed the remote from his bedside table. He stabbed the button and changed the station. Commercials there, too.

Jared switched back to Channel Four and waited tensely for the news to return. He dreaded hearing it, but he had to know.

What if he and his friends had left some kind of evidence? Maybe something had fallen from one of their pockets. And what if those two security guards discovered that he and his friends *hadn't* been working on the food stand? They'd start putting two and two together. We are in big trouble, Jared thought. Major trouble.

"Hey, Jared, turn that stupid television off!" Kevin pleaded for the hundredth time. "If the police thought we were messed up in Gunther's death, they would have been banging at our doors already!"

"He's right," Steve agreed, restlessly twisting his ponytail around a finger. "We're in the clear, man."

"We were in the clear, anyway," Joey reminded them. "We didn't push the jerk off that cliff, remember?"

"No. But we . . ."

"Shut up!" Jared snapped. "The news is back."

The newscaster's expression turned grim. "The

82

body of Stephen Gunther, aged forty-five, was discovered last night at the bottom of a cliff in the Fear Park Wild Animal Preserve. The preserve manager's body was horribly mauled by lions, although an examination showed that he was killed in the fall, and not by the lions themselves."

The scene switched to an interview with Jason Bradley. "Mr. Gunther was a valued employee," Bradley claimed in a solemn voice. "His death was a tragic accident, and we'll miss him."

The newscaster returned. "The weather forecast—right after these messages."

"See? The Bradley guy said it was an accident," Kevin declared as Jared turned the TV off. "Nobody blames us."

"How could they blame us?" Joey asked, "Nobody knew we were up there."

"Rob Fear knew it," Jared reminded him.

"Oh." Joey's face fell. "Right."

"Man! I forgot about him!" Kevin pounded a fist into the couch cushion. "You think he thinks we did it?"

"I don't know. But if he does, we have to set him straight." Jared stood up and grabbed his car keys. "Come on. We've got to go to Fear Park and tell him."

Robin Fear has to believe us, Jared thought as he and the others drove toward the amusement park. He's the only one who knew we were up on that cliff. He's the only one who might suspect us of killing Gunther.

But we didn't do it!

He has to believe us!

Cars lined both sides of every street for blocks. The public lot was jammed. Jared had to park twelve blocks away. As he and the others hurried toward Fear Park, his heart hammered so hard and fast he thought it might explode.

Breathless, Jared dashed up to the admissions booth. An older man with thick glasses sat inside. "How many tickets?" he asked in a quavering voice.

Jared shook his head. "We don't want to go on any rides or anything," he told the man. "We're here to see a friend—Rob Fear. He runs the Ferris wheel."

"Pardon?" The man peered at Jared through his glasses. "How many tickets did you say?"

"We don't need tickets. We just need to talk to somebody," Jared repeated.

The guy shook his head. "Sorry, son. Can't let you in without a ticket."

"How many times do I have to tell you? We don't want to use the stupid park," Jared declared through gritted teeth. "We only came to talk to Rob Fear."

"I can't take your word for that, can I?" the man

asked. "If I let you and your friends in, who's to say you won't decide to sample every ride for free?"

"*I* say!" Jared insisted. Behind him, he heard coins jingling as his buddies went through their pockets. He turned around and glared at them. "We're not paying!" he snapped. "Put your money away. We're not riding, so we're not paying!"

"Then you're not getting into the park," the old man told him.

"We have to!" Jared yelled. "We have to talk to Rob Fear!" In a rage, he reached across the counter, grabbed the man by the front of his shirt and yanked him to his feet.

"We have to talk to him! We don't want to ride anything!" Jared shouted. He shook the man. "Can you hear me now? We have to talk to Rob Fear!"

Out of control, Jared kept shaking the guy. He heard his friends shouting at him, but he didn't care. He just kept yelling and shaking the old guy.

"Are you going to let us in now, huh?" Jared screamed. "Huh? You going to let us in?"

The man's head wobbled wildly. His glasses flew off. Jared kept shaking. Harder. Harder.

And then the man's head slumped.

Jared stared at him, gasping for breath.

"You *killed* him!" Joey cried. "You killed him, Jared!"

chapter
14

Jared froze. I couldn't have killed him! he thought. I didn't shake him that hard!

The guy wasn't young, though. And his neck was kind of skinny. It wouldn't take much to snap a neck as skinny as that.

Did I really do it? Jared wondered. Did I really kill him?

"Hey!" A voice cried out from nearby. "What's going on there?"

Jared glanced toward the walk leading out of the park.

Two Fear Park security guards rushed toward the admissions booth.

"Oh, man!" Steve groaned. "We're toast!"

I didn't mean to kill him! Jared thought. He just wouldn't listen to me!

Too late to run. Too late.

"What's going on?" one of the security men

repeated as he and his partner ran up. "What's the matter with Mr. Jenkins?"

"I . . ." Jared swallowed. "I think he's . . ."

"Ooohhh!" A weak voice moaned. "Oh, my head. My neck!"

Jared spun around.

The old man was alive!

"My neck!" Jenkins moaned again. As he turned his head back and forth, he felt around for his glasses and stuck them on his nose. He blinked a few times, and then his pale-blue eyes focused on Jared.

"You!" he cried.

"What about him?" one of the security guards asked.

"He didn't want to pay for a ticket!" Jenkins complained. "He tried to break my neck!"

"I didn't!" Jared declared. "I didn't *try* to hurt him!"

The first guard clamped a hand on Jared's shoulder. "On your way, buddy," he growled.

Jared tried to shrug him off, but the guy tightened his grip. "You can't kick us out," Jared argued. "Not if we pay for tickets."

The second guard laughed. "You should have paid for them in the first place, pal. Now, take a walk."

The two husky guards herded Jared and his

friends away from the booth and stood watch until they were out of sight.

Jamming his hands in his pockets, Jared strode ahead of the others. Fear Park! he thought bitterly. The whole place stinks. I wish I could turn it upside down!

Jared stumbled on a rock in the middle of the sidewalk and almost lost his balance. Furious, he gave the rock a swift kick. It clattered off the pavement and came to rest near a hole in the fence surrounding the park.

A hole in the fence. Jared stopped and studied it for a moment. Slowly, a grin began to spread across his face.

He had an idea.

Excited, Jared hustled his friends back to the car and quickly drove them to his house. Up in his room, he rummaged through his closet and pulled out a green metal box.

"Are you going to tell us what you're doing or do we have to guess?" Kevin asked impatiently.

"Yeah," Joey agreed. "What are you smiling about, anyway? What's so funny?"

"Nothing's funny—yet," Jared told them. "But I figured out how to get us inside Fear Park. And once we're in there, we're going to have ourselves a whole lot of fun!"

Grinning again, Jared opened the box.

* * *

There's still plenty of time, Robin thought as he finished his final shift. The park will be open for another two hours. All I have to do now is find Dierdre and get her on the Ferris wheel.

He pushed his way through the crowded park. But he stopped when he spotted Jared Malone and his buddies by the House of Mirrors.

Hey—they're not waiting in line to get in, Robin realized.

The four guys are sneaking in through an emergency exit door.

What are they up to?

Robin waited until the last one had disappeared. Then he quickly followed them inside.

Laughter and shouting echoed through the maze of mirror-lined hallways. Robin hung back until Jared and his friends turned a corner. Then he hurried to catch up.

Rounding the corner, he saw the four guys at the end of a line of people. But they weren't staring and laughing at their distorted images like everyone else.

Still hanging back, Robin saw Jared reach into his pocket and bring something out. Then he knelt down and placed it at the foot of the mirror.

His buddies snickered.

Robin smiled.

A firecracker. Jared had just planted a firecracker.

Hidden, Robin watched as Jared planted a dozen more firecrackers. By then, he'd seen enough. As he turned to leave, he stumbled and fell against one of the mirrors.

The glass didn't break, but it rattled loudly enough to catch Jared's attention.

Jared took one look at Robin and hustled his friends around the corner and out of sight.

Scared I'll tell on him, Robin realized.

But I've got something much more interesting in mind.

Making his way through a line of people mugging at the mirrors, Robin ducked out of the building and glanced around, searching for Dierdre again.

There she was, over by the hot dog stand!

"Dierdre!" he shouted, waving.

Dierdre broke into a smile as he hurried over to her.

Robin gave her a quick kiss. "Hey, have you checked out the House of Mirrors yet?" he asked excitedly. "I was just in there, and it's really awesome!

"Listen," he continued. I left my jacket at the Ferris wheel. Why don't you go through the Hall of Mirrors while I run and get it? I'll be waiting for you when you get out. You're going to love it!"

As he spoke, Robin steered Dierdre toward the entrance to the Hall of Mirrors. He couldn't wait to get her inside.

THE LOUDEST SCREAM

Watching Jared and his friends plant those fire-crackers had given Robin an idea.

An excellent idea.

A perfect way to turn Jared's juvenile little prank into something much more interesting.

A major tragedy.

chapter

15

"**Y**ou'll love it, Dierdre!" Robin nudged her closer to the entrance.

But Dierdre stopped in her tracks. "I can't go in there," she told him. "I have to run an errand for Dad. Channel Five wants to interview him. They have a minicam crew here. Anyway, he asked me to get him a tie from his office."

She stood on tiptoe and quickly kissed Robin on the cheek. "I'll be back in a few minutes, and then we'll have some fun!"

Wrong, Dierdre, Robin thought as he watched her run toward her father's office. You won't have any fun at all.

But I will.

I'll have a blast!

Robin turned back to the House of Mirrors.

He could hear the people inside, shrieking with laughter.

Too bad Dierdre isn't with them, he thought. But I can't wait for her. I can't pass up such a perfect chance.

Robin closed his eyes. He shut his ears to the sounds of the park. The crowd swirling around him. The carousel's organ music. The barkers shouting on the midway.

"Jadot kalisto," he whispered softly. *"Jadot exto kalisto."*

As Robin chanted a spell from one of the ancient books, he could feel its strength begin to build.

It's working! he thought.

"Exto denota."

The power of the chant continued to grow, until Robin could practically feel it around him in the air. Now for the final line, he thought.

"Denota jadot kalisto!"

Robin snapped his eyes open.

For a split second, everything remained the same as it had been.

Robin waited tensely.

The air vibrated.

The ground trembled.

The whole world seemed to tilt.

And then a deafening explosion shook the ground as the House of Mirrors blew.

Robin stared at it. At his beautiful handiwork.

Sharp, deadly shards of glass shot through the

air, slicing into the screaming, terrified crowd trying to escape.

You *can't* escape! Robin told them silently.

Shrieks of horror, of pain, echoed through the park.

Music to my ears, Robin thought.

A body with no head landed with a thump at Robin's feet. Blood poured from the jagged open neck, darkening the ground. Robin stepped aside so he could keep watching the deliciously gruesome spectacle.

An arm. A leg. A hand. Ragged pieces of flesh. Legs chopped off at the knee. People stabbed and bleeding. Crying and moaning. Screaming for help.

People dashed around in a panic, shouting for ambulances. For doctors. For help of any kind.

Robin knew that some would survive. But more were dead.

Or would die soon.

A sudden shout caught his attention. Robin turned and saw Jason Bradley racing toward the horrifying scene, a blue-striped tie flying from around his thick neck. Dierdre ran a few feet behind him, her face twisted in horror.

Bradley must have been getting ready for the TV interview when disaster struck, Robin thought. He forced back a smile. What would Bradley say for the cameras now? Would he promise to refund everyone's ticket money?

As Bradley gazed at the cut and bloodied bodies, his eyes widened in shock. His face drained of color. He staggered as if someone had punched him in the stomach.

Robin almost laughed. Looks as if your opening night just got spoiled, Bradley!

There's nothing you can say.

And only one thing you can do—close down Fear Park.

It's your last chance to do it while your daughter's still alive.

Robin watched Dierdre for a moment. Her entire body shook with horror.

You're lucky, Dierdre, he told her silently.

Robin stood quietly, gazing around at the bleeding, crying crowd. He glanced at a group of guys huddled together near an exit gate. Glanced away. Then quickly looked back at the guys.

Yes. It was Jared and his pals.

They appear so confused, Robin thought happily. They know their puny little firecrackers could never have caused such a disaster. But they can't figure out what did.

Robin almost laughed as Jared and his friends broke their huddle and bolted through the gate.

They're afraid, he thought. They know they didn't do anything, but they're afraid anyway.

So use that fear! Robin told himself. Go on—do it now, while you've got the chance.

Putting on an expression of horror and determination, Robin sprinted over to Jason Bradley. "Mr. Bradley!" he cried. He gasped, as if he'd been chasing someone. "I think . . . I saw . . ." Robin broke off and panted some more.

Bradley grasped his arm. "I know what you saw," he muttered in a shaken voice. "We all saw it. It's terrible . . . terrible!"

"No, that's not it!" Robin gulped in some air. "Listen to me! I got a good look at the guys who did this! There were four of them."

Robin paused, enjoying the dramatic moment. "And I can describe them to the police!"

chapter
16

Two medics rushed past Dierdre, carrying a body under a sheet on a stretcher.

Dierdre squeezed her eyes shut. But not before she saw the large, dark-red stains seeping and spreading onto the sheet.

So much blood everywhere, she thought.

So much death.

Shutting it out was impossible.

She took a shuddering breath and opened her eyes.

Her father strode toward her, shaking his head.

Behind her, Dierdre could see Rob. Three police officers surrounded him.

All wore the same grim expressions as her father.

"What's going on, Dad?" she demanded when her father reached her side. "What do the police want with Rob?"

"Rob saw who did it!" Jason Bradley announced.

"The explosion?" Dierdre cried. "Who, Dad? Who was it?"

Her father shook his head. "He doesn't know them. But he got a good look at their faces. The police have a sketch artist. Rob is going to the station to give her their descriptions right now!"

Dierdre craned her neck and watched as the police officers hustled Rob away to a waiting car.

"This is an unbelievable break!" Mr. Bradley declared. "We're going to get them, Dierdre. We're going to get whoever did this!"

"That's great, Daddy." It *was* great, but Dierdre couldn't feel happy or enthusiastic. The destruction and death had already happened. Catching who did it wouldn't make it disappear.

Tears blurred her eyes as Dierdre gazed at the scene. Red and blue lights on police cars and ambulances flashed across cut and bleeding bodies. A severed leg. Ragged pieces of flesh. Dead eyes staring sightlessly at the sky.

Glass crunched loudly as medics rushed by with stretchers. Doctors and nurses shouted orders in hoarse, shocked voices. Moans and sobs still filled the air.

Dierdre shuddered.

Her father put his arm around her shoulder. "Go on home, honey," he told her. "There's nothing you can do here."

"Are you sure?" she asked.

He nodded. "The whole town has turned out to help. You go on home," he insisted. "Try to get some sleep."

Sleep would be impossible, Dierdre knew as she trudged away from the park. How could anyone sleep after what had happened?

Images from the nightmare scene kept whirling through her mind. She couldn't shut them out. She'd never forget them.

If only she could be with Rob, she thought as she passed his house on Fear Street. She wanted to feel his arms around her. To hear him tell her everything would be okay.

But Rob's house was totally dark. He wouldn't be back from the police station for hours, probably.

Besides, he couldn't tell her everything would be okay.

Nothing would be all right again. Not after this.

The night was warm, but Dierdre felt cold and shivery. As she turned up the front walk to her house, she decided to get into bed with five blankets. She wouldn't sleep, but at least she'd be warm.

She pushed open the front door.

An envelope lay on the floor at her feet. Someone must have slipped it under the door. Probably some kind of junk mail, she thought.

Dierdre picked it up and carried it down the hall and into the kitchen. She tossed the envelope on the table, then opened a cabinet and took out a box of cocoa packets. She'd have some hot chocolate first, then go to bed.

A couple of minutes later, Dierdre sat down at the table with a steaming mug of microwaved cocoa. She took a sip and immediately burned her tongue.

Tears flooded her eyes. She pushed the mug away and buried her face in her hands. But as soon as she closed her eyes, she saw the screaming, wounded people again.

Dierdre sat up and wiped her eyes. Would she ever get those pictures out of her mind?

Don't think, she told herself. Do something. Do anything to keep from thinking about it.

She reached for the envelope and ripped it open. Junk mail would distract her, at least for a few minutes.

But the envelope didn't contain junk mail.

Instead, Dierdre pulled out a newspaper clipping. An old one, obviously. The paper had yellowed, the black print had faded to pale gray.

Curious, Dierdre carefully spread it open on the tabletop.

BLOODBATH! the headline screamed at her. SHADY-SIDE YOUTH HATCHET ONE ANOTHER TO DEATH!

The date on the article was 1935.

This is definitely not what I need to take my mind off things, Dierdre thought. I already know what happened back in 1935. I already know the kids were supposed to chop up tree stumps and clear the land for Fear Park. But they went wild for some mysterious reason and started hacking away at each other.

As Dierdre started to crumple the article up, the photo caught her eye. The caption beneath it read, SECONDS BEFORE THE TRAGEDY, DOOMED TEENS SMILE FOR THE CAMERA.

A group of about twenty cheerful-looking kids stared out at Dierdre. One aimed his hatchet at a tree, a grin frozen on his face. Another had her hatchet slung over her shoulder. Several waved at the camera.

Most of them blurred into the background scenery of tree stumps and bushes.

But the boy in the foreground stood out clearly.

Dierdre shivered as she gazed at his face, frozen in time more than sixty years ago. At the straight brown hair. At the dark eyes.

The dark, serious eyes of Rob Fear.

chapter
17

The police officer pulled the cruiser to a stop in front of the huge stone house on Fear Street.

He turned to Robin, who sat in the passenger seat. "Thanks for spending so much time on this."

"Hey, no problem," Robin told him. "I just hope it helps you catch those guys."

"Your descriptions were good. Lots of detail," the cop assured him. "We'll have pictures up all over town by tomorrow. The newspaper will run them and they'll be on TV, too. Somebody will recognize them."

"I hope so." Robin opened the door and stepped onto the sidewalk. "Thanks for the ride, officer."

"You bet. Thanks for your help," the cop repeated. He pulled the car away from the curb, giving Robin a friendly wave as he drove off.

Robin smiled and waved back. Sucker! he thought.

As soon as the car rounded the corner, he threw his head back and laughed out loud.

He'd done it!

He'd closed down Fear Park.

Bradley wouldn't dare reopen it, not after tonight. Not with so many killed and wounded.

People would be outraged.

Robin could hear them protesting now. Fear Park is jinxed, they'd say. They'd scream that no amusement park was worth all that blood and all those deaths.

Jason Bradley would have to listen.

Whistling softly, Robin trotted up the steps and through the massive double front doors.

Why was the foyer so dark? Meghan always left a light on for him.

As Robin fumbled for the light switch, he realized the entire house was dark. No light spilled out from any of the rooms.

"Meghan?" he called. "Why are all the lights off?"

No answer.

"Meghan?"

The sound of his own voice echoed back at him.

He flipped the foyer light on. The rest of the house seemed even darker now.

"Meghan, where are you?" he shouted.

No reply.

The house is too quiet, he thought. It feels deserted. Where's Meghan? Why isn't she waiting for me as she always does?

He stood still for a moment, holding his breath. Listening carefully.

For a few seconds, all he heard was the wind stirring in the trees outside.

Then, a distant, muffled sound.

Footsteps?

An icy shiver ran down Robin's spine. Was someone in the house? Someone who didn't belong?

Robin let his breath out quietly and began to tiptoe down the long marble hallway. First door on the left—the dining room. Moonlight filtered in through cracks in the curtains. The high-backed chairs cast eerie shadows across the floor. Robin flipped the switch and the room blazed with light.

Empty.

"Meghan?" Robin called. "Meghan!"

Still no answer.

Where was she?

Robin passed through a door at the back of the dining room and into the pantry. Beyond that lay the kitchen.

Both rooms were empty.

The side door leading out from the kitchen was locked. Bolted from the inside.

But something's wrong, Robin thought. I can feel it.

Standing still in the middle of the gleaming tile floor, Robin tilted his head and listened again. All he heard was the noisy drumbeat of his heart.

He crept quietly out of the kitchen and glanced down the hall toward the front door. The only light came from the rooms he'd already been in.

As quietly as possible, Robin pushed open the door to the library and reached for the light switch.

The room appeared normal. Books on the shelves. The urn on the mantel. The leather chairs arranged near the fireplace. Nothing seemed disturbed or out of place.

But the house was dark when I came in, Robin thought.

And Meghan isn't here.

Why? Where is she?

An earsplitting scream tore through the silence.

Robin jumped. His heart thundered painfully against his chest.

The scream echoed down the hall again. Robin raced out of the library.

"Oh, no! I don't believe it!" a woman's voice shrieked. "I just cannot believe this!"

The woman screamed again.

And then she began to laugh.

Standing in the hall, Robin heard others join in, laughing and clapping and shouting. Music rose above the voices.

The cheerful, bouncy music of a TV game show. The TV!

Robin ran down the hall and into the living room. No one sat on the couch or the chairs. No one stood at the windows. The room stood empty.

A woman's smiling face peered out from the big-screen TV on the far wall. She wrapped her arms around the host's neck and jumped up and down as the studio audience cheered.

Robin dashed across the room and punched the television off.

Silence.

"Ahhhgh!" Another scream tore through the room. A scream of fury and rage.

A murderous scream.

Robin spun around. "Meghan!"

Meghan stood in the doorway, her face twisted with hatred.

Her hand gripped a gleaming kitchen knife.

"Meghan! No!" Robin cried again as she rushed toward him.

With a shrill scream, she raised the knife over her head and brought it down like a hammer.

Robin gasped as he felt the blade plunge deep into his chest.

chapter

18

The knife sank easily into his chest. Meghan shoved it in, down to the handle.

Robin gasped in shock.

"I'll never forgive you!" Meghan screamed. She twisted the blade in his chest. "Liar! Liar! I'll never forgive you!"

With an angry cry, Robin heaved her away. She stumbled back, caught her foot on a table leg and sprawled onto the floor in front of him.

Robin reached up and grabbed hold of the knife handle with both hands.

Once he had a good grip, he tugged.

Slowly but steadily, the knife began to slide out of his chest.

Robin smiled coldly at Meghan. "There's no blood, see?" he said. He kept pulling until the blade slid all the way out. "No blood and no pain."

He took a step toward her. "Did you forget that

I'm immortal? That we both are? What's the matter with you, anyway? What did I do to deserve this attack?"

Meghan scrambled to her feet and gazed at him angrily. "You made us immortal!" she cried. "I've given my life to you—and you lied to me! You betrayed me. I'll never forgive you!"

"What are you talking about?" Robin demanded.

"About that girl!" Meghan screamed back.

"What girl?"

"The pretty one, with the dark hair," Meghan told him. "You were kissing her at the park earlier tonight. I saw you!"

Dierdre. Robin's mind raced as he tried to come up with a good story.

"I couldn't stay here tonight," Meghan explained. "I had to be with you. I was afraid for you, out there fighting the curse. All alone." She laughed bitterly. "Or so I thought!"

"Meghan, please." Robin had his story now. "Listen to me."

"Why should I?" she demanded.

"So you'll understand," Robin told her. "That girl's name is Dierdre Bradley. *Bradley.*"

"You mean she's . . ."

Robin nodded. "Jason Bradley's daughter. I got close to her so I could protect her family, don't you see?" He sighed gently. "Jason Bradley loves his daughter very much. And he listens to her. That's the important thing."

Meghan gazed at him, a confused expression in her eyes.

"So I figured if I got close to Dierdre, I could get her to persuade her dad to shut the park down," Robin continued. "That's what I'm working for, Meghan. To get the park closed before more innocent people die. You know that."

Meghan kept staring at him.

"I would never betray you," Robin insisted softly. "I would never *look* at Dierdre Bradley if there weren't so many lives at stake. You're the only girl in my life. The only one I care about. You believe that, don't you?"

Meghan took a shaky breath. Her shoulders slumped. She hung her head and gazed at the floor.

Robin stepped close to her. He tilted her chin up and stared into her eyes. "Don't you?" he repeated in a whisper.

Meghan nodded.

Robin wrapped his arms around her and pulled her to him.

Had she bought his story? he wondered.

Did she believe him?

He couldn't tell. She had nodded, but her eyes remained wary and unsure.

He couldn't believe she actually came at him with a knife! Of course, she couldn't kill him. But she could get in his way.

I don't need this, Robin thought. I don't need this at all.

In fact, I wonder if I even love Meghan anymore. I used to. That's why I made her immortal, too.

But that was a long time ago. Over the years, she's become so boring. She never changes. She just clings to me like a leech.

And she just tried to kill me!

Maybe I should get rid of her.

Robin rested his chin on Meghan's shoulder and stared down at his hands clasped against her back.

He still held the knife.

It won't hurt her any more than it did me, he thought. We're both immortal.

But there *might* be a way to kill her. I'll have to see.

The sooner the better.

chapter
19

Jared peered out the window of the old Cameron mansion. The streetlights had just come on. No one out there. "Where's Steve?" he demanded anxiously. "He was supposed to be here by now."

"Maybe he stopped for gas," Kevin suggested.

"He wouldn't be stupid enough to do that." Joey nervously cracked his knuckles. "I mean, he knows somebody might recognize him. I told him he should walk here and use the alleys. He said he would."

"Then where is he?" Jared repeated. He began pacing around the room. "We have to figure out what to do! We have to find a better hiding place. We're not safe anywhere in Shadyside."

Kevin and Joey exchanged glances. They haven't a clue how much danger we're in, Jared realized.

Steve doesn't either. We're all too scared to think straight.

He paced around for another minute, then flicked on the tiny TV Kevin brought with him.

"And now, here's Cindy with an update on the Fear Park bombing," the newscaster announced.

Kevin moaned. "Oh, man, I don't want to hear about this again!"

"He said an *update*," Jared declared. "We have to watch in case something new has happened!"

A serious-looking reporter appeared on the screen. Behind her Jared could see the ruined House of Mirrors. Park employees moved back and forth, still cleaning up.

"It has been almost a week since a bomb blasted through this Fear Park attraction, killing twelve people and wounding twenty more," the reporter announced.

A bomb. Jared shivered at the words.

"Behind me, workers continue to clean up," the reporter went on. "Meanwhile, the entire town of Shadyside is outraged by this senseless act of destruction. And police have mounted a statewide manhunt for the four young killers."

Jared felt dizzy with fear as the four police sketches appeared on the screen. He'd seen them before, but they shocked him every time.

The drawings on the screen were of Jared and his

friends. They weren't perfect likenesses. But they were pretty close.

It's unbelievable, he thought, his stomach twisting into a knot.

The whole town thinks we're bombers.

Killers.

The whole town is after us!

"Shortly after the bombing, a witness came forward and described these four young men to the police," the reporter continued. "They have since been identified. They were seen fleeing the park minutes after the explosion. Police are asking anyone with information to call the following number—555–2662. That's 555–BOMB."

But we're not bombers! Jared thought in a panic. We're not killers. All we did was plant a few tiny firecrackers!

Jared wanted to run into the street and shout his innocence. But he was too scared. Ever since those sketches had appeared two days ago, he and his buddies had been in hiding.

The whole town is out for blood, Jared thought, his heart racing. If they find us, they'll probably lynch us!

Behind him, Kevin moaned again. "Oh, man, we are in major, major trouble! What are we going to do?"

"My uncle has a cabin upstate," Joey told him.

"It's in the middle of nowhere. We could hide out there."

"How are we supposed to get out of town?" Kevin pointed to the television, which now showed the highway patrol questioning drivers at an exit to the freeway. "They've got roadblocks up all over the state. The airport and train station are crawling with cops." His voice rose in panic. "What are we supposed to do—get *beamed* out of here?"

"Okay, okay. Don't freak out," Joey said. "It was just an idea."

"Yeah, well, it was a *dumb* idea," Kevin shot back.

As his friends argued, Jared kept staring at the TV. He hoped the update might bring some good news. But it didn't.

Nothing has changed, he thought. *We're still being hunted.*

He jammed his hands in his pockets and began to pace again.

Should we turn ourselves in? he wondered. *Tell the cops what happened—that we planted firecrackers? That we didn't set any bomb? That we ran because we were scared?*

It's the truth, he thought. *They have to believe us!*

Yeah, sure, Jared! he told himself in disgust. *They might believe you. But by then it'll be too* late. Because they'll shoot first and ask questions later!

The television picture switched back to the reporter, who was interviewing Jason Bradley. Bradley talked about how the workers had been cleaning up night and day. And about reopening the park as soon as possible.

The camera panned over the cleanup crew.

Zoomed in for a closeup.

For the first time in days, Jared felt a twinge of hope.

The camera focused on a member of the cleanup crew that Jared recognized—Rob Fear.

Rob can help us, Jared realized.

He saw us in the House of Mirrors.

He knew we planted firecrackers.

He knows we didn't plant a bomb.

I have to talk to him, Jared thought. He's the only one who knows the truth! He's the only one in Shadyside who can save us!

He punched the remote and turned to his buddies. "I think I have some good news!" he told them excitedly. "Remember when we—"

A loud knock on the bedroom door interrupted Jared.

"Open up!" a voice shouted from the other side of the door. "It's the police!"

chapter
20

Jared's heart raced. Beads of sweat prickled his face.

It's too late! he thought. The cops already found us!

He glanced at Kevin and Joey. They huddled in the corner, their mouths open in terror.

"Open up!" the voice repeated.

Jared's eyes shot to the window. No. No way. You can't escape, he warned himself. They probably have the place surrounded. You have to open the door and take your chances.

Jared sucked in a deep breath and walked unsteadily to the door. His hand shook as he reached for the knob.

Slowly, he eased the door open a crack.

"Gotcha!" Steve cried, leaping into the room. He went into a crouch and pointed an imaginary gun. "Up against the wall, turkeys!"

Jared slammed the door so hard the walls shook. "You jerk!" he screamed. He grabbed Steve by the front of his T-shirt, then shoved him backward against a chair. "You dumb, stupid jerk!"

"Hey, it was just a joke!" Steve protested, sprawling onto the floor.

"Yeah, well, your timing stinks," Kevin snarled.

"You think this mess is funny?" Jared demanded. "Twelve people died and everybody thinks we did it!"

"Okay, I'm sorry," Steve mumbled. He scrambled to his feet and straightened his shirt.

"You were lucky," Jared insisted. "So stop playing games!" Jared breathed deeply again to calm himself down. "Okay, listen. I think I figured out a way to get us in the clear. Remember when we were planting the firecrackers?"

The others nodded.

"Well, Rob Fear saw us," Jared told them.

"Yeah, he saw us planting firecrackers," Kevin reminded him. "That's not so good."

"Don't you get it?" Jared replied. "If he saw us planting firecrackers, then he knows we didn't set off any bomb. He can tell the cops they're looking for the wrong guys."

"Why hasn't he set the cops straight already?" Steve asked.

Jared shrugged. "He probably hasn't even seen the police sketches. They said on the news that workers have been working around the clock to clean up the park. And Rob is one of them. So here's what we do—we wait until it's really dark, then we sneak back into the park."

"Oh, man, that's the last place I want to go!" Joey declared.

"Me, too," Jared agreed. "But we have to. Because Rob Fear is the only one who can help us."

Robin swept a mass of glass and rubble into a large pile, then leaned on the broom and wiped his forehead. He was tired, but he actually enjoyed the work. It gave him a chance to admire his handiwork up close.

Jason Bradley strode by and patted him on the shoulder. "I appreciate all you're doing, Rob," he said wearily. "You're a big help."

"It's the least I can do, Mr. Bradley." Robin shook his head in frustration as Bradley walked away. *The guy still looks like he's in shock,* he thought. *But he hasn't given in yet.*

He hasn't announced that he's shutting down the park.

No matter. I'll just keep hitting him with one disaster after another. An explosion here. An "accident" there. A few more deaths.

Smiling, Robin lifted the broom and began sweeping again.

118

Sticking it to the Bradleys was the most fun he'd had in a long time.

"Rob?"

He turned to see Dierdre striding toward him, clutching a piece of paper in one hand.

"I haven't seen you for days, Rob," Dierdre declared. "You haven't even called."

"I know. I'm sorry." Robin gestured at the cleanup operation. "I wanted to, but I've been really busy. I've only gone home once, and I fell asleep the second I sat down in a chair. I didn't even make it to my bed."

Dierdre gazed at him suspiciously.

What does she want, anyway? Robin wondered. As far as she knows, I'm knocking myself out to help her father. She should be grateful.

"I've been busy, too, Rob," Dierdre told him. She held up the piece of paper. "Busy wondering about *this!*"

Robin's mouth went dry as he stared at the old newspaper photograph of himself.

"Somebody slipped this under my door," Dierdre told him, jabbing at the photo. "Look at it. It's you, Rob! What on earth is going on?"

Robin's mind raced in panic. Who sent that old photo to Dierdre? Who was trying to expose him, to bring him down? Who even knew the connection between the Rob Fear of today and the Robin Fear of 1935? Nobody!

Nobody except Meghan.

Robin's blood ran cold. Meghan did this! She *didn't* believe my story about Dierdre.

And now she's out to get me!

Dierdre tapped her foot. "Well? What's going on?" she repeated. "I mean, this *is* a picture of you, right?"

"It . . ." Robin paused, trying to come up with an explanation. Finally, he had one. He swallowed his anger at Meghan and faked a laugh. "It sure looks like it. Weird, huh?"

"Very weird," Dierdre agreed.

"Yeah." Robin laughed again. "I can't believe how much I look like my grandfather!"

"Your grandfather?" Dierdre quickly studied the photograph.

"Who else?" Robin asked.

Dierdre nodded. "I guess I should have realized it couldn't be you," she murmured. "When I got this, I was so confused and scared, I didn't even think it might be your grandfather."

"Hey, it surprised me, too," Robin told her. "I mean, the two of us could have been twins. I'm definitely a better dresser, though," he joked. "Look at those overalls—they don't even reach his ankles!"

Dierdre snickered. But then her expression

turned serious again. "I don't get it. Why did somebody send this to me?"

Robin shrugged. "Maybe it was a joke," he suggested. "Or maybe somebody wanted to cause trouble between us." He smiled at her. "It didn't work, I hope."

"Well, it *almost* did," Dierdre replied thoughtfully. She stuffed the article into the pocket of her denim shorts. Then she wrapped her arms around his neck and kissed him. "I'm sorry, Rob." She kissed him again. "Forgive me?"

"You don't even have to ask," Robin insisted, kissing her back.

"Gotta go," Dierdre told him, giving him one last kiss. "I know how hard you've been working. But call me when you can."

"You know I will." Robin waited until Dierdre was out of sight. Then he dropped the broom and strode angrily to the telephone beside one of the equipment sheds. His fingers shook with fury as he dropped in the coins and punched the number to his house.

"It's me," he snarled when Meghan answered the phone.

"Robin, hi. What's your problem?" she asked. "You sound weird."

"I don't *feel* weird," Robin replied through gritted teeth. "I feel betrayed, Meghan!"

"What do you mean? Who betrayed you?"

"You did! You sent that photo to Dierdre!" he cried. "How could you do that to me?"

"Robin, I didn't do anything to you!" Meghan protested. "What photo are you talking about?"

"Don't play dumb!" Robin screamed. "You know which photo—the one from 1935. The one that shows me standing in the woods with you and your friends."

"This is crazy!" Meghan cried. "I didn't send *anything* to Dierdre! I don't even have any photo to send!"

Can I believe her? Robin wondered.

"Robin, I didn't do it!" Meghan insisted.

Robin slammed down the receiver.

I have to get rid of Meghan as soon as possible, he decided. She definitely has to go.

Still, she sounded awfully convincing. And she was never a good liar, he reminded himself.

But if Meghan didn't send the old photo to Dierdre, who did?

Someone else who knew, he thought. Someone else who was alive then.

Had someone else followed him from 1935?

Robin's heart pounded with fear.

As he moved away from the telephone, he heard a sudden rustling sound from the equipment shed.

He started to turn.

Too late.

A hand shot out and grabbed him from behind.

An arm pressed against Robin's throat like an iron bar.

"Don't make a sound," a voice hissed into his ear.

chapter
21

Robin tried to struggle, but it was no use. The arm dug deeply into his throat, choking him as he was dragged roughly into the darkness of the equipment shed.

When they reached the very back of the shed, the attacker finally let go.

Robin fell against the toolbench. He sucked in a great gulp of air.

Someone moved behind him. Robin clenched his fists and slowly turned around.

Jared and his three buddies stood in front of him.

"What were you trying to do—strangle me?" Robin rubbed his throat.

"Keep your voice down!" Jared glanced fearfully toward the shed door, then back at Robin. "Sorry, man," he whispered. "I told Kevin not to hurt you.

But I had to get you in here without anyone spotting us!"

"Next time, try asking me," Robin angrily snapped. He rubbed his neck again and frowned. "Okay. What's this all about?"

Jared pulled a police flyer from his pocket and handed it to Robin.

Robin studied the four drawings carefully. Pretty good likenesses, he thought. I wonder why these idiots haven't been picked up yet.

"The cops think we set that bomb!" Jared whispered hoarsely.

"Yeah, but we didn't do it," the ponytailed one declared. "And Jared says you know we didn't."

"That's right," Robin agreed. "I saw you planting firecrackers, not a bomb. This is ridiculous. I haven't seen these drawings before, or I would have said something."

"So will you say something now?" Jared pleaded. "You have to! You're the only one who knows the truth!"

"Be cool," Robin told him. "Sure, I'll help you. I'll go to the cops right now."

Jared heaved a sigh of relief. "That's great. That's really great! You don't know how scared we've been!"

But I can imagine it, Robin thought happily. "Okay, you guys wait here," he told them. "I'll put a padlock on the outside so no one can get in. And I'll be back as soon as I've talked to the police."

Jared grabbed Robin's hand and pumped it gratefully. "Thanks, Rob. Thanks a lot. We owe you big time!"

You sure do, Robin thought.

A sly smile spread across his face as he stepped outside and snapped the padlock onto the shed door.

He just thought of a way for Jared and his buddies to pay him back.

Still feeling embarrassed, Dierdre ripped the yellowed news article into pieces and tossed them into the wastepaper basket in her father's office.

I should never have doubted Rob, she thought. Of *course* that was a picture of his grandfather! She was stupid to think anything else!

Sitting at the desk, she tilted the chair back and glanced around. The place was a total mess. Cups half full of cold coffee. Dried-up sandwich crusts. Papers scattered over everything.

Daddy has been working too hard, she thought. I have to make him get some rest. As soon as he comes in, I'll grab him and drag him home with me.

The phone rang. Dierdre picked it up, expecting another reporter. Or maybe the police. "Hello?"

"Stay away from Robin Fear," a hoarse voice whispered.

Dierdre's hand tightened on the phone. "Who *is* this?" she demanded.

"Never mind," the voice replied. "Just stay away from Robin. He's not your friend!"

"Who *is* this?" Dierdre repeated. Her heart beat fast and hard. "Did you send me that old photo? Who *are* you?"

"We have to talk," the voice whispered urgently. "Do you hear me? We have to talk—before it's too late!"

"Who . . .?" Dierdre gasped.

The line went dead.

Robin spun the padlock and yanked it open. As he pulled open the equipment shed door, he put a panicky expression on his face and pretended to be out of breath.

"What happened?" Jared demanded anxiously as Robin burst into the shed. "Did you tell the cops it wasn't us?"

Robin nodded. "Yeah," he gasped. "I told them." He paused for breath, enjoying their suspense.

"And?" Jared demanded.

This is so much fun, Robin thought as he brushed his hair off his forehead in a dramatic gesture. He wished he could drag this out for a few more minutes. But he had other things to do.

"Come on, Robin, tell us what happened!" Jared cried. "What did they say? We're in the clear, right?"

"I told them over and over. But they didn't believe me!" Robin announced. "They think you did it. They're coming after you and they're not going to give you a chance."

"Huh? What do you mean?" Jared demanded.

"They've got instructions to shoot first," Robin told him. "They're going to kill you all!"

chapter
22

Jared's face drained of color.

The other three guys looked ready to pass out, too.

"This is a joke, right?" Jared demanded. "Come on, Robin, you're making a bad joke. You have to be!"

Robin shook his head. "Do I look like I'm joking?"

"But why didn't the cops believe you?" Kevin demanded.

"Who cares?" Joey's voice was hoarse with fear. "We don't have time to stand around asking questions! You heard what he said—the cops are going to shoot first!"

Jared turned to Robin. "Did they follow you?" he asked in a tense voice. "Do they know we're hiding in here?"

"I don't think so," Robin told him. "But I can't be sure."

"We're sitting ducks in this shed. We have to split—now!" Joey cried.

"Keep your voices down!" Robin ordered. "And use your brains. Running is the worst thing you can do!"

Steve clenched his fists. "You got a better idea, Fear?"

Robin nodded. "As a matter of fact, I do."

Jared jammed his hands in his pockets. "Okay. What?"

"The police don't want to hear what you have to say, right?" Robin asked. "Well, what if they don't have a choice? What if you arrange it so they *have* to listen?"

"How are we supposed to make this *arrangement?*" Steve asked skeptically.

"Simple," Robin told them. "You take a hostage."

"Are you kidding?" Steve cried. "If we grab somebody, the cops will kill us for sure!"

"No they won't," Robin said. "You've seen all those hostage shows on TV, right? The police do everything they can to keep people from being hurt. Besides, all you're asking them to do is *listen* to your story."

Jared frowned. "And you figure once we tell our side of it, they'll let us go?"

"Sure. Because I'll back you up," Robin lied. "The TV and newspaper reporters will check everything out, too. You'll be in the clear."

Come on, Robin urged them silently. *Go for it.*

But Jared's expression remained doubtful. "What about taking the hostage? I mean, won't we be in trouble for that?"

"You're not going to hurt anyone," Robin explained. "And cops are human. They'll know you did it because you were desperate to clear your names. Besides, they'll still have the real bomber to catch. They won't have time to bother with you anymore."

Robin paused and watched the four guys exchange glances. They didn't look so panicky now. They were actually starting to look hopeful.

"Of course," he continued, "it's important who you take as a hostage."

"Yeah. Who do we grab?" Kevin asked. "A little kid?"

"That'll make everybody too angry," Robin told him. "I have a much better person in mind. Dierdre Bradley."

"Hey, yeah!" Joey agreed. "Her dad will make sure the cops listen to us!"

"I can get Dierdre here for you," Robin told them. "Once I get her into the shed, you pretend to knock me out. I don't want her to know I'm in on this. Then you grab her and hold her hostage. What do you say?"

"Are you sure this will work?" Jared asked nervously.

"It's better than hiding out or running for the rest of your life," Robin replied. "Trust me. In a few hours, you'll be totally free."

Jared took a deep breath. "Okay. It's worth a shot. Let's do it."

"Good. You guys stay here while I get Dierdre. And don't worry," Robin added. "Everything's going to work out great."

Robin eased the door open a crack and peered outside. No one around. He glanced over his shoulder, gave the guys a thumbs-up sign, and slipped out of the shed.

Everything is going to work out great, he repeated happily to himself.

For me, *that is.*

The Bradleys will have another disaster on their hands.

Then all I have to do is figure out a way to kill Meghan, and life will be perfect!

First things first, though. Get Dierdre to that shed and let the "tragic" hostage situation blow up in everybody's faces.

Robin glanced up and down the path. Bradley's office trailer stood several yards away. As Robin watched, Jason Bradley trotted down the steps. Behind him stood Dierdre.

Bradley strode off. Dierdre waved to her father, then moved back inside.

Perfect timing, Robin thought. She's all alone. And she complained that she hasn't seen me enough. I'll just drop in and suggest a little moonlight stroll.

Robin glanced at the office. He could see Dierdre's silhouette in the lighted window.

A moonlight stroll would be fun, actually. After all, he enjoyed Dierdre. Hanging out with her, holding hands with her.

Kissing her.

If he got rid of Meghan *and* Dierdre, he'd be lonely.

Nobody to talk to. To kiss. Nobody to put her arms around him and tell him how great he was.

Should I kill Dierdre? he wondered.

Maybe.

Maybe not.

Such a tough decision.

Choose, he told himself.

Keep her?

Or kill her?

chapter
23

"It was so creepy!" Dierdre declared, as she and Rob left her father's office. "This dry, whispery voice saying these awful things. Warning me about you!"

Robin put his arm around her shoulder. "And you don't have any idea who it was?" he asked.

"No. That was the worst part," Dierdre replied. "It didn't sound like anyone I know."

Dierdre leaned against Rob and shivered. She kept trying to wipe the voice from her head, but it kept repeating its warning. Telling her to stay away from Robin Fear.

She glanced up at Rob. He stared straight ahead, a concerned expression on his face.

Concerned for me, she thought.

He *is* my friend, no matter what that voice said. More than a friend. Much more.

He always will be.

"I'm so glad you came by the office," she told him. "I couldn't tell Daddy about the call. He has enough on his mind. But I wanted to talk to somebody!"

"Mmm." Robin squeezed her shoulder. "Maybe it was just a prank call, you know? Anyway, a walk will wipe the whole thing out of your mind. Except it's starting to rain."

"Just a little drizzle." Dierdre smiled and wrapped her arm around his waist. "It's kind of nice and misty, actually. I don't mind it."

Robin kissed the top of her head. "Your hair is already wet," he murmured.

"I don't care. I want to be with you." She turned her face up and gave him a long kiss.

The rain began to come down harder.

Dierdre laughed. "Looks as if we'll have to go back after all."

"Why don't we just wait it out in there?" Robin suggested. He pointed toward an equipment shed a few yards up the path. "It'll be cozy and warm." He kissed her again. "And romantic," he added.

Dierdre took his hand. "Let's go."

Breathless and spattered with raindrops, Dierdre scooted into the shed in front of Robin. "It's so dark in here!" she cried. "There must be a flashlight somewhere."

The door slammed shut. Dierdre heard a scuffling noise behind her. Then a loud gasp.

She spun around. "Rob!" she screamed.

Rob lay on the floor, his eyes closed.

"Rob? Rob?" she cried. He didn't move.

Slowly, Dierdre raised her eyes from Rob's face.

Jared Malone and his three friends stood against the front wall of the shed.

Dierdre's heart thundered in her chest. Their faces! They were the same faces on the police drawings of the bombers! She'd seen them for days, but it hadn't hit her until now. Until she actually saw them in person.

Jared. Paul's brother. A killer.

"You're the ones!" she shouted. "You killed all those people! You set that bomb!"

She glanced down at Rob. He was so still, so pale. "You killed Robin, too!"

"Shut up!" Jared snarled. "Robin is okay! Everything will be okay—if you just shut up and listen to us!"

"No!" Dierdre screamed. She raced for the door.

"Get her!" Joey yelled. "Don't let her out of here!"

Strong hands grabbed Dierdre from behind and dragged her away from the door.

"Nooo!" she wailed. She lashed out with her foot, but kicked only air.

A hand clamped itself against her mouth. Dierdre pulled her lips back and sank her teeth into the boy's flesh.

136

He yelped.

Dierdre jabbed back with both elbows and heard her attacker cry out. Twisting and turning, she finally broke free.

I have to get out! she thought. She tossed her tangled hair from her eyes and raced for the door again. I have to get out of here! They're killers. Killers!

She reached for the door handle.

And pain exploded in her head.

Blinding, searing pain.

Dierdre's stomach heaved.

Her knees crumpled.

The door handle seemed to be at the far end of a black tunnel.

The tunnel grew narrower and narrower as the darkness closed in.

They've killed me, too, Dierdre realized, as everything went black.

chapter
24

Slowly, Dierdre turned her head.

Pain hit her like a blow from a hammer.

She tried to cry out, but she couldn't open her mouth. She moved her lips. Felt something thick. Rough. Tight.

A gag!

I'm gagged!

She tried to reach for the gag. Something stopped her. Her hands were behind her. She couldn't move them.

Her hands were tied!

Dierdre's eyes snapped open. The pain washed over her. She shut her eyes quickly, breathing hard through her nose.

Slowly, the pain in her head faded to a dull thud.

A sharp pattering sound came from above.

Rain, Dierdre thought. It's still raining. It started when Rob and I . . .

Rob!

She opened her eyes again and glanced around.

She was still in the equipment shed. Leaning against the far wall, deep in the shadows of a tall storage closet.

Rob lay on the floor next to her. His hands and ankles were tied.

His eyes were still closed.

He's dead! Dierdre thought. Jared killed him!

She started to sob and almost choked on the gag. Don't be sick! Don't be sick!

Swallowing hard, Dierdre let her eyes drift shut again.

The rain had let up. It sounded soft now.

No. It wasn't the rain. It was someone whispering!

She opened her eyes a slit and peered through her lashes down the dim length of the shed. Four figures huddled together near the door, holding a whispered conversation. Jared. Kevin. Steve and Joey.

The whispers sounded fierce and frantic.

Finally, Dierdre made out some words: ". . . *get rid of her!*"

Her heart stopped, then began racing.

They're talking about me! They're going to kill me, too!

A cry of panic rose in her throat. She forced it down.

Don't moan or whimper! Don't let them see you're awake!

Moving only her eyes, Dierdre glanced around. A few feet to her left, she saw a dusty-paned window. To her right, the storage closet. Its door was open, partially blocking her from the view of the killers.

Tools filled the closet and hung from hooks on the inside of the door. Pliers. A spade. A coiled hose.

And a pair of long-bladed hedge clippers. Sharp and shiny.

Perfect for cutting.

Dierdre shifted her gaze to the other end of the shed. Jared and his friends still huddled together, whispering urgently.

She held her breath, then scooted an inch to her right. Paused. Scooted another inch.

The whispering continued.

They haven't seen me, she told herself. Keep going!

Another inch. Another. Sweat beaded on her forehead and rolled into her eyes. Keep going!

At last she felt the cold blades of the clippers against her fingers. Silently, she tugged them from the hook. She fumbled for the catch and pushed it up.

The blades snapped open with a sharp, metallic click.

Dierdre froze. Incredibly, nothing happened. No angry shouts. No footsteps running toward her.

She wedged the clippers against the base of the closet. Then she began to rub her bound wrists against the edge of an open blade.

Back and forth. Back and forth. The rope gave a little. Dierdre kept rubbing.

A strand broke. Then another and another.

Dierdre twisted her wrists, pulled against the fraying rope. More strands broke. The rope stretched and loosened.

Loosened enough for her to slide her hands all the way out.

She rubbed her arms, got the circulation going again. Then she rose quietly to her feet, and pulled the gag from her mouth. She shoved her hair out of her eyes and glanced worriedly at Rob.

His head moved slightly. His chest slowly rose and fell.

Dierdre almost gasped out loud with joy. He's not dead! They didn't kill him!

We can both get out!

Keeping one eye on Jared and his friends, she moved silently to Rob's side and began to untie the ropes on his wrists.

Rob started to groan.

Dierdre covered his mouth.

His eyes opened.

Silently, Dierdre put a finger to her lips.

Rob stared up at her for a moment, confused. But finally, he nodded.

He understood.

As quickly as possible, Dierdre finished untying him and helped him sit up. She pointed to the window.

Rob nodded again. "Go!" he mouthed silently.

Dierdre gathered her courage. Shot a last quick glance at Jared and his friends.

She stepped out from the shadow of the storage closet.

And leapt for the window.

Could she get out before they saw her?

Could she get away?

"Hey!" Jared shouted.

chapter

25

Dierdre grabbed the window handle.

Footsteps slapped against the gritty cement floor.

Dierdre tugged up, panting with fear.

She turned to see Rob beside her, helping her.

The window resisted for a second, then shot up as if it were greased.

Cool, moist air flowed onto Dierdre's face.

And then Rob disappeared from her side.

Rough hands grabbed her arms and yanked her backward.

"No!" she screamed. "No!" She twisted and kicked, battering her feet against someone's legs and screaming again. "No!"

"Cut it out!" Jared growled in her ear. He wrapped a hand around her mouth and used his other arm to wrestle her away from the open window.

Steve stepped up and slammed it shut.

Jared flung Dierdre away from him, across the shed. The window was our only chance, she thought, as she stumbled and fell onto the floor next to Rob.

Our last chance!

Beside her, Rob mumbled something. He must have hit his head again! she thought.

"We have to get out of here!" Jared cried, turning to his friends. "Now!"

Dierdre helped Rob to his feet. Standing close together, they braced themselves against the wall.

All four guys turned and stared at them.

This is it, Dierdre thought. They're going to kill us!

She gulped in some air. The guys still stared at her.

No. Not at her, she realized.

They were staring at the smoke.

Purple smoke, twisting and curling along the floor of the shed.

Rising and billowing.

"Rob!" Dierdre cried. "What is it? What's happening?"

Rob's eyes were wide as he gazed at the smoke. "It's just like in the old story," he murmured in a terrified voice. "Remember? In 1935, when all the kids came to clear the land for the park. The purple smoke appeared then, too." He swallowed and closed his eyes.

Dierdre stared in horror as the smoke continued to rise and billow through the shed.

"And right after it did, the kids chopped each other up with their hatchets!" Rob continued.

Dierdre shuddered.

"Something horrible is going to happen, Dierdre!" Robin warned. "Something we can't control!"

Dierdre shook as a cold wave of fear ran through her. She stared in horror at the thick purple smoke, snaking around the shed.

Wrapping itself around Jared. Around his friends. Slithering along their arms and legs. Floating around their throats.

"Nooo!" Jared moaned in a terrified voice. "Get it off me! Nooo!"

His friends began to groan, too. All of them grabbed at their faces, moaning and crying.

Dierdre gasped.

Their skin is stretching!

Tighter and tighter against their skulls! It's going to split apart!

With a loud *pop*, the skin cracked on Jared's forehead, revealing white, shiny bone.

"What's happening?" Dierdre shrieked. "What is happening?"

"They're coming apart!" Rob cried. "The smoke is pulling them apart!"

Joey's cheekbones jutted out like rocks.

Kevin's arms began to stretch from his side. He bellowed in terror and pain—as they snapped loose and fell to the floor.

Jared's neck stretched higher and higher—until his head broke off.

Dierdre screamed.

The purple smoke grew thicker. Swirling. Twisting around heads and arms and feet and legs.

Pop. Another boy broke apart.

His ribcage exploded and his arms and legs tumbled to the floor.

The smoke twisted and surged.

Shifted direction.

Began to float toward Dierdre and Rob.

"It's coming for us, now!" Rob cried. "It's going to rip us to pieces!"

Dierdre screamed as the smoke touched her. She felt its warmth. Felt it twine around her ankles and creep up her bare legs.

Higher. Thicker.

Picking at the skin on her legs and arms.

Stretching it.

Pulling at it.

Creeping higher and higher.

Swirling completely around her.

chapter
26

"Rob!" Dierdre screamed. "Rob, help me!"

No answer.

She could see nothing through the wall of purple smoke.

It got him, too! He's dead!

And I'm next!

Dierdre shut her eyes and pressed against the rough wall of the shed.

No way out!

I'm going to die like the others. I'm going to stretch and stretch until I rip into pieces.

She waited for her skin to tighten.

To split open over her bones.

No way out!

The smoke brushed over her lips. Curled against her eyelids.

Pressed against her face, her arms, her hands, her fingertips.

And then it drifted away from her.

I can't feel it, Dierdre thought. I can't feel a thing!

Am I dead? Did it kill me?

Cautiously, she opened her eyes. And blinked in surprise.

The smoke had vanished completely.

Dierdre jumped as a low moan echoed through the shed.

She lowered her eyes to the floor.

"Rob!"

She shoved away from the wall and rushed to him. "Rob—are you all right?"

Robin pushed himself to his knees and glanced around. "I'm okay, I think," he groaned. "But the smoke—I thought for sure . . ."

"It almost got us!" Dierdre helped him to his feet, then wrapped her arms around him. "And then it disappeared."

In horrified silence, she gazed around the shed.

Body parts littered the dusty cement floor.

Chunks of skin.

Legs and arms torn from their sockets.

A skull that had exploded into a dozen jagged pieces.

An eyeball, blue as a marble, perched atop one of the skulls.

Jared's eye.

Dierdre shuddered and held on to Rob. "My father has to close the park!" she cried. "He has to, Robin! He *has* to!"

"But, Dierdre—" Robin started to protest.

"I mean it!" Dierdre raised her head and stared at him. "There *is* a curse on this land! I didn't believe it before, but I do now! I have to convince my father to shut this park down for good!"

"Take it easy, Dierdre," Robin told her. "I'll help you convince him."

"You will?"

"Of course." He pulled her close again. "We'll do it together. He'll have to listen to both of us."

Dierdre leaned her cheek against his shirt. "But what if he doesn't?" she asked. "What if we can't convince him? I-I'm so worried, Rob."

She felt Rob's arms tighten around her.

"I'll help you, Dierdre," Robin said softly. "Then I'm going to take care of you. Real good care of you."

TO BE CONTINUED . . .

About the Author

"Where do you get your ideas?"

That's the question that R. L. Stine is asked most often. "I don't know where my ideas come from," he says. "But I do know that I have a lot more scary stories in my mind that I can't wait to write."

So far, he has written more than a hundred mysteries and thrillers for young people, all of them bestsellers.

Bob grew up in Columbus, Ohio. Today he lives in an apartment near Central Park in New York City with his wife, Jane, and son, Matt.

THE NIGHTMARES
NEVER END . . .
WHEN YOU VISIT

**Next, the horrifying conclusion
to the FEAR PARK TRILOGY:**
THE LAST SCREAM
(Coming mid-September 1996)

All Robin Fear's attempts to close down Fear Park have
failed. There is only one thing left for him to do—kill
Dierdre Bradley. He has a terrifying plan he is certain
will mean death for Dierdre.

But Robin doesn't know that someone is watching him.
Someone knows his plan—and has a plan of their own.
A plan that will destroy Robin Fear.